THE
EDGE
OF
FOREVER

THE EDGE OF FOREVER

MELISSA E. HURST

Sky Pony Press
New York

Sky Pony Press books may be purchased in bulk at special discounts for sales promotion, corporate gifts, fund-raising, or educational purposes. Special editions can also be created to specifications. For details, contact the Special Sales Department, Sky Pony Press, 307 West 36th Street, 11th Floor, New York, NY 10018 or info@skyhorsepublishing.com.

Sky Pony® is a registered trademark of Skyhorse Publishing, Inc.®, a Delaware corporation.

Visit our website at www.skyponypress.com.

10 9 8 7 6 5 4 3 2 1

Library of Congress Cataloging-in-Publication Data is available on file.

Cover design by Rain Saukas
Cover photo credit Thinkstock and iStock

ISBN: 978-1-63220-424-0
Ebook ISBN: 978-1-63220-892-7

Printed in the United States of America

For my family. I love you always and forever.

THE
EDGE
OF
FOREVER

1

BRIDGER
MARCH 11, 2146

THE cadets surrounding me are wilding out. Most of them are peering out the shuttle windows at the decay of Old Denver stretching below us. Their excited voices grind into my skull. I wish they'd be quiet, but I really can't blame them. This is my class's first time trip out of our own century. We're going to record a presidential assassination.

But I'm numb. Just like I've been for the last month.

My girlfriend, Vika, is sitting next to me. Her clear blue eyes are clouded with worry as she asks, "Are you all right?"

"Yeah, why wouldn't I be?" A sliver of guilt slices through me from the lie.

"Well, you've haven't said anything since we left the Academy."

She's right. I'd pulled up the mission schematics on my DataLink as soon as we boarded the shuttle and pretended to study them. I should've known she'd realize something was wrong with me. Even though we've only been dating for six months, she can read me like I'm broadcasting my feelings on a Jumbotron.

I brush back a strand of blonde hair that's curling across her cheek. "I'm fine," I say, forcing a smile.

"Are you sure?"

Before I can reply, a loud voice says, "Attention, cadets." All talking stops. Professor Cayhill is standing in the middle of the aisle. He's dressed in the same black and gray uniform we're all wearing. I swear it always startles me when I hear him. Cayhill is a puny-looking guy, yet his voice is really deep. "Please settle down now. We will arrive at the Old Capitol Building ruins in exactly two minutes."

After Cayhill takes his seat, a few cadets begin to whisper again. Even though it's quieter now, an excitement still fills the shuttle.

"I can't believe we're really here." Vika's eyes are huge as she stares past me out the window. "We're really going to do this."

Suddenly I'm overwhelmed with guilt. I've been a jerk to her all morning. I wish I could wrap my arms around her. I want to bury my face against her neck. I want to breathe in the cherry scent that clings to her. She's the one person I can always go to when I feel like I'm suffocating from sorrow. She's the one person who makes me feel alive.

But I can't do that now. Not on a time trip.

Instead I entwine my fingers with hers and squeeze. "I'm just glad they partnered us this time. I don't think I could do this without you."

It was hard dragging myself out of bed this morning. Hard getting dressed and going through the motions of prepping for a time trip. Vika commed me first thing to make sure I wasn't going to back out. I snapped at her. But she was right. I've already missed two time trips in the past few weeks. I can't miss any more. Not if I want to make it to the next level of study at the Academy.

Vika grins at me. Her face is flushed, making the few freckles sprinkled across her nose stand out. "You know, I think I'll love you until the day I die. Maybe longer."

I don't know why, but a chill creeps over me. Probably because she said she loves me. We haven't gone there yet. And I don't know what to say. "Yeah, I know what you mean."

That was lame.

The shuttle begins to descend. I glance out the window at the Old Capitol Building ruins. I've seen holograms of it when it was still intact, with white granite and a gold-topped dome. Another casualty of the Second Civil War.

The outer door slides open with a hiss, but Professor Cayhill holds up a hand before anyone can move. "Disembark in an orderly fashion and report directly to your team leaders."

After the team leaders exit, the cadets begin to file out. Vika tugs on my hand, and we join them. A cold wind blows as we exit the shuttle, whipping at the weeds and trees that have spread across Old Denver like cancer. I blink against the biting chill as I wait for the thrill of an impending shift to spark.

But the thrill never surfaces.

"My team over here," Professor March calls out. He's leaning against the back of the shuttle, next to the black ACADEMY FOR TIME TRAVEL AND RESEARCH lettering.

The cadets who've already exited the shuttle disperse to their assigned team leaders. There are not many of us—eighteen total, divided into three groups.

Professor March clears his throat and taps the antiquated watch he wears. The gold band gleams against his brown skin. "Time's ticking and we have a mission to complete." We hurry over to the small group huddled around him. Once we're there, he says, "Now that you're all assembled, are there any questions?" Silence greets him. "Okay, here are the comm-sets. You know the drill."

He picks up a black case resting next to him and flips open the lid. Inside are the thin communication headsets we use on our trips. I grab one and slip it over the top of my head. Then I make sure the ear and mouthpieces are in place before rotating the eye lenses forward. It takes another few seconds to punch in a code on my DataLink so it can sync with the comm-set.

Now the Academy can officially witness everything I see and hear. Or they will, once we activate the comm-sets after the shift.

Back at the Academy, a panel from the Department of Temporal Affairs will evaluate everything we record today. The cadets with the best footage will advance early to the next level of training at the Academy. I grit my teeth and force myself to focus. I can't screw up today. Not if I want the DTA to assign me to the military division of study.

"Okay, let's roll," Professor March says when everyone is ready. Then he looks at me. "Hold up, Bridger, I'd like to speak to you in private."

I close my eyes for a second. I was hoping he wouldn't do something like this. But yeah, I should've known better.

My teammates cast curious glances in my direction. Vika grabs my hand and gives it a tight squeeze. Professor March stares hard at everybody until they head toward the hill in front of us. That's where the ruins of the Old Capitol Building rest. When everyone is out of earshot, he asks, "How are you holding up?"

"I'm fine, sir."

"You sure about that? You look a little out of it."

"I didn't get much sleep last night." That's not the whole truth, but maybe it'll be enough to get him to leave me alone.

He lets out a puff of air. "Bridger, what am I going to do with you?"

I stay quiet. My dad used to say sometimes the best answer is to keep your mouth shut. I'm not so sure how that's going to work with the professor. He's known me since I was born. He was Dad's best friend, since their days at the Academy.

"I realize things haven't been easy for you, but I need to know that I can trust you. There's no room for error on a time trip."

"I'm fine. Really." I force myself to look him in the eye, force my hands to stay steady.

"If you're not ready, then please let me know. Nobody at the Academy will hold it against you."

"I need this," I say before he can continue. "Please. Dad wouldn't want me to sit around doing nothing." My throat constricts.

All of the fear, the failing to attend the other time trips, the unfocused way I'm behaving . . . it's for one reason. This is my first time trip since Dad died last month.

Professor March stares at me for what seems like an eternity. Then he rubs his hand across his buzzed hair. "I can respect that. But tell me if you think you won't be able to complete the assignment. Okay?"

"Yes, sir. Thank you."

I walk with him up the hill and through the crumbling outer wall of the ruins, grateful that we don't have to talk anymore. All of the cadets are inside, along with the other two professors. Nobody says a word. The only sounds come from the wind whistling through cracks and our footsteps crunching over broken chunks of marble. We find our team, and I move next to Vika. She gives me a questioning glance. I just fake smile at her again.

Professor Cayhill clears his throat. "Attention, cadets. I'd like a word before we depart."

I stifle a groan. Here we go. Cayhill loves his pompous lectures. He does this on every mission. For some reason he feels the need to flaunt his position as the department chair for our class. I send a silent thanks to whoever assigned me to Professor March's team.

"This is a momentous occasion, your first trip outside of this century. As such, I hope you take this responsibility seriously. The assassination of President Foster was one of the events that led to the Second Civil War. As you complete your assignments today, ponder the sacrifices made, the bloodshed, and the hard work involved in rebuilding our country. Remember, you are a spectator, nothing more. No matter what you may witness today, do nothing to intervene. The timeline is sacred."

Yeah, like we haven't had that pounded into our brains a million times.

Professor March looks sharply in my direction and frowns. I wonder for a moment if he somehow read my mind, then I look away, feeling stupid. He's only a Time Bender. Nobody has more than one Talent.

As the speech concludes, I catch Professor March sighing and checking his watch. The act brings a smile to my face. So I'm not the only one sick of listening to Cayhill.

We split off and follow our team leaders to our assigned departure coordinates. Professor March doesn't go far, leading us to a partially standing wall. "Okay, folks, check your settings. We're shifting to July 4, 2076. Time will be exactly oh nine hundred hours."

I lift my right arm and activate the interface on my silver Chronoband. A small holo-screen hovers over it and I quickly scan the data, making sure the time and date have already been programmed. Techs back at the Academy do this, but we always double check. Talk about a messed up situation if we miss our target time.

"Remember, this is the largest gathering you've ever shifted to," Professor March says when we're all finished. "You will undoubtedly get shoved, so it's imperative you stay with your assigned partner at all times. If you witness any suspicious activity conducted by other unknown Time Benders, alert me. Understood?"

We nod.

"Good. Let's do this. Activate cloaks."

I press the tiny gold button on my collar, along with everyone else. A faint shimmer surrounds our bodies. Most people would think we vanished, or they might see a ripple in the air like that over a flame. The comm-sets allow us to see anyone who's cloaked.

"Fixate date and time in your mind."

I picture the numbers in my head like a calendar.

"Engage Chronobands on my mark."

My fingers float over the activation button and twitch slightly. I force myself to breathe deeply, knowing what comes next. My heart begins to race.

Professor March's voice rings clear and strong. "Three, two, one. Engage."

I press the button.

Instantly I'm swallowed by the Void. It's as if I'm standing in a pitch-black room that's shrouded in silence. I squeeze my eyes shut and hold my breath. My chest tightens and my lungs constrict. I want to breathe so badly, but there's no air. I want to touch something—anything—but I can't. You can't feel anything when you're in between times. It's like I'm alone. Like I'm the only person in the universe.

When it seems like my lungs are about to burst, I emerge in 2076. I blink and wait for time to refocus. The past is bright and alive. Noise floods my senses. Colors swirl. And the smell . . . the dust and decay from moments before is replaced with something musky. It reminds me of the old books I saw once at the Academy's museum. I stand perfectly still, forcing myself to breathe slowly.

My teammates stand frozen as usual. I'm not sure why we're always so quiet after shifting. It's not like the people in the past can hear us. In addition to keeping us hidden, our cloaks mask any sounds we make. Well, stuff like talking and coughing. Nothing we can do about our footsteps or running into objects. Something I figured out fast when I wasn't paying attention and slammed into a glass door on a previous time trip. It scared a woman who was standing nearby.

"This is your last chance to ask any questions," Professor March says. He pauses to peer at each of us. When nobody answers, he replies, "Good, a prepared team . . ."

"Don't screw up," we finish.

Professor March laughs. "Exactly. Okay then, if you don't have any questions, let's head out."

As we step away from the now-intact wall and cross the shiny marble floor, I can't help but check out the place. It's so different from our time. Fancy portraits line the walls. I have to tilt my head up to see the top of the dome hovering above us. There were holograms in my mission schematics, but they can't replace actually being here. It's amazing. A few people are talking in excited tones. I'm surprised they're even in here. I'd figured everyone would be outside.

One of my teammates, Zed, lets out a low whistle as we pass two women. "Damn. Now I'd like to observe *them* for a while."

Vika shoots a withering look at him. "Really Zed? You shouldn't be looking at them like that."

"Why not? It's not like they can hear me. And they'd probably be flattered if they could."

"It doesn't matter if they can't hear your stupid comments," she says, rolling her eyes. "It's rude. Besides, not every female finds you irresistible."

"They don't?" Zed asks in mock anguish. He runs his pale hands through his black hair. "Methinks I must try harder."

Another teammate, Elijah, lets out a snort-laugh. "Man, if they could see your scrawny butt they'd die laughing. Now if they saw me, that'd be a different story." He flexes his muscles to prove his point and grins. His teeth flash in contrast to his dark skin. I might be laughing along with Zed and Elijah, but I'm surprised at how irritated I am. Zed always makes comments like that. But the people in here—and all the people we're about to see—are dead. Ghosts. Whistling at ghosts is messed up.

But what can I say? They're my best friends.

"Settle down, cadets. Focus on the mission," Professor March says with a scowl.

Outside, the landscape is transformed. The crumbling buildings are intact. Red, white, and blue streamers and flags are suspended from every structure. The whole area is packed with people. A man's voice rings out over the speakers, singing the old national anthem. My mouth parts, and I quickly snap it shut. No need to act like a starry-eyed newbie even though this is the biggest event we've been allowed to record. I've seen the old news feed records from this time period. But they didn't prepare me for this. For actually being here.

I try not to gag when we enter the thick of the crowd. I don't know what it is about people in the past. They always have this strange, stale scent clinging to them. The closer we get to the stage set up in front of the Old Civic Center Building, the more we have to push through the ghosts.

"We're almost there," Professor March calls out.

Ahead, I can make out Cayhill and his team climbing the stairs leading up to the stage. They get to record President Foster's death up close. Cayhill's team always gets the best assignments.

We're stuck recording from the audience.

The DTA says crowd shots are important. They give the consumers in our time the "authentic feeling" of being in the past. If the footage recorded today is good enough, DTA techs will splice all of it together to make a more impressive experience for participants of the History Alive Network. Or for those who enter a Sim Game. All they have to do is sit on their asses and pop on a pair of Virtual Lenses. Then they get to pretend they're here. Minus all the work.

"Time to pair up with your partners and assume your positions," Professor March says once we reach our break-off point. "And don't forget to activate your comm-sets once you're there."

Zed squeezes past me and glances at Vika, snickering. "You two lovebirds better behave."

He joins his partner, and they melt into the crowd. Elijah and his partner follow suit.

"Problems?" Professor March asks.

"No, sir," I reply.

Vika just gives him a tight-lipped smile.

"Excellent. I think I'll observe you two first since I have a feeling I'm going to be needed elsewhere soon." He casts a weary look in Zed's direction.

Vika's fingers wrap around mine, and she leads me away. When we're far enough from Professor March, she whispers, "Are you sure everything's all right?"

I give her a quick nod. "I already told you everything's fine."

"Okay, but remember, I've got your back. Always." She gives my hand a reassuring squeeze.

I squeeze her hand back before we separate and activate our comm-sets. I begin to scan the area for other Time Benders. At first nothing shows, but then a light blinks in the corner of my lens. The outline of a body flashes white. That indicates a cloaked Time Bender standing in the distance. Since frequencies are changed every few months, our comm-sets won't be able to penetrate the cloak. "I've got one Unknown to my left, approximately sixty-four feet away," I say, reading the info flashing across the bottom of my lens.

"None here," Vika says.

I continue to scan the area, but I still wonder about the Unknown. I wonder what year he or she is from. We run across them on occasion on our time trips. The DTA rarely overlaps visits to the same time. That doesn't mean someone from our future couldn't be here. I almost wish I could talk to the Unknown, but that's forbidden. It could contaminate whatever point in the timeline they're from.

"Let's begin phase two," Vika says after another minute.

"Be careful," I reply as a man bumps into me. It's a little unnerving being here. There are so many people around us.

We spread out and observe the audience while our comm-sets record. The excitement in the air is contagious. The void inside me doesn't feel as empty now.

The singer finishes and a large man dressed in a black suit hurries across the stage. A hush settles over the crowd as they await the main event.

"Ladies and gentlemen, may I have your attention. I would like to present President Kathleen Foster."

Frenzied cheers erupt when a slender, red-haired woman in a dark blue dress emerges from the Civic Center and steps up to the stage. She waves both hands and flashes a brilliant smile. It's easy to see why the country loved her. I wonder for a moment what would've happened to the country if she didn't die today. How different things would be now.

Vika's voice crystallizes in my ear. "I'm going to move a little closer to the stage."

"Don't go too far," I reply. Exiting our parameters will result in points being deducted from our grade.

"I just want to get some better footage. You know I like to live on the edge," she says, flashing me a smile.

Professor March cuts in. "I need to check in with the others. Maintain position and watch each other's backs. You're doing great so far."

He threads his way through the crowd, toward Zed's area.

I return my attention to the stage. President Foster's voice is almost hypnotic as she speaks. Yeah, I could definitely trust her if I lived in this time. I glance at the info screen on my DataLink.

It's 9:17.

She'll be dead in less than five minutes.

My stomach clenches. I don't know why I'm feeling like this. She's a ghost. She's already dead. All these people are dead.

Just like my dad.

The familiar lump swells in my throat. I try to swallow it back down.

"Have you taken any rear crowd shots?" Vika asks.

I haven't. I've been too busy watching the woman who's about to die. I swivel around and record the sea of eager faces, drinking in the president's shiny words of encouragement. Then I turn back toward the stage.

I spot another Unknown about thirty feet away. I wonder if it's the same one from before. But then the cloak wavers, revealing a male of medium height and build—like me. His brown hair is lighter than mine. He's dressed in a gray jumpsuit.

My heart feels like it's stopped.

"Dad," I whisper. No, it can't be him. I blink a few times, expecting to see nothing but a bunch of dead people. But he's still there, staring at me. Then he turns and slips through an opening in the crowd.

"No!" I yell, taking off after him. "Dad, wait!"

"What are you doing?" Vika asks. "You're not supposed to leave!"

I ignore her. I have to get to Dad. I have to find him before I lose him again.

A small part of me knows I'm sabotaging my grade, but I don't care. I shove my way through the crowd and concentrate on the back of Dad's head. He suddenly stops and whirls around.

I'm maybe five feet away when he says something.

"What?" I call out.

"Save Alora, son."

Then he vanishes.

My eyes dart around. Where did he go? Did he shift back to whatever point in time he came from? Why was he even here? And who is Alora?

My breath comes out in ragged gasps. I spin around, searching for him. He has to be here somewhere.

He *has* to be.

A popping noise sounds, followed by another. President Foster's speech stops. I twist around as she sinks to the floor. Screams shatter the stunned silence.

Chaos erupts as people try to get away, which is pretty much impossible. I remember Vika is alone.

A chill crawls over my skin as I search through the crowd for her. I don't see her. "Vika, where are you?" I yell.

She doesn't answer.

It seems like an eternity of me shoving against people trying to flee the stage area. I glance up at the stage. Ghosts surround President Foster. A few of Cayhill's cadets squeeze around them, getting close-up shots of the president.

But there's something going on near the stage. I make my way over there, nausea rolling inside me. A few people are pointing at the ground. A woman moves to the side, and I finally see what's happened.

Vika is lying on the ground, unmoving.

"No. *No.*" I push my way through, my mind racing. Why did I let her go closer to the stage? I should have stopped her. Everyone closest to the president would have been even more frantic to get away after the shots were fired.

Then I realize something else. Ghosts were looking at her. Her cloak has been deactivated.

I keep moving, but before I get to her, I notice a shimmer floating over her.

An Unknown.

Icy fear rips through my body.

By the time I get to Vika, the cloaked Time Bender is gone. I kneel and pull her crumpled body close. I don't even care that a few ghosts are still gawking at her. "Vika! Can you hear me? Wake up!"

Professor March arrives. "What happened, Bridger?"

I think of Dad's appearance. The message he gave me. Did it really happen? Or did I imagine the whole thing?

"I don't know," I say, looking back at Vika. Her broken comm-set lies next to her head. Blood trickles out of her nose. Her face is scratched. And she's so still.

Professor March gives me a hard stare as he searches for her pulse.

My heart is about to burst from my chest. Please let her be okay. Please.

Professor March's eyes widen. He presses the all-call button on his comm-set and shouts, "Emergency shift! I repeat, emergency shift!"

2

ALORA
APRIL 8, 2013

The steady noise filling the cafeteria fades away as a picture forms in my mind—an image of a man with bloodstained hands and two women. One with blonde hair several shades lighter than mine, and one with hair as dark as the midnight sky. My chest tightens. I dreamed about them last night, just like I have for years. The man is my father, and the only reason I know that is because of the pictures Aunt Grace has of him. I wonder if one of the women is my mother. I don't have a clue. Aunt Grace doesn't have any pictures of her.

Yeah, I know that's weird, but I've been living with Aunt Grace since I was little. I have a few hazy memories from before then, but not much. Flashes of me running in a wooded area. The smell of lavender as my mom would tuck me into bed at night. Little things that don't tell me anything.

And I'm pretty sure I used to live in a big city. Sometimes I get these images of tall buildings that seem to touch the sky, as if I'm in the midst of them looking up. Now this backwoods town is home, including all the small-minded people who inhabit it. Anyone who deviates from their idea of normal is considered too weird to associate with.

Lucky me.

"Earth to Alora. Are you even listening to me?"

A hand waves in front of my face, and I blink several times before turning to my best friend, Sela. "Sorry. What did you say?"

The two girls sitting across from us, Sela's new friends, laugh in a high-pitched twittering that makes me want to stab my ears. Or them.

"Are you okay? You're acting weird," she says.

For an instant, I consider telling her about the dream, but I change my mind. There's no point because I can't remember any details. "I'm okay. I didn't get much sleep last night."

That's close enough to the truth. On the nights I dream about my dad and the mystery ladies, I always wake up with a feeling of dread. Of course, sleep is impossible afterward.

"Right," Sela drawls. She takes a bite of her salad before continuing. "Anyway, I asked if you wanted to practice with us this afternoon. Jess and Miranda decided to try out for the squad too, so I thought we could all work on some cheers together."

"Yeah, Laura, it'll be fun," says the one on the left, Miranda.

"It's Alora," I reply through gritted teeth.

"Oh, right. Sorry." From her tone, I can tell she's not.

I don't understand what Sela sees in Jess and Miranda. They're as deep as a mud puddle. All they do is talk trash about everybody, what guys they like, and clothes. Plus they try to dress matchy all the time. Like now, they're both in tight capris and off-the-shoulder shirts, and last week they each dyed a blue strip into their hair. Seriously. But Sela's mom wormed her way in a local women's club a few months ago, and next thing I knew Sela had two new besties.

I take a deep breath and lean closer to Sela. "I don't know. I really need to study. Aunt Grace will kill me if I fail another test. And I might have to help out at the inn after school." I look at the ignored history book on my lap, feeling guilty. Aunt Grace told me she didn't need any help this afternoon. We aren't expecting any guests.

When I peek at Sela's face, she's wearing an expression that reminds me of an impatient parent dealing with an irritating kid. "You said you would."

"I know, but I'm not good at that kind of thing."

"How do you know that? You've never tried."

Jess rolls her eyes and sighs dramatically. "Oh, come on, Sela, you're acting like her mom."

I bite my lip. That hurts because I have no clue how my mom would react in this situation.

"She knows what I mean. And didn't you say your aunt was okay with you trying out?"

"Yeah, but she wants me to keep my grades up too." That's the truth. Aunt Grace wasn't sure about me going out for the squad, but Sela kept asking her and she finally said it might be good for me. Maybe I can get Aunt Grace to tell Sela that she changed her mind. Or something else. Like the fact I'm barely passing history.

I failed my last two history tests, and Aunt Grace threatened to ground me if I didn't make at least a C on this one. She says I never did that badly when she homeschooled me, which isn't exactly true. I don't know what's wrong. I'm making good grades in all of my other classes, but when it comes to history, no matter how much I study, very little sticks.

Sela runs a hand through her auburn hair, tucking it behind her ear. "Well, I think you should come with us. You know you want to."

I want to tell her I don't want to, but I stay quiet. Sela has been bugging me nonstop for weeks to go out for the squad with her. Her mom's been preaching how she'll have lots of new friends if she makes the team—like Mrs. Perkins had when she was in high school. Never mind that I was the only person who would have anything to do with Sela when her family first moved here back in November.

"Well, this has been fun, but we've gotta run," Jess says. She exchanges a glance with Miranda and they both stand.

"Yeah, I'm gonna puke if I have to stay in here another minute. This place reeks," Miranda says, patting her perfectly straight hair. "You coming, Sela?"

Sela seems torn. Finally she says, "Y'all go ahead. We'll catch up to you in a few minutes."

After they're gone, I say, "You didn't have to wait for me."

"I know, but I want to. You really look out of it."

"Wow, thanks, but if you wanted to go with your friends, you could have." I poke around at my salad, not wanting to eat any more of it. I'd kill for a cheeseburger and fries right now, but Sela's been on this super health food kick for a few months now, trying to lose an extra twenty pounds. She talked me into trying her way of eating since I've felt so crappy lately.

"They could be your friends, too, if you gave them a chance."

"I've tried. They don't like me."

"That's not true."

"Really? Do they ever ask to hang out with me? Do they ever text me? No." I hate how whiny I sound, but it's the truth. I just don't understand why Sela doesn't see it.

She starts to say something else, but instead cocks her head to the side and looks behind me. Grinning, she props her elbows on the table, laces her fingers together, and rests her chin on her hands. Then she proceeds to stare at me.

"So," she drawls out after a few seconds. "What's the deal with Trevor?"

"What're you talking about?"

"He was totally checking you out just now."

I shake my head. That's impossible. Trevor Monroe would never check me out. He and his evil sister Kate hate me because their mother hates Aunt Grace. I remember how he and Kate spread lies about me when I first started school this year. Things like I was some poor white trash who Aunt Grace took in years ago, and that she wasn't even my real aunt. "Nope. Hell would freeze over first."

Sela leans back in her seat, grinning. "No, my dear, he was definitely looking at you."

"No way," I reply, looking at my faded jeans and plain pink shirt. "And even if he was, there's nothing sexy here."

"Are you kidding? I don't understand why every guy here isn't fighting over you."

Something Aunt Grace would call *an unladylike snort* pops out of me. "Fight over me? That's a good one."

She huffs and crosses her arms over her chest. "Well they should. Of course, they'd never pay any attention to me."

I shift uncomfortably in my seat. It bugs me when Sela puts herself down. She's worked to lose weight since moving here, but she has a hard time seeing the change because she's not a stick like Jess and Miranda.

"Well, if Trevor was looking at me, it's probably because he's trying to figure out another way to start some crap."

"Aw, come on." She pauses to think, biting on her lip like she does when she doesn't know what to say. "You're an awesome person. I think you should talk to him."

"Oh, no. I'm not even going there. Besides, Naomi would flip if she thought I had a thing for him."

"I heard they're splitsville again." She raises her eyebrows at me, expecting a positive response.

"Please drop it, okay?"

"You need to live a little. Quit worrying all the time."

I wish I could, but Sela doesn't know everything. Sure, she knows how much I hate this stupid town. Other things, no. She doesn't know how much I need a scholarship to go to college. How Aunt Grace worries all the time about how to pay the bills. How I can't even remember what my parents look like. Those are things nobody knows, and I'm so sick of having to keep them to myself. Suddenly it seems like the cafeteria is shrinking, and I can't get enough air.

"Um, I forgot something at my locker," I manage to say. I grab my backpack and tray and stand so quickly my chair almost flips backward.

"You okay? You look sick." Sela's face contorts in worry.

"I'm fine. I'll see you in class."

When I pass Trevor's table, I hear laughter. I risk a peek and lock onto a few guys staring in my direction, including Trevor. Warmth blooms over my face, and I duck my head. I always turn an obnoxious shade of pink when I'm embarrassed.

That's when I promptly run into Naomi Burton—Trevor's girlfriend. Her tray flies to the floor with a crash, drawing everyone's attention in the cafeteria.

Kill me now.

Naomi whirls around and hisses, "You stupid idiot!"

"Hey, Alora, do you need to go back to kindergarten to learn how to put your tray up right?" someone asks. I glance up, and of course it's Kate, sitting a few feet away with her friends.

If I thought I was red before, I must be scarlet by now. Laughter thunders in my ears. I mumble an apology and try to help Naomi clean up. The remains of her salad are strewn all over the place, and one piece is stuck to the front of my shirt. I peel it off, horrified to see I'm stained with dressing.

"Just go," Naomi says, slinging the last bits of lettuce back on her tray.

Before I can apologize again, I glance at her face and stop. It's splotchy and her eyes are glassy, like she's been crying. Realizing it would probably be a good idea to leave, I quickly throw away my trash and rush out of the cafeteria.

I don't stop until I get outside. The air is as thick as a hot soup, but I don't care. I breathe deeply. The smell of freshly cut grass tickles my nose, and I sneeze several times. Still, it's better than being inside. I can't believe I crashed into Naomi. I can just imagine what everyone will say once I get to my next class. They'll call me Clumsy Alora or something equally stupid. It'll be the beginning of the school year all over. All that work at trying to blend in destroyed in seconds.

I check my phone. Class starts in ten minutes. Jeez, I wish I had more time out here. Or better yet, I wish I could just leave.

I pass a few students while heading to my favorite tree on the front lawn and sit on the side facing the street. I like it that way—it makes me feel invisible. The bark is scratchy through my shirt, so I lean forward and prop my elbows on my legs.

I try to forget everything, but that test still looms in my mind. I should study some more, but I just don't want to. Instead, I pull my purple sketchbook out of my backpack and flip to the last drawing. It's an unfinished one of my dad. I'm proud of how it's turning out, but it needs more work.

I started drawing when I was around eight or nine. Those sketches were okay. Then Aunt Grace let me take some art classes, back when she could still afford stuff like that, and after that my drawings got way better. I work for a few minutes before the heat saps what little energy I have. I put away the sketchbook and yawn.

Stupid school. Three more hours and then I can leave. I wish I could go home now and take a nap. That would be heavenly.

Leaning my head back against the tree, I close my eyes and concentrate on the soft birdcalls serenading me, on the voices drifting over the gentle breeze. I picture my bed, hear it calling my name. Yeah, I wish I was there right now. I wish this day was over.

That would be so nice.

"Alora! Where on God's green earth have you been?"

My eyes fly open, and I sit up to find Aunt Grace standing over me. My eyes dance wildly from her worried face to my bedroom.

My bedroom!

Afternoon sunlight shines through the window, casting shadows across the pale purple walls. I breathe in the scent of lavender from the air freshener Aunt Grace keeps in here. My fingers grip the soft comforter on my bed. It's real. I'm really here.

But how did I get here?

3

BRIDGER
MARCH 11, 2146

As soon as the shift is complete, I push my eye lenses back. The sun is shining too damn bright. Professor March yells into his comm-set, "I need a med team stat!"

I run my hands along Vika's face. "Come on, Vik," I whisper. "Please wake up."

Other than the scratches and blood trickling from her nose, she could be sleeping. Deep down, I know better. She's not moving. Or breathing.

Professor Cayhill and some other cadets gather around us. Their voices crash into me like a tidal wave. I block them out. All I can see is Vika, still unresponsive. All because of me.

I feel like I'm dying.

Someone tries to pull me away, but I jerk my arms back. They're not going to make me leave her.

"Bridger, control yourself," Professor March barks. He gets right in my face, so close that I can see the fear in his eyes. "I need you to move. The medics are here."

Three emergency medics have appeared next to us. Space Benders. I stagger to my feet and back away. They move in and kneel over Vika, trying to stabilize her until an emergency med shuttle arrives. It shouldn't take long. They're equipped to travel a hell of a lot faster than regular shuttles. I just wish one was here right now.

Elijah and Zed stand with the cadets on the other side of Vika. Elijah tries to break away from the group. Professor Diaz stops him before he gets two steps. Probably for the best. I don't want to talk to anyone right now. All I want is for Vika to wake up. I need Vika to wake up.

Professor Cayhill storms over, his face blotched red. "What the fure happened back there, Creed?"

I don't know what to say. I've never screwed up before on an assignment. Ever. I've always done exactly what the professors asked me to do. *Every single time.*

Except for today. And Vika is paying the price.

"Do you know what you've done?" Professor Cayhill asks, pointing a finger at me. "Now I've got to go back and erase the memories of all those ghosts thanks to you!"

The words are like knives cutting into my soul. I look down at the ground. Cayhill is right. Everything is my fault.

"Calm down. The cadets don't need to see you like this," Professor March says to him.

"How can I calm down? I've never had something like this happen. And where were you, Telfair? How could you let this happen?"

While Professor March says something else to the prick in a lower voice, a too-familiar sensation begins to build in my chest. The sense of heaviness. The sense of not being able to breathe. I walk away from the professors, snatching off my comm-set and running my hands through my hair. I freeze when my eyes flick to Vika again. The medics are still trying to revive her. It's the sight of her legs stretched out below them that pushes me too far. One is bent at an awkward angle.

I can't deal with this. I need to get out of here.

Now.

My feet move as if they're controlled by another person. I have to get away.

"Bridger, get back here," Professor March shouts.

I ignore him and keep running.

Footsteps pound behind me. The part of my brain that's still capable of rational thought screams for me to stop. I ignore it. I can't stay there. Not with everyone staring at me, trying to figure out what I did to screw up the whole mission.

For once, I'm glad Dad is dead so he can't see what I've done.

The thought of him makes me stop. He's the reason I left my post in the first place. I'd almost forgotten about that. I have to tell someone.

I turn around as Professor March catches up, glaring. "I don't know what's going on in that head of yours, but you're going to tell me exactly what happened back there."

Behind him, Professor Diaz shepherds everyone toward the Academy shuttle. For a second, I wish I could be with them, not tangled in this mess.

"Come on, Bridger, what happened? And don't even think about lying to me." He folds his arms across his chest like he does when he won't take no for an answer.

That stings. I've never lied to him or any of my professors. You can't if you want to be the best in your class. He knows that.

But what if he doesn't believe me? Before I can stop myself, I tell him everything. The expressions that flicker across Professor March's face would almost be comical if the circumstances were different. By the time I'm finished, he's shaking his head.

"So you think I'm lying?" I ask, feeling heat flush my face. "It's the truth. I swear. Dad was there. He told me to save some chick named Alora. If you don't believe me, check my vid feed. Or better yet, go back and see for yourself."

I don't know why I tell him to go back. The DTA has to approve all emergency shifts to investigate an event. Professor March couldn't just go because he wanted to go. That would be against the law. Just like it's against the law for Time Benders to shift to the past to witness any little thing.

Professor March runs his hands over his head. "I don't doubt that you *think* you saw him."

"I did. He spoke to me." My fist hurts from how hard I'm rubbing it. I force my hands apart.

Even though Dad was cloaked when he appeared, our comm-sets can detect his heat signature. I have proof.

"It's not that simple, Bridger." He takes a breath and says, "Look, I don't want you to say anything about seeing Leithan for now." The first thing that pops in my head is that's crazy, but he holds up a hand. "No, listen to me. There are some things I can't tell you about your father's work, but I need you to trust me."

"But—"

"I mean it, Bridger. Don't say anything yet. It's what your father would've wanted. Am I understood?"

I have no idea if that's true, but I do know he always told me to trust Professor March. Always. So I nod.

A relieved smile crosses his face. "Good. Now there's one more thing."

"What's that, sir?"

"You're not going to like this." He reaches out for my shoulder, but then his hand veers quickly toward my neck. I feel a sharp sting. "I've been ordered to sedate you."

I want to run away again, but the sedative is already coursing through my body. My legs turn to rubber. Professor March catches me as I fall against his chest.

"Trust me," he whispers as the world grows dark. "I promised Leithan I'd look after you. Everything will be fine."

"Mr. Creed, can you hear me?"

I blink a few times and try to focus on the man standing by my side. Dark hair, too-smooth skin, perfect teeth, dressed completely in white. Definitely a doc.

"I need you to keep still, okay?" His tone is friendly, but his eyes are cold. I feel like the lowest form of slime under his gaze. My mouth is dry as a desert, so I nod and try to sit up. The doc puts his hand on my chest. "Not yet. I'm running one last test."

My eyes flick down my body. I'm dressed in my black Skivvies and nothing else. Silver med patches are attached to my arms, legs, and chest. I examine the rest of the room. Everything is too bright. Bright white walls and floor. Bright lights. Completely familiar because we have to have a checkup after every time trip.

I'm back at the Academy.

So who's this guy? I've never seen him before.

Memories of the time trip fill my mind like I've entered a Sim Game. Only this is real. I let out a groan. This is a nightmare come to life. My girlfriend was seriously hurt, and I don't know how she's doing. Plus I saw my dead father. And Professor March doesn't want me to tell anybody. But I need answers. Now.

Before I can ask the doc what's going on, he begins tugging at the med patches. Each one stings as he snatches them off my skin.

I clear my throat. "Do you know what's going on with Vika Fairbanks?"

He yanks the last patch off particularly hard. "I'm not at liberty to discuss anything."

What the hell? The docs here usually are full of questions. They want all the details of our time trips. One even confessed to being jealous because she can't travel like we can. She said she wasn't lucky enough to inherit one of the Talent Genes—those that allow some people to travel through time, travel anywhere with just a thought, or read minds.

I sit up and swing my legs off the side of the exam table. My vision swims from moving so fast. I close my eyes until the room quits tilting.

"Be careful," the doc says. "I gave you a dose of Calmer while you were sedated."

I guess I should be grateful. With everything that's happened today, I'd be wilding out without it. "Thanks. So, can I go now?"

"No. Chancellor Tyson is on his way to see you."

My mouth drops open. "Why?"

Even though Chancellor Doran Tyson is the head of the Academy, we rarely see him on campus. He's always at public functions that promote the Academy. Huge banquets put on once a month when new Sim Games are debuted or another Virtual Trip is about to be uploaded to the History Alive Network. Dad said that Chancellor Tyson loves pissing off the Purists by flaunting the positive effects of time travel on our economy. But dealing with day-to-day matters is something he usually leaves to his assistant chancellors or the professors.

Unless something bad is about to go down.

The doc's eyes seem to harden even more. "I said I'm not at liberty to discuss."

"Fine," I snap. What a prick. It wouldn't kill him to tell me something.

Then it occurs to me that things with Vika might not be so good. She wasn't breathing the last time I saw her. No, it can't be that.

It can't.

The doc taps something on his DataPad and inclines his head toward a small table next to the wall. "You can get dressed."

He leaves the room without another look at me. I hop off the table and unfold my uniform. It smells faintly like sweat and Vika's favorite perfume. I inhale the cherry scent, feeling sick. I can't get the image of her lying on the cracked pavement out of my head. I want to see her smiling and laughing. Alive. She can't be dead. Maybe she's in critical condition and Chancellor Tyson wants to tell me personally since Dad died last month. I hope that's the worst it could be.

After I'm dressed, I walk by the door, but it doesn't whoosh open automatically like it should when I get within a foot of the sensor. Definitely not good.

There's nothing I can do. I'm locked in here. I don't have my DataLink, so I can't talk to anybody or look up any info about the trip in the DataFeed. Then again, it wouldn't be on there. Chancellor Tyson would see to that. You never see negative news about the Academy.

I've probably done a hundred laps around the room by the time Chancellor Tyson enters. He's dressed in his usual black Academy uniform.

Professor March is with him. I feel a weird mix of resentment and relief. Mad that Professor March sedated me the way he did. Glad that he's here to buffer whatever Chancellor Tyson has to say.

The last time I spoke to the chancellor was at Dad's memorial service. He firmly shook my hand and told me if I ever needed anything to not hesitate to ask.

I'm hesitating now.

His face is like a storm of anger and sorrow. He stands in front of me, hands on hips, and stares. Again, I feel like the lowest form of life on earth.

"Mr. Creed, we have some questions for you."

The door opens again and a gray-haired man dressed in a navy military uniform enters. I blink and glance at Professor March, trying not to look surprised. It's General Thomas Anderson—the head of the Department of Temporal Affairs' military division. He was Dad's superior officer. He's also the jerk who refused to tell us how Dad actually died because his final mission was classified.

General Anderson shakes hands with Chancellor Tyson and Professor March. I want to ignore him when he stretches his hand toward me. But I can hear Dad's voice telling me to man up.

"Bridger, son, it's been too long since I've seen you."

My teeth grind together when he says *son*.

"I won't keep you long. I just need you to answer a few questions, then you'll be free to go."

Really? I thought Chancellor Tyson was in charge at the Academy.

General Anderson coughs in his hand before saying, "Now, it's come to my attention that you thought you saw Leithan while you were on your time trip. Is this correct?"

My eyes flick to Professor March. His face is blank. No help there. So do I tell the truth or lie like Professor March wanted? And I wonder why they're even asking me. Surely they've already sent an investigative team back to observe the events. They should already know Dad was there.

"Bridger," Chancellor Tyson interrupts. "We heard what you said on the vid feed. Did you really see your father or did you *think* you saw him?"

"Why are you asking me this? Haven't you investigated already?" I ask.

Chancellor Tyson and General Anderson exchange an odd glance with each other. I frown, wondering what is going on.

General Anderson says, "We did send a team back, but they didn't note any evidence of your father being there."

My mouth opens and I quickly shut it. That can't be right. I know what I saw. My dad was there. He *was*.

Or was he? What if I just imagined the whole thing? They want to know what I *thought* I saw. If I'm crazy or not. That's why Professor March asked me to deny seeing Dad. He's looking out for my career. The Academy can't have a nutso Time Bender. But, still, I hate lying.

"It's understandable if you imagined seeing him. After all, you lost him recently." General Anderson's voice is smooth and reassuring. Just like it was when he refused to give me any answers after Dad died.

I wonder why he's even here. What does it matter to him if I saw Dad on this time trip? Does it have anything to do with the classified mission Dad was on? I have to find out. "Was Dad at the Foster Assassination for his last assignment?"

General Anderson's lips flatten to a thin line. "I can't divulge the nature of Leithan's last mission, but I can reassure you he never shifted to the Foster Assassination at any point during his education or career."

I'm not sure what's going on, but I don't believe him. Still, I don't want them to think I'm insane. "Maybe you're right. Maybe I just thought I saw him. It was really crowded."

General Anderson smiles. "That's what I thought. And can you tell us your version of the events that happened there?"

I want to ask why doesn't he just question his team that went back to witness everything, but I don't. Instead I quickly relate how I left my assigned position, and how I discovered Vika was hurt.

Chancellor Tyson asks, "Is there anything else you want to add?"

"No, sir."

"Okay, that's all I need," General Anderson says. He shakes hands with Chancellor Tyson and Professor March again. "Good to see you two, though I wish it wasn't under these circumstances."

After he leaves, Chancellor Tyson gives me a long, hard look. "There's something else we need to discuss before you're dismissed."

I begin to rub my fist. This is bad. I shake my head and step back. "It's Vika, isn't it?"

"I'm afraid so. I wanted to be the one to inform you that Miss Fairbanks is in serious condition. The med staff is doing everything they can for her, but she's in a coma and there is little chance she will regain consciousness."

No. This can't be happening. Not to happy, smiling, always-there-for-me Vika. She has to wake up. She *has* to. "I don't understand. How could this happen? Can't you do anything else for her?"

Chancellor Tyson shakes his head and says, "Bridger, she was trampled by hundreds of ghosts. Her injuries are quite severe."

"This . . . this is all my fault," I choke out.

Professor March is suddenly by my side. "Bridger, it's not your fault. She left her position on her own free will, and she wasn't trying to follow you. It looked like she was trying to get a better view of the president."

I hear what he's saying, but it doesn't help. If I hadn't followed Dad—if it *was* Dad—I could have made sure Vika didn't go too close to that damn stage. She'd be fine.

I wish I could change things. Before I can stop myself, I blurt, "Let's go back. We can stop all of this from happening. Not a lot of time has passed yet."

"No," Chancellor Tyson says. "You, better than anyone, should know that's not an option."

My hands shake, so I ball them at my sides. He's right. That's the first rule of time travel. The timeline is sacred. Nothing can be changed, ever. After Dad died, I wanted to go back and save him too. Just like a lot of people wanted to go back and save their loved ones before me. It was a huge source of conflict a few years before the turn of the century when the public learned that genetic manipulation had resulted in people who could travel to the past.

Then the Department of Temporal Affairs was established. Rules were created and order was imposed. All emergency trips to the recent past have to be completed by a special team from the DTA who only observe the events. The past has to stay the same or the world we live in today could be destroyed.

It doesn't make the hurt any easier, though. Pain rips through my chest, one stab after another. Professor March said it wasn't my fault, but it doesn't feel that way. It should've been me.

My voice sounds hollow as I ask, "Can I see her?"

"I'm sorry. Only immediate family can visit her." Chancellor Tyson says, then he clears his throat. "And there's one more thing."

Professor March scowls at Chancellor Tyson. "Do you have to sentence him now?"

Sentence? What sentence? I look between them. It's like a bad dream, like I'm not really here.

"I have to," Chancellor Tyson says. "Bridger, I'm sorry, but because you violated orders and left your position, and because your partner was seriously injured, I have to suspend you from the Academy, pending a full investigation."

4

ALORA
APRIL 8, 2013

"Well, are you gonna answer me or just look around the room?" Aunt Grace asks. Her hands are on her hips and the worried expression she wore moments before has morphed into one that screams I'm in trouble.

I close my eyes. The last thing I remember was sitting under the tree at school. I don't remember going to my afternoon classes, or how I made it through the history test. Not even riding home with Sela after school. A sick sensation churns in my stomach.

"Don't even think about lying, young lady. I can practically hear the excuses racing through your head."

What can I say? *So, Aunt Grace, funny thing is I don't remember how I got here.* That'll go over real well. I glance at the alarm clock on the small table next to my bed. It reads 4:17 in neon green numbers. Jeez, I've lost nearly four hours.

Aunt Grace runs her hands over her light brown hair, trying to smooth the flyaway pieces back against the soft curls. "I nearly had a heart attack when Sela called wanting to know how you were."

"What? Why'd she do that?" I ask, even though I'm not sure I want the answer. I bet I made a complete idiot of myself.

"Don't play dumb, Alora. I swear, I can't believe you of all people skipped school."

Wait, I ditched my classes? This is worse than I thought. I cover my face with my hands.

"Do you know what you've put me through for the last hour? I'll tell you. Hell. First I got the call from Sela and she said you were acting weird at lunch. She thought you were sick and told me to pick you up early. Then the school called and said you didn't bother going to your afternoon classes. You have detention tomorrow, by the way."

Oh, this is getting better by the minute.

"I nearly went crazy trying to figure out where you were. I've been everywhere looking for you!" she exclaims, waving her hands all over the place. "I was fixing to call the police to report you missing."

Yep, I'm dead. Aunt Grace is going all drama queen on me.

"So, what do you have to say for yourself?" She finishes by crossing her arms and tapping her foot.

Silence louder than any screaming hangs between us. I can't believe I did this. Cutting class isn't something I'd do. It took a lot of convincing to get Aunt Grace to even let me go to public school this year.

I'm saved from having to answer by a shrill horn honking. Aunt Grace checks out my window. "Oh, shit."

This can't be good. Aunt Grace never cusses unless she's really upset. I hurry to her side. Parked on the circle driveway in front of the house is a gleaming white Cadillac. I try not to cuss myself.

It's Trevor and Kate Monroe's mother, Celeste. She also happens to be Aunt Grace's sister-in-law. Celeste's husband is the president of one of the banks in town, so she thinks she's too good for most everybody, especially us. She's been bugging Aunt Grace to sell this house back to her ever since Darrel, Aunt Grace's husband and Celeste's brother, passed away eleven years ago. She thinks it's a disgrace that Darrel and Aunt Grace turned the Evans family ancestral home into a bed-and-breakfast inn and she wants it back. Bad. Aunt Grace says hell will freeze over before she gives in to Celeste.

Aunt Grace whirls around, fixing her ice-blue eyes on me. "We're not finished."

I follow her as she heads out of my room. I don't want to be around Aunt Grace when she's in this kind of mood, but I don't want her to face Celeste alone, either. Celeste has a way of making Aunt Grace feel like crap. I should know. Kate does the same thing to me whenever she gets the chance at school. I close my eyes, remembering Kate's bitchy comment back in the cafeteria.

The doorbell chimes when we're halfway down the stairs. Aunt Grace's back stiffens, like she's getting ready to head into a fierce battle. I hope it's not that bad. Who knows? Maybe this time Celeste is here to make peace. Maybe she's decided to be nicer to her brother's widow.

Or pigs could fly.

At the bottom of the stairs, Aunt Grace fusses with the flowers on the antique foyer table and straightens the mirror hanging over it, and then she smoothes down her hair. "Do I look okay?"

I give her a reassuring smile. "Yes, you always do."

Aunt Grace nods and opens the door. "Hello, Celeste," she says in a too-high voice. "What brings you out here today?"

Celeste gives Aunt Grace a condescending smile. "Why, Grace, I tried to call you several times today but you never answered." She sweeps past Aunt Grace like she owns the place, her floral perfume filling the area. Kate follows her. Suddenly, coming downstairs with Aunt Grace doesn't seem like it was a good idea. I tug at my T-shirt, wishing it wasn't so wrinkled. Both Celeste and Kate look like they could have stepped out of a fashion magazine. Celeste is wearing a killer red dress and her dark hair is pulled up in a complicated style. Kate has on a pair of denim capris that hug every curve and a gold shirt that would probably look hideous on anyone else. Of course, it's perfect on her.

Celeste takes in the area and walks slowly toward the dining room that's just off the foyer. Her heels click on the hardwood floor when she steps off the oriental rug. "Anyway, Kate and I were running errands and I thought I'd stop by for a bit. I haven't seen you in a few weeks, have I?"

"No, I don't think so," Aunt Grace replies. She's wearing the fake smile she usually reserves for extremely annoying guests. "How have y'all been?"

"Oh, busy as usual. Rob and I just got back from the Bahamas last week. He took me there for my birthday. And Trevor and Kate have been great."

At the mention of her name, Kate glances up from her phone and gives us a thin smile. What a fake. Then she makes eye contact with me. From her look, I can tell she's just noticed I am in the room with them. A malicious smirk replaces the smile.

"Alora, where were you this afternoon? I didn't see you in history."

Heat floods my face. "I . . . wasn't feeling too well."

Do I have to sound so lame?

"Really?" Kate asks. "I heard that you cut class."

Celeste gasps. "Oh my goodness. Is that true?"

Just great. First I knock Naomi's tray out of her hands in front of the whole cafeteria, and now Kate is humiliating me in front of her mom. She probably thinks Aunt Grace doesn't know and wants to get me in trouble. I try to think of some brilliant comeback, something to illustrate her immaturity, but my brain won't cooperate.

"Alora wasn't feeling well." Aunt Grace's voice has a razor's edge as she stares at Celeste. I gape at Aunt Grace, both happy and mortified. I could fist bump her for standing up for me, yet I could die because she *had* to stick up for me. I can imagine what Kate is thinking. *Look at Alora, having to get her aunt to make excuses for her. How pathetic.*

"Right, she wasn't feeling well," Celeste echoes with a shrug. "Now if she did skip, I do hope you punish her. That's such unbecoming behavior, don't you agree? Of course, Kate would never do something like that."

Aunt Grace is as still as a statue. She takes a few slow breaths and says, "Of course not. Kate would never *think* to do something like that."

The two women stare daggers at each other, their smiles never leaving their faces. It's like a contest to see who can kill the other first by false friendliness.

Finally Celeste checks her slender silver watch and lets out a regretful sounding sigh. "Oh dear, time's gotten away from me. Kate has to be at tumbling practice by six. I'll be so glad when her car is fixed and I don't have to chauffer her around anymore." Celeste's gaze flicks from Aunt Grace to me. "Did you ever get Alora something to drive?"

"Not. Yet."

I want to melt into the floor. Celeste knows I turned sixteen two months ago. And I'm sure she knows Aunt Grace didn't have the extra money to buy me a car of my own.

"Oh, what a shame. Maybe you can get her something soon. Well, Kate, are you ready?"

Kate rolls her eyes. "Yes, Mama. I've been ready."

Celeste strides back to the front door, but pauses as she reaches out her hand to open it. "Before I forget," she says, turning to face Aunt Grace again. "Have you reconsidered selling the house? Rob got a huge bonus at work, so I can add another thousand to my last offer."

And there it is—the real reason for this so-called visit. Gag me.

"No, Celeste. I've already told you Darrel and I worked too hard to build up this business, and I have no desire to give it up." Aunt Grace isn't even trying to pretend to be nice anymore. Her words are coated with ice.

"Are you sure about that? I've heard business has been slow for a while."

I can't believe her nerve. With those words, Aunt Grace seems to visibly deflate. It makes me want to slap Celeste, but Aunt Grace would never let me.

"Things are fine, Celeste. I don't need your money."

"Oh, I think otherwise. You'll come around eventually." She opens the door and lets Kate out first. "I'll talk to you soon."

"Not if I can help it," Aunt Grace mutters. As soon as the front door closes, she slumps down on the bottom step of the stairs. "I know I say this every time she stops by, but I can't believe she and Darrel share genes."

I sit next to her and rub her back. At least this visit was better than the last. I remember how Celeste ranted the whole time about how the house should belong to her. Aunt Grace thinks Celeste is bipolar or something.

Anyway, Celeste is determined to get the house back. From what Aunt Grace told me, Celeste and Darrel's grandmother was the last owner of the house before she willed the entire estate to Darrel. Celeste was seriously pissed because her grandmother didn't leave her anything, but Aunt Grace said that's because Celeste never came around unless she wanted something. When Darrel died of cancer, Celeste thought Aunt Grace would turn the house over to her because it had been in her family for generations. Aunt Grace refused.

But what if Celeste is right? Money has been tight around here for a few years, but Aunt Grace never said anything about it being so bad that she'd have to sell the place.

I'm afraid to ask, but I have to know the truth. "Are things as bad as Celeste makes them out to be?"

Aunt Grace doesn't look at me. She stares straight ahead, unmoving for a few seconds, then she nods. "Yeah, things aren't so great."

My stomach twists more than a pretzel. "Are you going to sell the inn?"

"I don't know. I don't want to, but if business doesn't pick up soon, I'll have to do something. The bank doesn't care if I can't get customers. I have to pay, or they'll foreclose the property."

Even though Darrel inherited the house, there wasn't a lot of money in the estate. They had to take out a loan to cover the cost of the renovations for the bed-and-breakfast, which Aunt Grace is still paying for to this day.

I can't think of anything brilliant to say, so I stick with, "That seriously sucks."

"Yes," Aunt Grace says, rubbing her forehead. "It does suck."

I start to stand, but she puts a hand on my leg. "Hold up, missy. I haven't forgotten about your little stunt earlier."

Great. I was hoping she had forgotten. "Okay," I drawl out. "What are you going to do to me?"

She frowns at me. "Something's not right. I don't understand why you'd skip class. You've called me before when you didn't feel well. Why skip now?"

The truth fills my mouth, trying to force its way out, but I swallow it back. If I tell her what really happened—that I don't remember how I got home—she'll probably want to drag me to the doctor. That means lots of tests and bills she can't afford. I can't do that to her. Not when it's probably nothing. I haven't been sleeping well lately, after all.

So I lie. "I don't know. I really didn't feel well, so I just left."

5

It's my fault. All of it.

Those words pound in my skull with each step I take. I hurry down the hallway leading from the exam room to the elevators. I keep my head lowered, ignoring the few people I pass. But I can hear the whispers. Hear Vika's name on their lips.

By the time I get to the elevator, I want to tear my hair out. At least I'm alone. I don't know if I could stand having to ride with someone else. Even for the few seconds it takes to get from the third floor to the lobby.

The silver door shuts with a hiss. Then a feminine voice asks, "What level?"

"One," I snap. I check my DataLink for the time. It's almost five in the afternoon. After Chancellor Tyson suspended me, he returned my DataLink and told me I have one hour to clear off the campus. I don't plan to take that long. Most of the other cadets should still be in class or returning from whatever time trip they've been on today. I have no intention of staying around long enough to face them.

As I cross the grassy area between the Academy's glass and steel main building to my quarters in Phoenix Hall, I keep replaying the day's events. Chasing Dad. Seeing Vika lying on the ground. Suddenly I can't breathe. A cool wind blows, but I feel like I'm on fire. The doc should've given me a larger dose of Calmer.

I stop just before going inside my building and lean against the brick wall. Breathe in, breathe out. In, out, in, out. Focus. Just focus.

It's weird how my life is falling apart, but everything around me still seems normal. The girls' hall and the academic building still overlook the eastern part of the campus to my left. The Rockies still slice across my view to the right.

A few Nulls are weeding the flowerbeds between the buildings. My heart races as I watch the smooth rhythm in which they work. They're dressed entirely in gray. Their faces are covered by a shield that keeps them from being recognized. They're criminals. Those whose past actions can't be redeemed in the eyes of the North American Federation. They've had their minds completely wiped. They're now brainless drones. Little more than slaves for the government.

What if that's my sentence after the Academy finishes its investigation?

I check my DataLink again. I'm down to fifty minutes. I square my shoulders and hurry inside.

It doesn't take long to get to my apartment—it's on the first floor. I pause just outside the door, hoping Elijah and Zed aren't here. Facing them right now would be too hard.

No such luck. Both of them are sitting in uncomfortable silence on the black couch in the living area. They're watching a woman dressed in a navy suit talking to someone through her DataLink. It's my mother.

I close my eyes and swear under my breath. Why does she of all people have to be here? But I can't just stand here. I've got to get my things.

Elijah sees me first and springs to his feet. "Man, where have you been? Have you seen Vika?"

"Yeah, Creed, what happened back there?" Zed asks, joining us.

I almost answer them, but Mom spots me. Her face takes on a hard edge as she says, "He's here. I've got to go."

I shake my head and push past them. In my bedroom, I search through the top drawer of my dresser until I find the brown box containing my stash of Calmer. I grab a vial and inject the gold liquid in the right side of my neck. My muscles loosen up instantly. The pressure on my chest disappears.

Outside, I hear Mom ordering Elijah and Zed to leave even though they live here. I can't believe her nerve. She has no authority here. But tell her that. She's a big shot artifact retrieval expert for the Department of Temporal Affairs. She's used to getting her way.

That's one reason I haven't used a home pass in over a month. I can barely stand to stay in the same room with her, much less the same apartment. And now I'm about to have to do just that. I don't know if I can.

Mom's heels crash like thunder as she crosses the living area. This is one of the few times I wish I could bend space.

She stops in the doorway and studies my room. Her nose wrinkles like she's disgusted. I didn't make the bed this morning or pick up my dirty uniforms. "This," she finally says, her eyes snapping back to me, "is unacceptable."

"What is?" I ask. My face grows warm despite the Calmer I just took. That's the effect she usually has on me.

"Everything." She crosses the threshold and points at the mess. "I raised you better than this. Your room is a disgrace. And to top things off, I get called out of a very important briefing because my son decided to wild out on a time trip. Do you know how this could affect my position? Or what about your brother? He could get assigned to an inferior professor like Telfair because of this!"

Her voice has risen to a piercing screech by the time she finishes. The typical beginning of a Morgan Creed rant. I don't need this. Not now.

I try to tune her out and pack my clothes while she bitches. But one thing she says catches my attention. I drop the shirt I was holding and face her. My hands begin to shake, so I clench them at my sides. "What did you say about Dad?"

Her eyes narrow. "I said I can't believe you're still so hung up over your good-for-nothing father. He's dead, Bridger, and he's never coming back. So for you to think he visited you on your little trip is beyond ridiculous. Besides, he's not worth your devotion. In case you forgot, he left us for another woman."

I sink down on the bed and run my hands over my face. Unbelievable. After everything that happened today, she has to bring up Dad leaving her. I really couldn't blame him. All they did was fight for years. Mainly over the fact that Mom tried to control everything. But that's not all. Mom suspected Dad was cheating on her and flung it in his face all the time. He always denied it.

About three months ago Dad decided he couldn't take it anymore. He canceled their marriage contract and moved out. Mom claimed she didn't understand why. She dragged me and my younger brother Shan over to Dad's place to "talk some sense into him." We saw him hugging a woman outside his apartment. She had dark hair like Mom, but she was shorter. More delicate looking. Anyway, Mom wilded out on both of them.

"I knew it! You son of a bitch, you've been cheating on me!" Mom screeched as she stomped toward Dad and the woman.

Dad pulled her behind him and held up a hand to stop Mom. "Morgan, calm down. I never cheated on you and you know that."

"Like hell," she hissed, raising her hand.

Dad caught it. "Don't you dare start. Not now."

"Yeah? So I suppose the two of you are just friends? Give me a furing break!" She then let out a stream of obscenities and tried to move around Dad to get to the woman.

While trying to stop Mom, Dad managed to yell to me, "Get Shan out of here. Now!"

Until Dad had said that, I'd almost forgotten about Shan standing behind me. I'd been in shock. He looked so pale, like he was about to puke. I don't remember us leaving Dad's building, but I do remember ending up at a nearby Green Zone. It took forever to get Shan to stop crying. That was hard. He hadn't cried like that in years.

"Have you ever considered the reason Dad left was because of you? You're impossible to live with." It's difficult, but I keep my voice even. I refuse to act like her.

Mom flashes across the room and slaps me. It stings, but I don't show any emotion. Instead I say, "That proves my point."

I'm not finished packing, but I have to get out of here. Now. I grab my portacase and storm out of the room. Zed and Elijah can send the rest of my stuff later.

Mom follows. "Where do you think you're going?"

Without looking back, I snarl, "Away from you."

Outside, I walk south, toward the transport lot. The farther away I get from Mom, the better I feel.

I've got to hurry if I want to catch the six o'clock shuttle back to downtown New Denver. More cadets are out now. I don't look at them directly. I keep moving. Hopefully nobody knows what's happened.

I let out a deep breath once I climb on board. There are no passengers. Maybe nobody else will need a ride. Mom has her own private shuttle, so I don't have to worry about her needing a lift back home. Still, I'm not fully at ease until we're in the air.

I lean back against the plush seat and look out the window. The Academy grows smaller and smaller, gradually fading into the scenery west of the city. Ahead, New Denver's lights glow against the darkening sky. I'm not sure where I'll go once I get there. I just know I can't stay at Mom's apartment tonight.

My DataLink chimes, and I check the interface. It's Professor March. I think about hitting accept, but decide against it. I don't want to talk to anyone right now.

My thoughts shift to Vika, and my stomach twists. It doesn't seem real that she's in a coma and probably won't recover. I remember how excited she was this morning. How she practically glowed. Her last words echo in my head.

What are you doing? You're not supposed to leave!

I don't care what Professor March said about her just trying to get a better view by the stage. She would have never done that if I'd been there. It's my fault she's hurt. I run my hand over my face, but I'm still breathing evenly. The Calmer is working, or I'd be a mess. Especially after dealing with Mom.

I just don't get Mom. I never really have. At least, not since I've been old enough to understand what was happening between her and Dad. She always expected Shan and me to take her side, but I'm not stupid. It's all her fault Dad left. Who would want to be around a shrew like her?

I try not to think about her anymore, but something she said about Dad keeps bothering me. How he would never come back. Professor March thinks I saw Dad on the time trip because I wanted to see him. And General Anderson said the investigative team didn't witness Dad there at all. I don't know how Dad kept them from seeing him, but I know what I saw. I heard him. He *was* really there.

I'm not crazy.

But why did he tell me to save Alora?

How can I find out who she is?

The answer crystallizes in my mind as if someone downloaded it. Dad used to tell me everyone has secrets. And he once showed me the perfect place to hide things.

6

My fingers drum a restless pattern on my desk as I try to study my history notes, but I can't concentrate. I glance at the clock for what seems like the millionth time. It's 4:43. Two minutes later than the last time I looked. Seventeen minutes until I'm free of detention.

I've been suffocating since the moment I walked in this classroom—a.k.a. the Slammer. The room smells like someone's stinky shoes. Plus, there are nothing but slackers and future criminals in here. And that's not all. Trevor and two of his buddies got detention. Of course they're sitting right behind me.

I swear I'm dying.

"Is there a problem, Miss Walker?" the teacher asks. He peers over the top of his glasses before dropping his gaze to my fingers.

A blush warms my face as I snatch my hand off the desk. "No, sir."

"Then please refrain from making unnecessary noises."

"Yes, sir."

Several students snicker and the warmth on my face spreads through my whole body. I could probably burst into flames. Why can't it be five o'clock already? First thing I'm going to do when Sela picks me up is beg her to take me to The Gingerbread House so I can get some donuts. I need sugar.

I really should study for the history test. At least the history teacher had to go out of town on a family emergency, so there's a sub for the rest of the week. Hopefully I won't have to make up the test until Monday.

"Don't let him get to you," Trevor whispers, his hot breath tickling the back of my neck. "He has major control issues."

I'm positive my face is as red as my shirt.

Keeping my eyes on the teacher, I whisper, "I'm not." My heart is hammering so loud, I'm sure he can hear it.

As the last few minutes tick by, I wonder why Trevor even spoke. He's barely acknowledged my existence in the past except to lie about me. Why would he be nice to me now?

"You're dismissed," the teacher announces as soon as the bell rings. I sling my purse over my shoulder, grab my books, and bolt out the door.

I'm already past the neighboring classroom when someone calls out, "Hey, wait a minute, Alora."

I freeze at the sound of Trevor's voice. Slowly turning, I wait for him to catch up to me. Behind him, his buddies stand outside the Slammer, grinning like they're in on some big secret. This can't be good.

I try to ignore the sinking feeling in my stomach as I search his face for signs of an impending insult, but there's nothing. He's wearing a smile that makes most girls melt when it's directed at them. Not me, of course. His eyes, a blue that almost matches the sky, are locked on to me.

"Hey, are you okay?" he asks, turning up the smile wattage to extra-bright.

I step back before answering, "Um, yeah." Oh, way to sound intelligent, Alora. "Why?"

He shrugs. "I was just checking. You seemed a little upset in there." He inclines his head back toward the Slammer.

"I'm fine."

"You sure? I'm pretty good at reading people, and you look like something's bothering you. Anything I can help with?"

I want to ask him why he even cares, but I don't. Aunt Grace says classy is better than bitchy. "I said I was fine."

"Okay," he drawls. Awkward silence follows, then he says, "So, I heard you skipped school yesterday afternoon. I never thought you'd do something like that."

"I didn't realize you paid attention to me," I reply. I wish I could figure out what he wants, where he's going with this conversation.

"Oh, believe me, I do."

I'm not sure if I should be flattered or totally creeped out. "Look, I've got to go. My friend's waiting for me." At least I'm not lying. Sela *is* supposed to take me home.

I turn to walk away, but he grabs my arm and says, "Wait."

His fingers bite into me and I tell myself not to yank myself away. He probably doesn't realize he's gripping me so hard. I try to keep a shocked expression off my face as I ask, "What do you want?"

He closes the already too-small distance between us and leans in, surrounding me with the spicy scent of his cologne. "I've had my eye on you for a while. I figured you'd like to go out with me sometime."

My first instinct is to laugh. Trevor wants to go out with me? No. Way. He's up to something. And even if he hadn't been such a jerk to me for so many years, I wouldn't touch him for anything. Trevor is a player. He's officially dated Naomi all year, but he's been after other girls too. Girls who are more than willing to play whatever game he wants. I'm not interested in being one of them.

"I thought you and Naomi were together."

His face hardens for a moment before the smile returns. "Don't worry, I broke up with her yesterday."

Sela was right, but still, I'm not buying that he's interested in me. "Okay, but why do you want to go out with me?"

He places both of his hands on my arms. "What can I say? I'm tired of phony girls, and I don't think you're like that."

Just great, he's going cliché on me. Rolling my eyes, I say, "Oh please, don't try that line on me. I think I'll pass."

I shrug off his hands and head toward the exit, hoping he'll drop his act and leave me alone, but he catches up and falls in step beside me. I notice a few surprised looks from students still lingering in the hall. I know exactly how they feel. He opens the door for me and I step into the cooling afternoon. Clouds hang low overhead, threatening to pour rain.

"All right, that was cheesy. I'm sorry. So how about this? We go to Java Jive tomorrow after school and hang out."

He's got to be kidding. I think back to my first day of school here after years of being homeschooled by Aunt Grace. Trevor and Kate could have helped me out and introduced me to their friends since we've known each other since childhood. But they didn't. In fact, they went out of their way to make sure everyone ignored me.

So, of course, I say, "I don't think so."

Trevor tilts his head and scratches his chin. "Let me sweeten the deal. I know you're having trouble in history, right?"

I try not to groan. Our history teacher takes great pleasure in sharing everybody's test scores.

"That's one of my best subjects. Since you missed the test yesterday, I could help you study. I've seen the questions."

Normally I'd laugh out loud. Who's ever heard of a jock offering to tutor someone? But, thanks to the history teacher's big mouth, I happen to know Trevor isn't joking. He actually likes that kind of stuff. And I need all the help I can get so I won't fail the class.

I let out a sigh. "Fine, I'll do it. But I'll meet you there and we keep it to thirty minutes."

His grin is dazzling. "Deal. So how about three thirty?"

"That'll work."

"Great!" He looks to his left, toward the student parking lot. "Do you need a lift anywhere?"

"No, thanks," I say, glancing over my shoulder to where Sela has parked her red VW Bug in front of the school. "My ride's already here."

"Ah, that's right, you said that already. I swear, my memory sucks sometimes. Well, then, I'll see you tomorrow."

As I stare at him walking away, a cold uncertainty curls around me. What was I thinking? There is no way Trevor is doing this to just be nice. Maybe I should cancel on him. The last thing I want or need is to be the butt of somebody's joke.

Sela beeps her horn. As I cross the lawn to her car, I'm suddenly overwhelmed with a weird feeling—like someone's watching me. I peer around. Trevor's already in his truck, pulling out of the parking lot. The girls tennis team is practicing on the courts. Across the road, a tall man wearing glasses is pumping gas in a gray sedan. Shrugging it off, I figure it's just my nerves from talking with Trevor. And I hope Sela didn't see me talking to him, or I'll have to face a million questions from her and some I-told-you-sos.

I should know better.

She rolls down the window before I reach the car and, after turning off a screeching heavy metal song, squeals, "Were you talking to who I think you were talking to?"

I briefly consider lying, but that's pointless. Sliding into the passenger seat, I say, "Yes." Before she can ask anything else, I ask, "Did you have to wait long?" I notice her damp tank top. She's been working out at the local gym after school every afternoon.

"Oh, no. I had a few errands to run for Mama," she answers, polishing off her bottle of water. After pulling away from the school, she continues my torture. "So, what did he want? A date or something?"

The need for sugar is overwhelming. I deserve some after this afternoon. Sela won't like it, but I decide to negotiate. "I'll tell you everything if you take me by The Gingerbread House first."

She wrinkles her nose. "I thought you couldn't go anywhere."

She's right. Aunt Grace grounded me for a week after my "little stunt" yesterday and told me to go straight to the inn. Which isn't a big deal to me because it got me out of practicing cheers with Sela and the Brainless Twins. Still, a short detour won't hurt. "It'll only take a few minutes."

"Yuck. Why do you want to keep eating that junk?" She scowls, looking down at my stomach. "You know, it's so not fair. You eat whatever you want and never gain an ounce. I should hate you."

"Sorry. I can't help it."

"Fine, I'll assist with your addiction this once. Now gimme the deets."

As I fill her in on my conversation with Trevor, her mouth keeps opening wider and wider. Pretty soon, I'm sure she could fit her whole fist in there.

"Oh my *gawd*! I knew he was checking you out yesterday." She flashes one of those I-told-you-so smirks.

"There's no way. He probably bet his friends that he can hook up with me. I'm just going because he's a whiz at history and I need all the help I can get to pass the test."

"Alora! Have you considered that he might actually be into you?"

"Nope."

"Maybe all that's about to change. I know you're a great person, and if you give Trevor a chance, he'll see that too. Besides, if you two start dating, then you could set me up with one of his friends," she says with a wink.

"Right," I say, thinking it will never happen. I can't shake the feeling that he's up to no good.

Sela parks in front of The Gingerbread House, and I hurry inside. It's a small old house painted a chocolate brown and trimmed in white with a variety of candies painted on the exterior. No one appears to be here other than the owner, Mrs. Randolph. I look forward to a few minutes of peace and quiet while I pick out my poison.

After I buy some donuts, I chat with Mrs. Randolph for a few minutes, but on the way to the exit I get that weird feeling again. My skin prickles as I reach for the door handle. I swear someone is watching me. I twist around and scan the small shop, but no one's here except for Mrs. Randolph. She's already turned back to her small television, engrossed in a soap opera, so she doesn't see me looking around like a crazy person. Still, the feeling is there, like I'm standing right next to somebody.

And then I feel something, like a hand touching my arm.

I scream.

"What's wrong, hun?" Mrs. Randolph asks, hurrying around the counter.

I stumble back from the door. "It's nothing. I'm okay."

"No, you're not. You look like you've seen a ghost."

Or felt one.

7

BRIDGER
MARCH 11, 2146

After arriving at the shuttle port, I plow into the crowds sifting through downtown New Denver. It takes another fifteen minutes to get to Dad's apartment. I stop in front of the retina scanner next to the door. A red light flashes in my eyes, indicating it's identifying me. I never used to pay attention to the light. Now it reminds me of blood. I wonder if Dad was covered with blood when his body appeared back in our time after he died. I'll never know. General Anderson wouldn't let us see his body until the memorial ceremony.

The door slides open, and I step inside. It's like a punch to the gut, knowing Dad isn't here. I place my portacase on the nearest chair and examine the room. This is the first time I've been back since his memorial ceremony. Mom has put pressure on me and Shan to sell the place. Shan doesn't care. But I don't want to let it go. I realize Dad's never coming back, but having his stuff here is comforting.

The apartment is huge—one of the perks of being a Time Bender—but nothing fancy. It's the standard white unit you'd find in new apartments. But his presence is stamped everywhere. The overstuffed black couch is accented with three throw pillows that are green—Dad's favorite color. Antiques from his past trips are scattered on shelves. Large digigraphs showing scenes from his favorite old films line the wall opposite a wide window overlooking the city. Smaller digigraphs of Dad, Shan, and me dot the black table in front of the couch.

I'm drawn to those like a magnet. My favorite shows the three of us when I was ten and Shan was six. We were on vacation, on a tour of the Washington, DC ruins. I run a finger along the side of the glass frame and watch as Dad, holding Shan on his shoulders, drapes his free arm around me. Then Shan and I wave at Mom, who was recording us.

There's even a digigraph of Vika and me. Dad recorded it at the Christmas party he hosted back in December. Vika opens my present, squeals, and gives me a kiss in front of everybody. I remember how embarrassed I was, hearing the hoots of laughter from Dad's friends.

I blink and swipe at my eyes, hating myself for being so weak. So not like Dad. He never would've been caught standing around crying like a baby. It's time to man up.

I head to Dad's bedroom but stop at the doorway. It still smells like him in here. His woodsy scent, though faint, fills the room. I let out a few deep puffs of air and force myself to enter. I keep my eye on my goal—the antique desk.

It's not one of those cheap replicas you can find anywhere. It's the real thing, made of maple. When the Department of Temporal Affairs has information about the exact date and time a property is to be destroyed, they'll send in a retrieval team to confiscate artifacts if they're worth saving. This desk is one of those. Built in 1850, it was salvaged when the house it was in burned. Dad asked to keep it since it wasn't the main objective of the mission. General Anderson agreed because Dad was one of his best operatives.

The first time I saw the desk, I was less than impressed. The wood was chipped and had smoke damage. Dad insisted that I help him restore it. That was pretty wild because we discovered some hidden compartments in the desk. Six to be exact. If Dad had anything he wanted to hide, it would be in one of those compartments.

A few minutes pass as I search through the first five. They're the easiest ones to get to—the false bottoms in all of the drawers. There's nothing in them. With each empty discovery, my stomach twists a little more. There has to be something in the last one.

Before I can slide the middle drawer open, a chime sounds throughout the apartment.

I groan. Who could that be? I hurry out of Dad's bedroom as the door opens. Professor March enters the apartment. I stop as if I've run into a force field. "What are you doing here, sir?"

"I tracked your DataLink," he says as he sits on the couch. "You haven't answered any of my comms, and I wanted to talk to you."

I ignored them. "Yeah, well, I'm not exactly in the mood to chat right now."

"I can imagine."

I take one of the seats across from the couch and stare at Professor March.

"So," he says, leaning forward, "how are you doing?"

"How do you think, sir?"

"Bridger, I know this is rough on you. That's why I'm here. I thought you needed someone to talk to."

I want to tell him that's the last thing I want, but I keep that to myself. "What's there to talk about?" I ask, my heart thrumming in my chest. "Everybody thinks I'm crazy, and my girlfriend is in a coma because of me. So things aren't great right now."

Professor March nods. "I stopped by your quarters before coming here. Zed and Elijah told me your mother was there earlier. What did she say to you?"

"Oh, the usual. She was more worried about how it would affect her or Shan. Then she blamed everything on Dad."

"So Morgan was riding her broom again, huh?"

"Always."

A sad look crosses Professor March's face. I wonder what he's thinking, but I can guess. He misses Dad too. They were roommates back in their Academy days and used to do everything together. Even after Dad went military and Professor March went civilian for their careers, they still made time to hang out. That used to irritate Mom endlessly.

"It killed me when I found out Leithan had died," he says in a hoarse whisper. "He was like my brother. I was closer to him than my own sister. So I know what you're going through."

"Yeah," I say, feeling my throat close. I swallow hard a few times. "I know we have those time traveling rules for a reason, but I don't get why it would be so bad if you go back right away. Just before the moment someone is supposed to die and save them. How much could that affect the timeline?"

"Nobody knows for sure, Bridger. But would you really want to take that kind of risk?"

He's right. I just don't want to admit it. The pain is too much. All I can do is stare at the floor and hope I don't wuss out in front of him.

After a few moments, he says, "Sometimes I wish cloning tech would've worked out. That would be better than nothing."

I slowly nod. I want to have my dad here more than anything, but I don't know if I like the idea of him being a clone. Around the year 2103, scientists developed a way to replicate bodies at an accelerated rate. For the right price, someone could have their genetic material stored. Then upon their death, the person's consciousness would be downloaded, and within days they would be alive again. It seemed like the perfect way to cheat death. But there was just one problem—the clones always went crazy. A few years of dealing with that led to cloning being outlawed by the government.

Neither one of us says anything for a while. Finally Professor March asks, "Where are you staying tonight?"

I shrug. "I don't know. Maybe here. I can't handle Mom right now."

"Do you think that's a good idea?"

"It's mine and Shan's apartment now." It surprises me how much saying that hurts. Yet another reminder Dad is gone.

Professor March looks down, taking a few deep breaths, then back at me. "I don't think you're ready to stay here. Not alone, anyway. Leithan hasn't been gone long. It might be too overwhelming."

"Where else can I go?"

"I don't mind if you stay with me for a while. I'm not due to go back on Warden Duty for another two weeks."

The professors at the Academy rotate staying in the residential halls with the cadets, to make sure we "behave like proper trainees." Most of them let us do what we want as long as we don't do anything stupid. But some of the professors actually enforce all the rules. Like Professor Cayhill.

"Okay," I reply. "I'd like that."

Professor March stands and claps his hands together. "Good. I don't know about you, but I'm starving. Are you ready to go?"

I almost tell Professor March that I want to finish searching Dad's desk, but I bite back the words. He didn't believe me when I said I saw Dad at the Foster Assassination. He'd think I really am crazy.

But I can't leave without checking the last compartment.

"I need to go to bathroom first," I lie. Not the most original excuse, but it works.

"Sure, I'll wait."

Back in Dad's room, I fly to the desk and ease out the middle drawer. I set Dad's things on top of the desk and run my fingers along the right side behind the inkwell. It takes a few tries before I find a depression in the wood and press it. The back side of the inkwell pops out with a soft click, revealing two small hidden drawers. My fingers tremble as I check the first drawer. It's empty.

The second one better have something, or I might wild out. I will my pulse to slow as I slide the second drawer out and reach inside. I can't find anything at first, but in the back corner I touch something. Feeling relief, I snatch it out. It's an old-style envelope. I tear it open and nearly fall over when I check the contents. The envelope is stuffed with hundred dollar bills. Those went out of circulation when the North American Federation was formed and credits were designated as the new currency. I'm so shocked to see the money that I almost miss the DataDisk tucked in the envelope. I'd give anything to check it out now. But I can't keep Professor March waiting.

I slide the envelope into a leg pocket of my uniform and replace everything in the drawer before rejoining Professor March. We're on the way out of the apartment when my DataLink chimes. I check to see who is calling and let out a groan. "I wish she'd forget I exist."

"Morgan?"

"Yeah, I don't want to listen to her anymore today."

Professor March frowns. "I know you don't want to hear this, but she's your mother. And since you're a minor and she's your only legal guardian, you need to talk to her. She could make things really unpleasant for you."

I want to tell him what I think of her, but once again he's right. Better to just go ahead and find out what she wants so she'll leave me alone. I accept the comm and try to keep a neutral expression on my face as her image appears above my DataLink. "What are you doing at your father's apartment? I thought I made it clear that you were to come to my place."

Here we go. "I don't remember you saying that."

"I most certainly did. I want you to get over here immediately."

"I can't, Mother. I'm a Time Bender, not a Space Bender."

"Don't be a smart-ass."

"Would you rather I be a dumb-ass?"

Mom lets out a stream of very un-Morgan-like words. I smile, but Professor March's expression wipes the smile away. He's standing in the doorway, arms crossed, scowling at me.

"What?" I ask, not happy with the way he's acting.

"That's your mother, Bridger. Show her a little respect."

"Are you serious?"

"I am."

"Who are you talking to?" Mom asks.

"Professor March is here with me," I say, feeling a split second of satisfaction when her lips curl in disgust.

"Telfair? What does he want?"

"He actually cares about how I'm doing, and he said I can stay with him."

Mom shakes her head. "Oh no, you're coming here."

Anger courses through my body, but I keep my voice calm. "I want to stay with him, Mom. Just for a few days so I can think things through."

"I said no."

"Don't you care about what I want for once? Dad was right, you're selfish." The words are out before I can stop them. Maybe I shouldn't have said them, but I'm glad I did.

Mom recoils like I slapped her as Professor March barks, "Bridger, that's enough."

"She never thinks about what's good for me. It's always what's good for her or Shan," I protest. I don't get it. Why is he defending her? I thought he was on my side.

"I know," Professor March says. "But you've been suspended from the Academy for a month, and you're going to be investigated. I suggest you do whatever she says. You don't need any more blemishes on your record, and Morgan could do that if you defy her wishes."

I want to scream at how unfair it is. Why should she be allowed to control my life when she doesn't care about me? But a very small part of me knows Professor March is right.

"Bridger, I'm giving you exactly one hour to get here, or I'll report you as a runaway," Mom says.

"Why are you doing this?" I ask.

"Because contrary to what you think, you're my son and I do love you." Her voice is softer, more like the one I remember from my childhood, back when our family was still intact.

It's an act. She hasn't shown any affection for me since the divorce. Not since I supported Dad when he decided to leave.

"Bridger, don't do anything stupid," Professor March warns.

"Fine," I snap. "I'll go."

8

ALORA
APRIL 9, 2013

After Sela deposits me at the house, I plunk my books and bag of donuts on the porch and sit in one of the white rocking chairs. I rub my arm where I felt the touch back at The Gingerbread House as if I can make the memory disappear. I don't know why I keep thinking about it like someone actually did touch me. Nobody was there except for Mrs. Randolph, and she was too far away from me when it happened.

What if I'm losing my mind? First I skip school and can't remember what I did or how I got home; now I'm imagining invisible people grabbing me. Next stop, the loony bin.

I wish I could tell Aunt Grace what's going on, but she'd freak out and drag me to the emergency room. Besides, I *think* I have an idea of what could be happening. The dream I've had with my father and the two women are ones I've dealt with on and off for years, ever since I came to live in Willow Creek. Usually I just have them once or twice a month.

But I've had that dream every night for the past two weeks. Could this be a side effect of my memories trying to resurface?

I can't remember why I came to live with Aunt Grace when I was six years old. She just said that my dad left me with her and wouldn't tell her what was going on. I don't believe that for one minute. It seems weird for him to have left me without telling her why, but for some reason Aunt Grace doesn't want to talk to me about it.

"I'm home," I yell once I'm inside.

"Back here," Aunt Grace replies.

In the kitchen, I find Aunt Grace peeling potatoes by the sink.

"What's for supper?" I ask as I place my books on the small table to my left. I extract a donut from the bakery bag and take a bite.

Aunt Grace gives me a disapproving look. "Don't eat another one. I'll have supper ready in about a half hour. Shrimp, fries, coleslaw, hush puppies, and chocolate cake for dessert."

"That sounds good, but why are you cooking so much?" There are way more potatoes than Aunt Grace and I can eat.

"Because, my dear, we have a guest," she says, beaming at me. "Now can you take up those shrimp before they burn?"

"And you invited him to supper?"

"Yes. I thought it wouldn't hurt to show a little extra hospitality tonight."

I scoop the shrimp out and drop them on a paper towel–lined plate. "So, how long is the mystery guest staying? Long enough to pay some serious cash I hope."

"He's supposed to leave on Sunday, but he said he might stay longer if he gets another assignment around here. He's a photographer for a magazine in Atlanta, so be extra nice. We might get some free advertising out of this."

I allow myself to smile. That's good news for once.

After I polish off my donut, I ask, "Do you need me to do anything else?"

"Yes. Frost the cake."

Aunt Grace has a bowl of homemade frosting on the center island resting next to the cake. I grab the spatula and start spreading the chocolate goo across the bottom layer. We both work quietly for a while. I watch her, noting how relaxed she seems. Maybe I should strike while she's obviously in a good mood.

"Aunt Grace, I need to ask you something," I say, placing the spatula back in the bowl.

"Uh oh, that sounds serious."

"Well, it's been so long since I moved in with you and I'm so grateful for you taking me in, but I was wondering if you—"

Aunt Grace shakes her head. "I can see where this is heading a mile away and the answer is still no."

"But you don't know what I was going to ask."

"Oh, I'm sure it's the usual 'Why did my parents leave me?' Am I right?" Her face is grim as she attacks the bowl of potatoes, slicing them into thick strips.

"Yeah, but I thought you would be willing to tell me what really happened now, since I'm older."

"I've told you a million times I don't know what happened. Your dad dropped you off and you were unconscious. He said there had been an accident and he needed you to stay here while he took care of things. He didn't have time to answer all of my questions. And that's the last time I saw him."

"But don't you think that's weird? That he shows up, dumps me off, and leaves without any explanation?"

Aunt Grace slams the knife on the counter and faces me. "I don't understand why you're asking all these questions now. It's been a long time since you've brought it up."

"I need to know the truth."

"Why don't you let it go? Whatever happened must've been bad if you can't even remember."

A sick sensation makes my stomach heave. I force myself to breathe slowly a few times before I speak. "I just don't understand why you don't want to help me remember. I know I've got the memories up here somewhere," I say, tapping the side of my head. "Please."

Her face softens. "Sweetie, it's more complicated than that. My brother would've never left you like he did without a good reason. Whatever happened to y'all must've been awful. And because of that, I'd rather you *not* remember. And besides, kids forget things all the time. I can't remember half the things I did last week, much less when I was young."

"But this is not normal. I can't even remember what my own mother looks like."

"Drop it, Alora. I'm done with this discussion."

"You're not being fair," I shout. "I'm not a porcelain doll. I won't break. I need answers."

"I'm sorry. I can't," she whispers.

"No," I say, hating how my voice quivers. "You *won't*."

My head feels like it could shatter into a million pieces. I have to get away before I say something I'll regret. I bolt out of the kitchen, ignoring Aunt Grace calling my name. I know she won't follow. She has to finish cooking for our precious guest.

I stomp up the stairs, not caring that I probably look like an angry toddler. I'm so busy thinking dark thoughts about Aunt Grace that I don't notice the guest at the top of the landing until I almost smack into him. "I'm so sorry," I say.

I have to strain my neck to look up at him. He's tall, with graying brown hair and an athletic build, probably in his late thirties or early forties.

He's actually kind of nice-looking for someone so old. But for some reason, he's staring at me with a shocked expression on his face.

"Is something wrong?" I ask.

The weird look is quickly replaced with a warm smile. "No. You just kind of remind me of someone."

"Oh, well, sorry I almost ran over you."

"Don't worry. I'm not hurt," he says.

Slipping around him, I mutter, "Well, okay then."

He reaches out and places his hand on my arm in almost the exact place I felt the touch earlier. I try not to jerk my arm away.

"Are you all right?" he asks.

I wonder if he heard my argument with Aunt Grace. Probably, with the way voices carry in here. "I'm fine. I just have a headache and I need to lie down for a while."

"That's a shame. Mrs. Evans said supper would be ready around six, so I'm heading downstairs a bit early. I haven't had time to check things out. I'm Dave by the way. Dave Palmer." He thrusts his hand out at me and I reluctantly take it. It's too warm and moist and I want to wipe my hands on my jeans as soon as I let go.

"I'm Alora. Nice to meet you," I mumble. "I better go. My head's killing me."

He steps to the side and waves me past. "I'm sorry. I didn't mean to hold you up."

I hurry down the hallway, past the guest rooms, to my bedroom—the last one on the left. Once inside, I flop down on the bed. My chest heaves as I try to calm myself. I wish today would hurry up and end. Aunt Grace's denying she knows anything about my past is driving me nuts. It doesn't make sense, hiding details from my life, and I hate how it makes me feel like a freak.

The more I think, the angrier I get. If Aunt Grace is going to keep lying to me, then I'll have to find out myself. Surely if there was a bad accident, it would've been reported in the news, or maybe Aunt Grace has some secret information she's hidden from me. If I could find something, it could jog my memories.

I massage my fingers over my temples. The pain is awful, worse than I've ever had before. If I had more energy, I could go for a run to the river—that always relaxes me and makes me feel like I'm in control, like I can leave my problems behind. My eyes are so heavy, though. I close them and succumb to sleep.

Chirping crickets and croaking frogs are the first things I hear when I awake. I stretch and then frown. I'm lying on something hard, something wooden. Alarmed, I bolt upright. It's night and a full moon hangs low in the sky, framed by stars. I'm on the pier at the river, behind the inn. Fear rips through my body.

What's happening to me?

9

The first thing I notice when I enter Mom's apartment is a burnt smell. Shan is standing in the doorway of the kitchen. His hair, light brown like Dad's, sticks up everywhere. At thirteen, Shan is as tall as me, but he's all arms, legs, and elbows.

"What happened?" I ask, wrinkling my nose.

"I overcooked the protein pie again."

I snort. "I take it you were in a Sim Game?"

"Yep. I was running for my life during the 2056 Cali earthquake. It was a blast." He takes a bite of a sandwich—probably a vegi-spread, his favorite—and says, "You might want to avoid Mom. She's in a mood."

"Yeah, what's new there?"

Shan shrugs. "Hey, just thought I'd warn you."

"Right. Thanks." I smile, but he's already turned away to head back in the kitchen. Shan has an appetite that could rival someone twice his size. That's typical. Talents manifest in kids when they're around thirteen or fourteen. One of the symptoms is they're always hungry.

A sickeningly sweet smell envelops me as I continue down the hallway. Mom's lame attempt at covering Shan's burnt supper.

The whole apartment is so different from Dad's. Mom's into what she calls Retro Classic, whatever that means. The furniture is weird-looking. Everything is white and black, and the walls are set to an obnoxious shade of red. At least she left my and Shan's rooms alone.

"It's about time you got here," Mom says when she spots me. She's lying on the white lounge in the living room, watching the news feed on the TeleNet screen.

I keep walking.

"I'm talking to you, Bridger," she says. She swings her legs off the lounge and stands with her hands on her hips.

I focus on putting distance between us. All I want to do is view the DataDisk in peace and avoid another fight with her.

But she won't leave things alone. I attempt to activate the lock command when I'm in my room. She overrides it and storms in.

"Oh, no," she says, pointing her finger at me. "You're not going to pretend I'm not here."

I decide to tell her what I know she wants to hear. "Okay, fine. I'm sorry. I shouldn't have talked to you the way I did. Are you happy?"

Mom crosses her arms and glares at me. "Oh, so you're sorry now? At least you can admit that, but it doesn't change things. You're in trouble and you don't seem to care."

I can feel my blood pressure shooting up. "I do care. Can't you cut me some slack? It's not all about me getting in trouble. Vika is in a coma! Or do you even care about that?"

"Of course I do! That's the whole problem. Chancellor Tyson explained everything to me, but what if they still hold you liable? Your career will be over, and there's no telling how that could affect me or Shan. There's so much at stake here and you seem oblivious to it."

I want to shake her. I need her to get out. Now.

"Mom, can I be alone for a while? Please."

She's quiet for a few seconds before she says, "Fine. And I am sorry about Vika."

"Thanks," I mumble. That was unexpected, her making a semi-caring statement.

She takes a step toward the door, then turns back to me. "I want your DataLink."

My head snaps up and I glare at her. "What did you say?"

"I said give me your DataLink. You're not going to disrespect me. Your father may have let you get away with that, but I won't."

Fure, she's got to be kidding. Before I can stop myself, I blurt out, "That's crazy!"

Her face flushes, but she continues like I never interrupted her. "You're grounded. After a week, I'll reevaluate based on your behavior. You will not communicate with your friends, and you will not leave this apartment other than to attend Academy matters. Is that clear?"

A string of curses crowd my thoughts, but I don't say anything. Instead I give her a look that lets her know what I think of her stupid punishment.

"I said is that clear?"

I nod slowly, hating her more than ever. She's said nothing but nasty things about Dad for years and I put up with it. This is beyond unreasonable. If I wasn't under investigation at the Academy, I'd leave without another thought.

"Now give me the DataLink."

My hands shake as I unfasten the DataLink and hand it to her.

She lets out a sigh. "I know you think this isn't fair, but you'll have children of your own one day and you'll understand."

After she leaves, I fist my hands, trying to keep them from shaking so hard. I want to punch something. Instead I sink on my bed and rest my head in my hands. I don't get her. It's like she's trying to do everything possible to ruin my life. She's just flaunting her authority over me because she knows I can't defy her.

All I want to do is check Dad's DataDisk. That's it, and she's taken away the thing I need to view it.

I'm about to give up when I think of Shan. Or rather, his DataLink.

I tear out of my room to the kitchen. Shan is still in there stuffing his face. Yeah, he can do some serious damage to anyone's food supply. Serves Mom right.

I check to make sure Mom isn't around and take a seat at the table next to him. He gapes at me as if I've suddenly materialized like a Space Bender. "S'up, Bridger?"

I study him for a moment. He's growing up fast. I can't believe this is the same kid I used to be so close to when I was younger. Lately we've grown apart, though. All because he's such a mama's boy. I hesitate just for a second, then finally say, "Can I ask you a favor?"

He raises an eyebrow. "That depends."

"I need to borrow your DataLink."

"What for?"

I'd forgotten how nosy he is. I haven't been around him a lot lately. He definitely gets that from our mother. "Not long. I need to ask Elijah something and Mom grounded me from mine."

"Ouch. Sucks to be you."

"Right. So can I have it?"

"Well, I might be persuaded to part with it if you do something for me."

I lean back in my chair, semi-impressed he's learned how to negotiate. "What exactly do you want?"

"I need more credits. Mom said I've used too much already this month and there's a new Sim I want to download. The 2011 Japanese tsunami."

That Sim hasn't been out long. It'll cost me more credits than I like. But it's worth it. "Okay, but only if you let me borrow the DataLink whenever I need it for the next week."

"Only in the evenings and it's a deal," he says.

He slips the DataLink to me, and I zip back to my room. I activate the lock again and sit at my desk. Sweat beads across my forehead. I quickly swipe it away and snap Shan's DataLink on my wrist, then pop in the Data-Disk. A holographic menu hovers over the band. Three files are displayed. I select the first one.

It's a copy of an article from an old-style newspaper called *The Willow Creek Tribune*. It's dated July 8, 2013. Adrenaline floods my body as I scan the first paragraph. It's about a sixteen-year-old ghost named Alora Walker.

That's the name Dad said to me.

I grin. So I'm not crazy.

I quickly read through the rest. Alora was found dead in an abandoned burning house on her aunt's property. She'd also been shot in the head. The case was declared a homicide.

I close the file and select the next one. When it opens, I recoil. It's Alora's obituary, but her picture is what I can't stop staring at—she could be Vika's twin. Or at least her sister. Alora's hair is a slightly darker shade of blonde than Vika's, and her face is a little rounder.

I realize there are people in the world who look alike, but this is too much of a coincidence.

Hopefully the last file will have more answers. I open it, and a short message appears.

Leithan, thank you so much for agreeing to help me. These are the only things I could find about Alora. Please save her.

I read the message several times. I can't believe it.

If it's correct, then whoever wrote this note asked my father to do something illegal. Something he would never do.

Only, he did.

A chiming sound interrupts my thoughts, indicating the door lock is being deactivated. I drop my arm as Mom enters my room. I want to shout at her for barging in again, but one look at her face silences me. There's nothing hostile there, only sadness.

"What's wrong?"

"I'm sorry, Bridger, but Chancellor Tyson just called. Vika is dead."

10

I sit on the dock and pull my legs close, rocking back and forth as I stare at the river. The night air is unusually warm, like a blanket wrapped around me, but I still shiver. I'm trapped in a nightmare, one that's starting to repeat itself. Why am I having these blackouts? *Why?*

I swat at the mosquitoes buzzing around my head as I stand. There's no telling how much time I've lost or if Aunt Grace is looking for me. I need to get back to the house.

My skin prickles once I'm in the forest. Usually I love being in the woods, but not at night. You never know what could be lurking in the shadows. A deer. A coyote. A serial killer.

I'm gasping for air by the time I reach the house. Aunt Grace is sitting on the back porch in one of the rocking chairs. She's giving me the stink eye.

"Where have you been and why haven't you answered your phone?"

She probably thinks I ran off to have a tantrum, or that I'm morphing into one of those emo kids who like to quote weird poetry and moan about how life is so unfair. But I can't tell her the truth. I can't give her any reason to consider selling the house to Celeste.

"I left it in my room," I say. "I decided to go running for a while. I'm sorry."

Aunt Grace crosses her arms. "That's all you can say for yourself? I told you earlier that our guest was joining us for supper. I kept him waiting while I looked all over the house for you, and then I had to make an excuse about why I couldn't find you. Do you have any idea how that embarrassed me?"

My face grows warm. I hadn't even considered how my disappearance would look with a guest around. "I'm so sorry, Aunt Grace. I just . . . I just had a horrible headache earlier, and I had a bad day at school, and after fighting with you I just needed to get away for a little while. I really am sorry."

Aunt Grace considers me for a few seconds. I can practically see the gears churning in her brain. "You haven't been acting like yourself for the past few days. Is there something going on at school that I need to know about?"

"No, ma'am, it's nothing. I'm just tired." My stomach twists. I hate doing this.

"I hope that's all." Aunt Grace heaves a deep sigh. "I'm worried about you, sugar."

Now I feel even worse. I focus on the porch, not wanting to look her in the eye. "I'm really sorry, Aunt Grace. I don't know what I was thinking."

"You know, you're starting to act just like Nate when he was around your age."

My head jerks back up. "What do you mean by that?"

Her eyes take on a faraway look. "He went through this phase where he skipped classes and ran off for hours at a time. It used to drive my mama nuts."

This is the first time she's mentioned anything about Dad when he was younger. Maybe if I can play things right, she'll open up more about him. Or even my mom. "Did he ever say why?"

"No, he did it for a while, then decided to grow up and stop acting so irresponsible." She pauses and gives me a pointed stare.

Okay, the bonding over Dad moment is finished. I paste on what I hope is a convincing smile. "Yes, ma'am. Lesson learned."

"Good. Now let's go inside. I've been waiting out here forever and mosquitoes have eaten me alive."

"What time is it?"

She withdraws her phone from her pocket. "It's eight twenty."

A sick feeling stirs inside me. So I've lost almost three hours.

As soon as we're inside, Aunt Grace wipes a hand across her forehead, wrinkling her nose. "I need a bath. Leftovers are in the fridge, so help your-self." She takes a few steps down the hallway then looks back at me. "Are you sure everything's okay?"

"Yes, ma'am. I'm sure."

My heart thrills. If she's taking a bath, that means she'll be in there for a while. Meaning I can get in her room and look for things. Things that might give me answers.

The man I met earlier, Mr. Palmer, is watching the television in the front parlor. I don't know if he's the kind of guest to get chatty, so I tiptoe past the doorway.

If anyone saw me right now, they would think I look ridiculous. I shouldn't have to sneak around in my own house.

When I make it to my room, I close the door, leaving it cracked so I can still see Aunt Grace's room. My heart pounds in anticipation. I rarely go in her bedroom. She says she needs her personal space, especially since we have to share the rest of the house with guests. I bite my bottom lip. Maybe I shouldn't do this. Maybe I should let it go.

No, I've got to find what she's keeping from me.

A few minutes later, Aunt Grace exits her room with her nightgown and robe draped across her arm and goes next door to our bathroom.

As soon as I hear the sound of running water, I dash across the hall into her room. The door clicks softly as I shut it. I wipe my palms on my shorts and survey the room. It's covered in ugly rosebud wallpaper and her furniture is dark and old. Aunt Grace says it's vintage. I say it's hideous.

Still unsure of what I'm looking for, I decide to check the closet first. Shoes line two shelves to my left in neat rows. Her clothes hang across the rear wall, and two large plastic storage boxes are stacked to my right. Ignoring another stab of guilt, I attack the boxes. They're full of old bills and receipts. Boring business-related stuff that makes my eyes glaze over. A single shelf is mounted over her clothes. I drag one of the plastic boxes over and stand on it, praying the lid will hold me.

A half dozen dust-covered boxes sit on the shelf, waiting for someone to discover what's hiding inside. I hold my breath as I reach for the first box and slide it toward me.

Shoes.

The second box has shoes, and so does the third. I check all of them to make sure there's nothing else. Just freaking great.

Grinding my teeth together, I put everything back in place, turn off the light, and step out of the closet.

Next is her dresser. It's tall—almost to my chest—and has a lace doily draped across the top, covered with pictures. There are two with Aunt Grace and her husband. The majority are of me. My most recent school picture and some she took of me in her garden, plus some from when I was little. The oldest picture of me was taken a few months after I came to Willow Creek. Aunt Grace has her arms wrapped around me and she's smiling as if she's never been happier.

Through the wall, I hear a thud and footsteps. Aunt Grace is getting out of the tub.

My fingers fly as I slide open each drawer and filter through the contents. Underwear, socks, old T-shirts, shorts. And a handgun. I snatch my hand back in surprise. Aunt Grace never told me she had one of those in here. But still nothing that could help me.

Please let me find something.

My hands shake as I slide open the bottom drawer. Unlike the carefully folded items in the other drawers, this one is littered with open envelopes and pieces of paper. I pick one up and unfold it. A picture slips out and falls to the floor. I snatch it up. Two guys are standing in front of a tank in what appears to be a desert. One looks like my dad when he was younger, maybe in his early twenties. He's dressed in a military uniform, with his arm draped over another soldier.

I quickly tuck the letter and picture in my pocket, close the drawer, and stand. Time to get out before Aunt Grace comes back.

I've only taken several steps when Aunt Grace appears in the doorway. Her face flushes. "Alora, what in the world are you doing in here?"

If I could rewind time, I would do it right now.

"I asked you a question, young lady," she snaps. "What in the world are you doing in my room? Snooping around?" Her eyes flick to the bottom dresser drawer.

Excuses fly through my mind. I could tell her the truth, but I don't want to fight anymore. Or I could tell her I heard a noise in here. She might buy that.

"I'm waiting." Aunt Grace strides in the room.

I bite my bottom lip. "I need a family picture for a school assignment. I forgot about it and didn't know how long you were going to be in the bathroom, so I thought you wouldn't mind me grabbing one of those." I nod in the direction of the pictures on top of the dresser.

Aunt Grace's eyes narrow. She stops in front of me, her fingers drumming along her hips. "You should've waited until I got out."

"I know and I'm so sorry," I say, looking down.

"Have you been in here long?"

"No, ma'am. I just got in here a minute ago."

"Uh, huh." She stares hard at me. After an eternity, she walks over to the dresser. "I suppose you can use this one." She picks up the picture of us taken in the garden. "Don't lose it."

"Thank you, Aunt Grace." I take the picture from her and give her a hug. She feels stiff. I have to swallow back the lump in my throat. I can't believe how much I've lied to her in the past few days.

I lock the door when I get back to my bedroom, then place the picture of Aunt Grace and me facedown on the desk. My fingers fumble against my pocket as I extract Dad's letter. I scan it, but there aren't any answers. It's only a short note telling Aunt Grace how he hated being stationed in the desert and how much he missed her and the rest of the family. No matter, the picture is what I want. I study it, trying to see myself in Dad. We definitely have the same color hair. I can't make out his eyes, but one time Aunt Grace mentioned they're blue, like ours.

It's weird how the few pictures Aunt Grace has of Dad are all like this one, taken when he was probably in his twenties instead of more recent ones. She said my parents never gave her any.

I concentrate on Dad's face in the picture, trying to merge this image with the one from my dreams, when his face is older and more haggard. But no matter how hard I try, I can't remember. I slam the picture on my desk. It's not fair. I just want to remember my parents. I'm sick of feeling like a freak, living as a ghost of a person.

I pick up the picture again. This isn't enough—I need more information. Aunt Grace has to have something else hidden from me. Why would she act so weird about me going in her bedroom? I think back to how she glanced at the bottom drawer.

I don't know what it is, but I'm going to find out.

11

BRIDGER
MARCH 16, 2146

I follow Mom and Shan from the transport lot to the Academy's main building. A large group of Purists are on the sidewalk in front shouting anti–Time Bender chants and holding picket signs. They disgust me. Using a death to promote their sick agenda.

We ignore them as they hurl insults at us and hurry inside. Mom lets out a relieved-sounding sigh. Ahead of us is our destination—the ballroom. Usually it's used for Chancellor Tyson's publicity banquets. Today it's the scene for Vika's memorial ceremony.

I'm hollow inside, like someone scraped out what was left of my soul. Dad's memorial ceremony was hard enough to get through. At least I had Vika, Elijah, and Zed to help me. Now Vika's gone because of me.

Mom and Shan stop outside the black double doors. She takes a moment to straighten her blue dress and smooth her hair. Muffled voices trickle through the doors. I even hear some jackass laughing. My hands fist at my sides. I wish I could leave, but I can't. Vika would wild out if she knew I wanted to skip her memorial ceremony.

"Are you all right?" Mom asks. It's weird, but she's been slightly nicer since Vika died. A hell of a lot more than after Dad died. She even gave my DataLink back yesterday.

"I'm fine," I mumble.

"You don't look fine. You look like a zombie," Shan says.

He's probably right. I doubled up on Calmer before leaving the apartment.

"Leave him alone, Shan," Mom says. Her brow creases as she looks at me. "Are you sure you want to do this?"

"Yes. Now can we go in? I want to get this over with."

Mom and Shan immediately melt in the crowd when we get inside. I freeze by the door. It seems all eyes have zeroed in on me. I try to ignore them as I check out the ballroom. Everyone is dressed in varying shades of blue—Vika's favorite color. Some people are crying; some are laughing. All around, large digigraphs of Vika are mounted on stands. I lower my gaze. I can't look at them.

I need to find someplace where I can be alone. The whispers dig in my back as I walk through the crowd. I know what they're saying. And they're right.

I end up in an unoccupied corner of the ballroom and slump down in one of the chairs lining the wall. I run my fingers over my DataLink as I picture the files on Dad's DataDisk. I've searched for hours trying to find more information about that ghost mentioned on those files. Anything to let me know what was so special about her. But I haven't found anything. Personal records from her time are rare unless the person was famous or important. Apparently, Alora Walker was a nobody. So why would Dad try to save her? It doesn't make sense.

"Man, where have you been?"

I look up and smile. Elijah and Zed are standing in front of me. This is the first time I've seen them since Friday. I didn't realize how much I missed them until now.

"I just got here. Mom took forever to get ready." I don't add how she wasn't sure if we should come. She decided at the last minute it would look bad for us to skip out since Vika's mom is a high-ranking DTA official.

They sit on either side of me. Instantly, I feel better. Not much, but I'll take it.

"How are you holding up?" Zed asks.

"I'm dealing."

"Uh huh," Elijah grunts. "You're stoned on Calmer."

"It's better than the alternative," I reply.

They can't argue with that. After Dad died, it took me wilding out three times over nothing before Mom agreed to let the docs give me the Calmer prescription.

"I don't know about you two, but I'm glad to get out of my parents' place for a while." Zed rolls his eyes and lets out a groan. "I'm actually ready for classes to start again."

Chancellor Tyson canceled classes this week to give everyone a chance to mourn Vika. Students were sent home except for those whose parents are stationed at DTA facilities outside New Denver.

"Tell me about it, man," Elijah says. "Mine act like they don't want me out of their sight. They haven't been this bad since that girl was kidnapped way back when we were kids."

"Yeah, I'd forgotten about that," Zed says. "Was she ever found?"

I shrug. "I don't think so."

It was a big deal when I was around seven years old. Someone broke into a Time Bender's apartment, shot her, and kidnapped her young daughter. Nobody ever found out who did it or why. But I remember how Mom never wanted Shan or me out of her sight after that. Dad said she was being ridiculous and overly dramatic. It's one of the few times she was actually protective of me.

"May I have your attention?"

Vika's mother, Colonel Halla Fairbanks, is standing on the stage at the end of the ballroom holding a microphone. She's dressed in a light blue two-piece dress and her ice-blonde hair is smoothed back from her face. She looks beautiful in a cold way. And not at all like she's sad.

"I want to thank you for coming to Vika's ceremony today. She would have loved seeing all of you here." She pauses to scan the room, smiling. "Attendants are now distributing Virtual Lenses. Please take a pair and I will present to you a showcase of my daughter's life."

"I can't." It's hard enough being here, but I can't sit through the virtual simulation of Vika's history. It nearly undid me at Dad's ceremony.

"We can go outside," Zed says.

"Good idea. I need some air anyway. There are too many people in here." Elijah grabs me just above the elbow and tugs. "Get your ass in gear, man."

We slip out of the ballroom before Vika's mom announces the start of the simulation, then exit the building. For the first time since I arrived on campus, I can breathe without feeling like a shuttle is sitting on my chest.

We set out across the grassy area behind the main building and take a seat on the nearest bench. I stare at the flowerbed across from us. It's full of pink, yellow, and purple flowers. Whatever they are, Vika always liked them.

"So what's been going on with you?" Zed asks. "You haven't answered any of my comms."

"Yeah, mine either," Elijah says.

I quickly explain all the drama with Mom and how she took away my DataLink. I leave out the part where Shan let me borrow his. I wasn't exactly in the mood to talk to anybody.

"Have I told you before how I really feel for you?" Elijah asks. "Because I do, man. Your mother is impossible."

"Truth," Zed says. He pats me on the back. "But at least you've got us. Now doesn't that make you feel better?"

"A little," I reply, looking from him to Elijah. Worry is written on their faces. The tight smiles, the concern in their eyes.

Sunlight glints off my DataLink, drawing my attention. I want to show them what I found. I can trust them. Still, I hold back. I don't know why. Probably because what Dad asked me to do is illegal. Or it could be because I haven't figured out who asked Dad to save the ghost in the first place. Or if he even went back to 2013. I could be wasting time fooling around with this.

This leads me to another question that's been bothering me. If he did an illegal shift to 2013, was that when he died? General Anderson said Dad's last mission was classified. What if that's just a cover? The DTA might not even know the truth themselves. That would explain why the general questioned me himself in the exam room.

I have only one way to find out the truth.

I have to go back to 2013 to see for myself.

The rational part of me screams in protest. If I'm caught, my time-bending career will be over. I'd most certainly receive a nulling sentence.

I jump when Zed asks, "Are you okay, Bridger?"

"I think so," I say, and before I change my mind, I spill the truth. If I'm going to do this, I'll need help. I don't tell them where the ghost chick was from or the exact year she lived in. If the DTA ever found out, whatever Dad was planning would be ruined.

Both are them are speechless.

Elijah manages to say, "Man, I don't know. Do you think it's a good idea to shift by yourself? And where are you going to get a Chronoband?"

"I could do a free shift."

"Oh, hell no," Zed says, shaking his head. "You know what could happen."

He's got me there, but that's something I'll have to risk. Before Chronobands were developed, Time Benders could only free shift. That meant utilizing the gene that allows us to manipulate time without the benefit of a device to deliver us to a specific time and date. Time Benders would arrive hours or even days before or after their intended target. Dad used to say with enough training we could learn to accurately free shift, but the Department of Temporal Affairs would never allow it. They prefer us dependent on their technology.

"What about your inquiry? Do you want to get permanently kicked out?" Elijah asks.

I want to argue, but everything they say is right. I have too much to lose if I'm caught. But how can I go forward with my life when Dad asked me to do this?

Voices drift across the green from the direction of the main building. The group from the memorial ceremony is moving outside. Colonel Fairbanks and the rest of Vika's family are in the lead. If Vika had a father, he would have been at the head of the procession with her mom. But Vika never knew who he was. Colonel Fairbanks used a sperm donation from an anonymous Time Bender to conceive her. I let out a sigh, remembering how much that used to bother Vika. She once tried to research who her biological father was, but her mom found out and had the records permanently sealed. That pissed Vika off so much.

The group makes its way toward the center of the green, where walkways leading to the different buildings on campus intersect. Elijah and Zed stand up and I reluctantly follow them as they head over to the crowd. Most everyone has reddened, tearstained faces. Yeah, I'm glad I didn't view Vika's virtual history. Even with the extra Calmer, I'm sure I'd be a mess.

We end up at the back of the crowd and wait for Colonel Fairbanks to speak. Hushed whispers circulate like a low hum. I keep quiet. This is the most important part of the ceremony, when Vika's family will deliver her ashes back to the earth. My heart is heavy. I'll never see her in person again. Her body is gone, destroyed in a fire that left her as nothing more than a pile of dust. I take several deep breaths. I don't know if I can make it through this.

Colonel Fairbanks begins her address, holding the silver urn with Vika's remains. She thanks everyone for coming to help celebrate Vika's life. Beside me, Elijah sniffs a few times. My own eyes begin to well up with more damn tears. I look down and wipe at them hard, then check out everyone else. I'm not alone in showing emotion, but I don't like it. Not in front of everyone. I turn around for a moment to calm myself.

That's when I see her.

Standing back at the main building is Vika. She blows a kiss and I take a step back. *No furing way.* That's not her. It can't be. I blink then look again.

Nobody's there.

12

ALORA
APRIL 10, 2013

My body tenses as Sela turns into the parking lot at Java Jive, then I sigh as the tension melts away—Trevor's truck isn't here. I yell over the music, "Okay, Trevor's not here. Let's go."

Sela turns the radio off. "Oh, no. You're not gonna bail. Besides, we're early. He said three thirty, right?"

Sela is practically glowing. You'd think she was the one meeting Trevor.

"Yeah." Trevor reminded me right after history class today. As if I could forget. "I'm not so sure about this. What if it's a prank?"

She rolls her eyes. "I swear, you're beyond exasperating. He said he was gonna help you study. How could that be a prank?"

"I don't know." I need all the help I can get with the history test, but my mind isn't here. I just want to leave. I plan to sneak into Aunt Grace's room again while she's cooking supper.

"Exactly, you don't know. He might be using this as an excuse to hang out with you. Or maybe ask you out on a date." Sela waggles her eyebrows.

"Jeez, no he won't. I'm not his type."

"Shows how much you pay attention. If you're female, you're his type." She parks the car close to the building. "Are you ready to knock his boots off?"

"Really, Sela, this is a bad idea. Just take me home."

"Nope. You've got to pass the test, remember? I'm tired of you being grounded already, and you said you'd try out for the cheer squad."

I scowl. Funny how her saying that makes me want to fail the history test.

She laughs and opens her door. "Oh, lighten up. You'll have fun, I promise. Now are you gonna get out or do I have to drag you out?"

I consider telling her I'd like to see her drag me out, but I did agree to meet Trevor. "Fine," I huff. "But don't expect me to have fun."

"I don't get you. Half the girls at school would kill to have Trevor notice them."

"Yeah, the half he hasn't already screwed behind Naomi's back," I mutter as I grab my history book and open the door. "Do I look okay?"

Sela glances at my skinny jeans and green shirt. "Girl, please. You could dress like a bum and still look good."

"No, I wouldn't, but thanks anyway." Leave it to Sela to make me feel a tiny bit better. "Well, I guess I better go."

"I'm sending you thoughts of rainbows and fairy dust and if that doesn't work, I'll even stoop to gummy bears and chocolate," she says with a grimace.

"If that doesn't work, nothing will." I try to smile, but my face feels frozen.

"You'll do great. I bet he wants to confess his undying love for you and promise to never leave your side again." She folds both of her hands over her heart and sighs.

"Now you're being ridiculous."

"You wouldn't have it any other way, would you?"

No, I wouldn't. This is the Sela I miss, the one who cracks jokes and wants to spend time with me without two idiots tagging along. It's selfish of me to think that, but I can't help it. Things were so much better before Jess and Miranda entered the picture.

A bell tinkles as we walk into Java Jive. We're enveloped with the scent of coffee and fresh pastries. I allow myself to relax a little. A few kids from school are already here. They barely acknowledge us as we place our order. I hope it stays that way. Why didn't I tell Trevor to meet me at the library?

I grab my order and head to a rear corner booth. Hopefully nobody will notice Trevor when he comes back here.

Sela chats nonstop while I sip on my mocha frappé. I can barely taste it. The bell on the door sounds again and again. I twist around, and my stomach sinks like a stone in water. The place is filling up with kids from school. More are in the parking lot.

Sela grins and waves at someone behind me. "Hey, over here!"

Oh God, he's here. I turn again, expecting to see Trevor, but instead I find Jess and Miranda heading toward us. Just great.

"Hey, girlie," Miranda says. She shimmies onto the bench next to Sela.

Jess gives me a thin smile as she sits with me. "Where's Trevor?"

My grip tightens around my cup as I my eyes flick to Sela. "You told them?"

She shrugs. "Everyone will know soon enough."

"But it's just a study thing. He didn't ask me out on a date."

"He hasn't yet."

I take a long sip of my drink to keep from snapping at her.

Miranda's nose wrinkles as she watches me. "I hate to think about how many calories are in there."

Jess nods. "Uh huh. Those things are so fattening."

I hate the way the Brainless Twins stare at me with those smug expressions and wonder for a moment how good it would feel to throw my fattening frappé in their faces. No more smug looks, that's for sure. But I don't do anything except take a big bite of my fattening chocolate chunk cookie.

Then I proceed to almost choke when Sela lets out a squeal. "Ooh, he's here!"

Reluctantly, I look out the store's window. Sure enough, it's Trevor. He parks his truck and jumps out, pausing to smooth his hair while studying his reflection in the side mirror.

"Awww, look at that. He's primping for you," Sela says. The Brainless Twins twitter.

I give Sela a withering glare. "Knock it off."

"Okay, no jokes." She grabs her drink. "All right, girls, let's clear out so Alora can work her magic on loverboy."

Jess snorts while Miranda shakes her head. I know what Miranda's thinking and I agree with her—there will be no magic-making from me. Hopefully I'll get out of here without becoming Willow Creek's biggest idiot.

The girls head to an unoccupied table near the exit. Even though I despise Jess and Miranda, I'd give anything to be with them now.

I grab my history book and flip to the chapter I need to study. I try to read over the first paragraph. Nothing sticks. All I want to do is watch the door, but I don't want Trevor to think I've been looking forward to seeing him. That's pathetic.

I'm so engrossed in pretending to study that I jump when Trevor says, "Hey, there you are." He places his hand on my shoulder. "Easy there. Are you all right?"

"Yeah, I'm fine." I search for something brilliant to say, but my tongue feels heavy.

He slides his history book on the table across from me. "I'm gonna get something to drink. You want anything else?"

"No, thanks, I'm good."

After he leaves, I try to appear relaxed. I cross and uncross my legs and rub my palms against my jeans. The noise level has gone up since I got here. The place is packed. And even worse, some of the kids from school must have noticed Trevor talking to me. They keep glancing in my direction like they've witnessed a supernatural occurrence. Sela catches my attention and gives me two thumbs up.

Somebody please kill me now.

"I'm set," Trevor says as he sits across from me. Then he slides a small bag across the table. "I figured you might want another one of these. I know how much you like them."

I open the bag and inhale the scent of another warm chocolate chunk cookie. I glance up at Trevor. "Um, thanks. But you really didn't have to do that," I say, feeling my face get hot.

Trevor smiles. "It's no big deal. I'm just trying to be nice, that's all."

"Well, thanks again." I take another sip of my frappé, but I can barely swallow it. I push the container away. "Before we get started, I wanted to thank you for offering to help me. I really need to pass this test."

"No problem." He glances around before leaning closer. "You know, I've wanted to ask you out for a long time."

Talk about direct. That's the last thing I expected to hear. "I can't believe that. You've been with Naomi for ages." And your mom hates my aunt.

He leans back, scowling. "Yeah, that's two years of my life I'll never get back. I wish I could forget."

"Really? I thought you two were pretty tight."

"With Naomi, everything is about appearances. It gets old."

"I kind of got that impression too." Especially since she's besties with Kate.

He bites a chunk off his donut and chases it with coffee. "It's time for me to move on. I've got better things to look forward to."

He holds my gaze for a moment. With his smile turned up to killer levels and all attention focused on me, it's kind of easy to see how girls might fall for him. Wait, what am I thinking? I tap a finger on my book. "So, are you ready to study?"

"Absolutely," he says, taking out his own history book. He opens it, extracts a few pages full of notes, and offers them to me. "And I came prepared."

I glance over the notes, taking in the neat handwriting of the detailed outline he made of the chapter. I peer at him over the pages, starting to feel guilty. He put a lot of work into this. Maybe I was wrong to be so harsh with my judgment of him.

He starts to speak again, but his face darkens as his eyes shift to something behind me. I get a sinking feeling as I turn around.

Naomi is standing at the door with Kate. They're both wearing tennis skirts and tank tops. Naomi's ash-brown hair falls in a braid over one shoulder, while Kate's hair is pulled up in a ponytail. Both have zeroed in on Trevor and me.

They march across the room and stop at our booth. Kate's lip curls in a sneer. "What are you doing with *her*?"

If I thought my face was burning before, it's on fire now, but I don't say anything. Naomi stares at me like she would choke me if she could get away with it.

"I don't remember inviting you here," Trevor says.

"I didn't realize I had to have your permission. This *was* our favorite place to go after school," Naomi says, turning her attention to him. "I figured you'd try to flaunt some new whore in my face, but I didn't think you'd start with trash."

"What?" I ask, hating how my voice squeaks.

Naomi places a hand on Kate's arm. "Oh, I'm so sorry. Aren't y'all related?"

"Hell no," Kate says. "She's from Grace's side of the family. No shared blood, thank the lord."

"Outside. Now," he says to Naomi through gritted teeth. Then he says to me, "I'll handle this. Don't go anywhere."

He takes Naomi by the arm and leads her away. She tries to protest, but it sounds feeble. Kate smirks and follows them. Just as they get outside, Naomi flashes a triumphant smile over her shoulder.

I close my eyes, wishing I could disappear. But it wouldn't solve anything. I'd still have to deal with this mess.

"What was that all about?"

Sela is standing next to me. At least the Brainless Twins didn't come over, too.

"Apparently Naomi didn't know Trevor was going to help me study today and she's not happy."

"So she wants to start some shit with you?"

"No. Yes. I don't know. I guess I can't blame her. Trevor said he's the one who broke up with her. I guess she's not over him."

"Girl, don't make excuses for that beyotch. She seriously needs to have her butt kicked."

I blink a few times. "Really? And who's going to do that?"

"You should. My mama says if you let someone run over you, they'll think they own you."

I want to tell Sela that she's being ridiculous, but I know she's right.

"I'm going to see what's happening out there." I grab my things and slide off the seat.

"Want some backup?" Sela asks.

I shake my head in alarm. "No. I've got to do this myself, okay?"

"Gotcha, but if those two jump you, I'm all over them."

She rejoins Jess and Miranda at their table, no doubt filling them in on my unwanted drama. It seems like everyone's eyes are on me as I head outside. My feet drag as if they know I'm heading into disaster.

I blink a few times at the bright sun and search for Trevor and Naomi. Kate is chatting with two girls at one of the outdoor tables. She calls out, "Where you going, Alora?" in a mocking voice. The other two girls laugh along with her.

I ignore them and keep looking for Trevor and Naomi. They're next to Trevor's truck. I had expected to find them arguing, but they're standing close, talking quietly. This can't be good.

I'm halfway across the parking lot when Naomi's voice rises. It almost sounds like she's pleading. Then she says, "Please, don't."

I stop a few cars away and crouch next to a gray sedan. I feel like an idiot, but I need to hear what they're talking about. Naomi says something else, but it's too muffled for me to understand.

Then I hear Trevor say, "It's a joke."

In that moment, a mixture of emotions rolls through me. How stupid am I for believing Trevor wanted to help me? I mean, why would he? He's a player and he tried to play me. I'm so pissed that I fell for it.

Sela and the Brainless Twins are probably glued to the window. I should go back and tell her what I heard, but I can't face them.

Before I can stop myself I sneak out of the parking lot. The inn is about three miles from here, so I can walk. By the time Sela realizes I've left, I'll be halfway home. She might get mad at me for leaving without telling her, but she'll understand when I explain why.

I've gone a block down Main Street when my eyes glaze with tears. I rub them away and blink back the rest. I won't cry over some stupid jerk. He doesn't deserve my tears.

I round a corner and glance back over my shoulder. A gray car is behind me, driving slowly. Unease creeps up me, and I walk faster.

A few moments later, the car pulls up next to me and the driver rolls the window down. "Hello, Alora."

Adrenaline floods my body and I almost take off running, but I finally recognize the man. "Hey, Mr. Palmer," I say, allowing myself to relax. "I didn't realize you drove that car."

He smiles and pushes his glasses back up. "Yes, it's nothing fancy, but it gets me to where I need to go."

"Oh, okay."

"Are you heading back to the inn? I could give you a ride," he says, patting the seat next to his camera. "I promise I won't bite."

I try not to take a step back, but that's exactly what I want to do. He might be a guest, but I'm not about to accept a ride from him. "No, thanks. I need the exercise."

His jaw flexes like he's chewing on what to say next. "Suit yourself. I'll see you soon."

My body is already covered in chills from the Trevor fiasco, but as Mr. Palmer drives away, they sink into my core, freezing me. All I can think about is his car as I clutch my history book against my chest. It's the same gray car I hid next to back at the Java Jive parking lot.

Is he following me?

Or am I just being paranoid? Lots of people go to Java Jive. Even if Mr. Palmer was there, this route is the quickest way to get back to the inn. I'm just being ridiculous.

I guess that's what I get for letting Trevor mess with my head.

13

The sun is barely peeking over the skyscrapers when I leave Mom's apartment. The brightness blinds me for a moment. I rub my temples, trying to ease the pressure. I didn't take any pain meds or Calmer. It'll take a clear head for what I'm about to do.

I grip my portacase strap as I thread through the crowd. Everyone is too noisy as they make their way to wherever they're going. Nulls silently pick up trash and clean storefront windows. Again I can't help but think that could be me if I'm caught.

I left early in case Mom changed her mind about me going camping with Zed and Elijah. She grew a heart last night and agreed to let me get away for a few days. I guess I looked like hell after Vika's memorial ceremony yesterday.

I almost feel bad for lying to her.

We're meeting at Elijah's house. From there we're supposed to take Elijah's family hover bikes to camp in the Rockies, like we usually do every few months. Zed and Elijah really are going up there. They're taking my DataLink in case Mom decides to track me.

I'm catching a hypersonic plane to Georgia. Hopefully I'll be back sometime tonight. Or at least in a few days.

The crowd parts long enough for me to glimpse a flash of blonde hair. Just like Vika's. I almost call out her name. Instead I close my eyes for a few seconds. That wasn't Vika. Just like it wasn't her at the memorial ceremony. Even though I was late, everyone else viewed her body before it was taken away for cremation. One of the possible side effects of taking too much Calmer is hallucinations. I know I've taken too much this past week.

After riding the maglev across town, I exit and walk the few blocks to Elijah's place. I've been this way countless times before, and yet I still stare in awe at the houses. They're all huge and sit on large landscaped lots. Like Dad used to say, you can't hide money. And Elijah's family definitely has it. His great-grandmother helped develop Chronobands.

A maid answers the door and informs me that Elijah and Zed are waiting for me in the game room, which is where we usually hang out. I have to pass several more rooms to get there. Each one is full of the latest tech gadgets or priceless historical artifacts.

I find Elijah sitting on one end of a dark blue, U-shaped couch. He's watching a vid on the giant TeleNet. Zed is sitting opposite him, wearing a pair of Sim Game glasses.

"Man, you sure you want to do this?" Elijah asks.

"Yes, I've got to," I say, leaning against the side of the antique pool table.

"But have you really thought this through?"

Zed slips off the glasses. "And what are we supposed to do if your mom comms you?"

"I don't know," I snap. Yesterday they were all supportive. They said I needed to find out the truth. I snatch off my DataLink and toss it to Zed. "Don't answer it. She'll probably comm one of you, so tell her mine is messed up or something."

Elijah frowns. "Do you think she'll buy that? This is your mother we're talking about."

I try not to roll my eyes. "I get what you're saying, but it's not like we're doing something unusual. We go camping all the time."

"Except you're not really going," Elijah mutters. He walks over to me and slips a new DataLink out of his pocket. "Here's the replacement. You owe me three hundred credits."

"Thanks," I say as I put it on. "Look, I've got to go. My flight leaves in less than an hour."

"I've got a bad feeling about this, man." Elijah places a hand on my shoulder. "Are you really sure you want to do this?"

"You sound like my mom," I say.

"Damn, Bridger. That's a cut," Zed says with a smirk. He stands and stretches.

Elijah looks from me to Zed and laughs. "For real."

"You guys, nothing bad will happen. Mom thinks I'm with you. I'll zip over to Georgia, shift back long enough to see if Dad's there, and be back before you know it."

"Yeah, you might be able to do that if you have a Chronoband," Elijah says. He glares at me, his jaw tightening.

He's right, but nobody has access to Chronobands unless you go through the Academy or the DTA. No exceptions.

As I reassure Zed and Elijah again, I ignore the small voice inside me telling me I'm lying. With free shifting, nothing is certain. It's something I'd never consider using under normal circumstances. But now it's the only option I have.

"Come on," I say, heading toward the door. "We have to leave together if this is going to work."

"Right," Zed says.

Elijah and Zed sling their portacases over their shoulders and follow me out. Elijah stops by the dining room to let his parents know that we're leaving. We're almost to the front door when a piercing shriek echoes through the house.

"Grams on the loose?" Zed asks Elijah.

Elijah starts to answer, but then footsteps thud behind us. We look back to find a woman running down the stairs. She appears to be middle aged, but I know better. The woman is Elijah's great-grandmother, the Chronoband pioneer.

She's also a clone.

My pulse thrums, seeing her like this.

After so many clones went crazy, most of them were forcibly institutionalized by the government. Those with enough money could afford to be taken care of at home.

"Somebody help me!" she screeches. "They're trying to kill me!"

Two more people are behind her—a young nurse and another woman. It's Elijah's grandmother. She looks older than her own mother. Talk about messed up.

Elijah's grandmother calls out, "Mom, please wait. Nobody is trying to hurt you."

Elijah heaves a deep sigh. "Just a minute, guys."

I feel helpless as Elijah goes back and waits at the bottom of the stairs. His great-grandmother stops running, her neck swiveling back and forth between Elijah and the women behind her. "Leave me alone! Just leave me alone!" Then she starts screaming.

The women finally reach her. Elijah's grandmother murmurs something soothing. The nurse extracts a tiny syringe from her pocket and stabs his great-grandmother in the neck. Within seconds, the screams stop. Elijah hurries up the stairs to hug his grandmother and kiss the other one on the cheek. She just stares blankly in the space ahead of her.

After they lead her back upstairs, Elijah rejoins us. "Sorry about that. You know how it is when Grandma and Grams visit."

Less than two hours later, I exit the hypersonic plane in Athens, Georgia. Like the New Denver terminal, it's crowded. The only difference is there are way more Purists here. It's not always easy to identify Purists, but the ones in here stand out like a Jumbotron flashing in the night sky. Obviously overweight, showing signs of premature aging or poor health, they've steadily refused the benefits of genetic modification. And they always reek of too much sweat. Bunch of idiots.

The Purists cast disgusted glances at me. Probably because I'm in my Academy uniform. I should have worn regular clothes, but I need the cloaking device when I get to 2013. If I could've gotten my hands on a Jewel of Illusion, or Jewill, I wouldn't need my uniform. Those were cloaking devices implanted in jewelry. The government outlawed them soon after they were introduced to the general population. They claimed Jewills encouraged criminal behavior.

"Abomination," someone says from behind me. I whirl around, but whoever said it doesn't confront me. Figures. Purists like to snarl and protest in large groups. Individually, they're cowards. They know anyone who's been modified can kick their ass.

It takes another half hour to catch a shuttle to Willow Creek. I was surprised to learn the ghost's house is still intact. It was a bed-and-breakfast in her time. Now it's a museum run by a historical society. And not even a good one. It's Purist controlled, meaning they give tours and lectures. No virtual sims of what life was like there in the past that would make the experience a million times better. Like I said, the Purists are a bunch of idiots.

I stand in front of the museum for a few moments. It's three stories tall, with wide, white columns along the front porch. It looks good for being so old. I guess the Purists cared enough to keep it in pristine shape.

A stone path cuts around both sides of the house. I take the one on the left that follows a narrow driveway. A group of tourists are standing on the rear porch listening to a lecture given by a pudgy, balding man. I don't understand how they're staying awake.

My DataLink chimes. It's Zed. What could he want already? I accept the comm and immediately know something is wrong. Zed's face is pinched in worry.

"Dude, your mom knows," he says in a rush. "She commed us and we told her you accidentally busted your DataLink. But she didn't believe it when we said you had gone to set up some fishing lines."

I close my eyes for a second and swear under my breath. "What did she do then?"

Zed takes a deep breath and then says, "It's not good. She sent one of her space-bending buddies over to check on you."

A dull ache starts to throb at back of my head. I can't believe it. Why does she always have to ruin everything?

"Then she blabbed to our folks that we're covering for you. They're seriously pissed. We have to be back in New Denver within the hour."

"Did you tell her where I went?"

Zed shakes his head. "We said you wouldn't tell us. But what if she gets a Mind Bender to question us?"

I want to die. I haven't experienced a mind probe, but I've heard it's like someone sticking knives in your skull. I didn't want something like this to happen. The only good thing is that I never told Zed and Elijah my target year.

"I'm so sorry," I say. I start to speak again, but freeze when three Space Benders materialize by the woods behind the museum. They're dressed in dark gray uniforms, meaning they're military. My mouth goes dry. Why the hell would military get involved? Immediately they spot me and start running.

You're supposed to find an isolated place to shift so you won't appear in the same space as a person or object, but I don't have time to do that. The Space Benders are pointing stunners in my direction. I've got to shift now.

Shaking, I close my eyes and repeat July 4, 2013. July 4, 2013. July 4, 2013. I hold my breath.

Then there's nothing but the Void. No light, no sound, no air.

My lungs are going to burst.

I open my eyes to blackness.

I've never shifted this far back in time, much less without a Chrono-band. I must have done something wrong. I'm going to die. I fight the urge to breathe.

Suddenly there's bright sunlight and oxygen. I gasp and suck in a lungful of air. Smells swirl around me—freshly cut grass and something floral. And there's a weird sound, like a mechanical sputtering, followed by the crunch of gravel. I look to my right. An old-style auto is a few feet away from me.

It's heading in my direction.

14

Brakes screech as I dive out of the auto's way. Pain shoots through my left side as I slam into the ground.

The engine shuts off. Then I hear a woman screaming, "Oh my God!"

Footsteps thud around the truck. I look down. Holy fure, I'm still visible. This can't be happening. I shrug off my portacase and roll on my back. A searing fire flares in my left knee. I hold still and wait for the pain to pass.

The ghost, a woman with curly light brown hair, kneels by me. "I'm so sorry, I didn't see you. Are you okay?"

"I'm fine," I say through gritted teeth. I have to get away from her before I contaminate the timeline. Talking to ghosts is forbidden.

"Are you sure?" She leans closer to peer at my face. "Do you think you broke anything?"

I shake my head no. I try to sit up, but the pain in my knee stops me. I lie back down and blow out a few puffs of air.

The woman searches through her pockets, muttering to herself.

Another voice calls out from somewhere behind the woman. "What happened?" It's a soft voice with traces of fear in it.

The woman glances over her shoulder. "I need you to call 9-1-1."

No way, I can't let her involve more people. "Please don't. I'm feeling better. I just need to rest for a minute."

What I need to do is try to walk and assess the damage to my knee. If it's not too bad, it will heal within a few hours. Thanks to all those genetic modifications the Purists hate so much. I start to sit up yet again, but I stop when I see who the woman was talking to. My mouth falls open. I must look as brainless as a Null, but I can't help it.

It's the ghost Dad wanted to save—Alora. And she looks so much like Vika that I can't breathe.

"Are you sure you're all right? You look like you've seen a ghost," the woman says, her eyebrows knitted together.

You have no idea, I want to say.

"I think you should see a doctor."

"No, really, I'm fine," I say, trying to ignore the cold clamminess of my skin. "Just let me walk it off."

She bites her lip and stands. "I don't know."

"Aunt Grace, what happened?" Alora asks in a firmer tone.

The woman, Grace, looks at Alora. "I was backing up and almost ran over him. I swear I didn't see him. It's like he came out of nowhere."

I let out a snort. Not so smart, but I can't help it. She's right and doesn't even realize it.

"So do I need to call 9-1-1 or not?" Alora holds up her phone. I gape at it, fascinated. I couldn't imagine having to carry around something like that. DataLinks are way more efficient.

"No," I answer before Grace can. I extend my right hand in their direction. "Could one of you help me?" They stare at me like I've grown a third eye, so I add, "Please."

Grace sighs and grasps my hand. My knee throbs as she pulls me into a standing position. I sway a bit but force myself to stay up. Getting on my feet is the best thing I can do. I turn away from Grace and Alora and take a tentative step. The pain is still sharp. I take a few more steps and stumble. I wish they weren't watching me. I wish they couldn't see me at all.

"Oh, for heaven's sake, you need to get off your feet," Grace says, now standing next to me. Her eyes flick to Alora. "Help me get him inside."

"Really, that's not necessary," I say as Grace gently takes hold of my left arm. Alora picks up my portacase before grasping my other arm. My first impulse is to shake them off, but Grace is giving me a look that says she won't take no for an answer.

Alora rolls her eyes and shakes her head. I stare at her, unable to look away. Her face is rounder, and her eyes are a lighter shade of blue, but the resemblance to Vika is unmistakable.

"You hush now," Grace says to me. "I almost killed you, so the least you can let me do is look after you for a bit."

The back porch stairs creak as we climb them. I hate to admit it, but I'm glad they're helping. Hobbling up those few stairs makes my knee hurt even more.

They escort me to a room at the front of the house made to replicate something from the late nineteenth century. I groan in relief as Grace helps me stretch out my legs on the couch and orders me to lean forward. She places a pillow behind my back.

Alora stands a few steps away, watching me. I smile at her, and she quickly looks away. That's definitely different from Vika—she would always stare me down. Even if I caught her looking at me first.

"There, how's that?" Grace asks once she's finished fussing over me.

"Good," I say.

"Does your knee still hurt?"

"No, it's fine as long as I don't move it."

"That's good." Grace clasps her hands together. "I bet you're thirsty. Do you like sweet tea?" I have no idea—I've never tried it. Before I can reply, she says, "I'll get some for all of us. It'll just take a few minutes."

Grace sweeps out of the room, leaving me alone with Alora. Alora's mouth parts slightly as she glances at the doorway. It's like she would rather do anything than stay in here with me.

Then she looks down at my portacase clutched in her hands. "I guess you need this," she says, setting it next to me.

"Yes. Thanks for bringing it in."

"No problem." She retreats to the other side of small table in front of the couch and sits in a green chair. "So, what's your name?"

"Bridger."

"Nice to meet you. I'm Alora Walker and the crazy lady is Grace Evans, my aunt."

I nod like I don't already know this. I shouldn't say anything, but I don't want to act like an ungrateful jerk. Alora and Grace are trying to be friendly. I should show them the same courtesy, even though I really shouldn't even be talking to them. "It's nice to meet you too."

We're both silent for a moment, checking each other out. Then Alora asks, "Where are you from?"

I close my eyes. I should have known she would ask something like that. And I have to give her an answer. I guess it's better to stick close to the truth. "Denver."

Alora leans forward. "I've always wanted to go there."

"Go where?" Grace asks as she breezes back in the room. She's carrying a silver tray with three tall glasses of tea. She places the tray on the table and hands a glass to Alora and me before sitting in a chair by Alora.

"Denver," Alora says, turning to Grace. "That's where Bridger is from."

"Oh, how lovely." Grace takes a sip of her tea and grins. "And what brings you to Willow Creek, Bridger?"

I twist the cold glass in my hand and stare at it. Why do women always want to know every little detail about everything? It doesn't matter what time you're in, they're all the same. I glance up and find Alora and Grace both waiting for my answer. "Um, I'm here . . ." What can I say? Then the answer pops in my mind. "I'm here because I'm looking for my father. He's missing."

"Oh my goodness, what happened?" Grace asks.

"He disappeared a few months ago."

"Why do you think he's here?" Alora asks.

Damn. It's like I'm having an inquiry hearing. "I found a message someone sent to him. It indicated that he might be here, so I thought I'd see for myself."

Grace makes a *tsk*-ing sound and sets her tea on the table. "That's awful. I really hope you find him soon."

"Yeah, me too."

"So I take it you're here because you want to rent a room?" Grace asks.

I almost blurt out no. But it would seem weird for me to show up at a bed-and-breakfast and not want to rent a room. But I can't stay. I clear my throat and say, "Well, I was going to see if you had anything available, but—"

"But nothing. You're staying."

I knew from the start that shifting to the correct date would be difficult. I brought a few changes of clothing, some Calmer, and the cash Dad left. That was supposed to be for things I might need since I'd planned to camp in the woods if I had to wait a few days. Staying at the inn was never part of the plan. Interacting with ghosts was never part of the plan. But bumming my knee was never part of the plan either. It'll heal quickly if there is no major damage, but spending the night in the forest might be too difficult.

"Maybe for one night," I find myself saying even though I know I shouldn't. I reach for my portacase. "How much will it cost?"

Grace waves a hand at me. "Not a dime. I almost killed you, remember? It's the least I can do."

Alora lets out a strangled sound. I guess she doesn't like the idea any more than I do. But at least I'll get to keep a closer eye on her tonight. Maybe I'll get an idea of what's so special about her and figure out who's supposed to kill her.

"Are you okay, sweetie?" Grace asks.

"Yes, ma'am. I choked, that's all." She fidgets with the glass before setting it on the table.

Grace checks her watch. "Oh crap, the post office is gonna close soon." She stands and looks at me. "That's where I was fixing to go when I almost ran over you. Alora, keep him company, will you? I'll be back in a flash."

After Grace is gone, Alora pulls out her phone again. She chews on her lower lip as she taps something on the screen. I find myself staring at her mouth.

What the hell, Bridger. Stop that, she's a ghost!

Alora slides the phone back in her pocket with a groan and stands.

"Anything wrong?" I ask. I know it's none of my business, but she doesn't look happy. Her face is scrunched up like she's either pissed or upset or both.

"It's nothing. My friend is mad because I left her and . . ." She shakes her head. "You don't want to hear my drama. You've got enough to deal with."

"No, I don't mind. It's not like I can go anywhere right now." I incline my head toward my hurt knee.

"True," she replies. "But I've got homework I need to do." She glances toward the doorway. "Just holler if you need anything."

I want to tell Alora to stay. But that might wild her out, coming from a stranger. "Okay. And thank you." She starts toward the door, but another thought occurs to me. "Hey, what's the date? I can't remember exactly."

"April tenth."

It's like time stops. I blink a few times. Did I hear her right? *April tenth*? No, that can't be right. It can't. I can't be three months before her death date.

My stomach tightens, but I force a smile and thank her again. Then I flop my head back against the pillow as soon as she leaves. This is the worst. I could try to shift right now, but that would be idiotic with a hurt knee. I have to wait a little longer. Then I run the risk of not hitting the right date again. Or worse, I could revert back to my home time and have to face the Space Benders that the DTA will undoubtedly have stationed at this location. If I had a Chronoband, I wouldn't have to worry about that.

I don't have a choice. I have to stay here, at least one night. I just hope I don't contaminate the timeline.

No matter what I do, I'm screwed.

15

ALORA
APRIL 10, 2013

As I climb the stairs, I glance back at the doorway to the front parlor. A small part of me wants to stay with Bridger like Aunt Grace asked. What if he needs something and I don't hear him calling? That would be bad, especially since Aunt Grace did almost run over him. Then there's the fact that he's really cute. I could stare at his dimples for hours.

I shake my head. Jeez, what am I thinking? The last thing I need to do is go mooning over a new guy. I mean, he doesn't even live here. He might stay a few days, and then he'll be gone. Besides, you can't trust good-looking guys. Look where that got me with Trevor. I can't believe I fell for his line about wanting to help me study. I might as well have the word *idiot* stamped on my forehead.

I stop in front of Aunt Grace's door, my fingers hovering over the handle. This is it. She'll be gone for twenty minutes or so—plenty of time to search the bottom drawer. But the moment I'm inside, my heart begins to thud furiously. "Get a grip," I mutter.

My legs can't carry me fast enough to the dresser. The drawer creaks as I open it. And for the second time today, I get that punched-in-the-gut feeling.

It's empty.

I should've known Aunt Grace would move everything. She doesn't trust me. Well, I've got news for her. I'm not about to quit. This proves she has information that could help me. I close my eyes. Where would she have moved the stuff? If she took the time to get those old letters and pictures out of here, she definitely wouldn't put them somewhere else in her room. And the guest rooms are definitely out.

Which leaves the attic.

I open my eyes and groan. Just freaking great. Aunt Grace always keeps the door to the attic locked. She says nobody at the inn has any business up there, including me. And the key to unlock the door is on her keychain.

I need something to pick the lock. Something like one of Aunt Grace's bobby pins. I cross to the mirrored dresser that doubles as Aunt Grace's vanity. There's a small wicker basket full of colorful ponytail holders next to her hair brush. I rummage through it, hoping a bobby pin is on the bottom, and nearly shout *yes* when my fingers close around one.

I fly out of Aunt Grace's room and down the hallway, stopping three doors to the left, and insert the bobby pin in the handle. I move the pin around gently, but the lock won't open. I grind my teeth together and try again and again. Nothing happens.

Finally after what seems like an eternity, I hear a tiny click and breathe a sigh of relief. The door creaks as I open it. I glance around to make sure I'm still alone before stepping across the threshold, stopping only to shut the door.

The air becomes stale as I climb the stairs. I shrink from the cobwebs hanging overhead and shudder, imagining the feeling of a spider crawling on me.

Sunlight spills in through the windows. It doesn't light up the whole space—just enough to make the shadows seem darker. More cobwebs fill every nook and crevice. I shiver again as I slowly walk around, searching for anything that could possibly hold Aunt Grace's secrets. The attic is full of old furniture, trunks, and other odds and ends, all coated with a thick layer of dust.

One of the trunks catches my eye. It doesn't look ancient like the rest of the stuff up here, and unlike everything else I've seen so far, fingerprints mar the surface. A weird, fluttery sensation fills me as I lift the lid. Please let this be it. Please.

The inside looks like a treasure chest for a young boy. On top are a few old baseball gloves, two scuffed-up bats, some torn comic books, and some faded shirts. I pick up a blue and white shirt. It's an old jersey with the name *Eagles* written across the front and the number three on the back, below the name Walker. It must have been my dad's. I hold it close and sniff, hoping for a hint of what he smelled like, what *he* was like. Disappointment washes over me—it's musty, like the rest of the attic.

A paper shopping bag is on one side of the pile. The paper crinkles as I open it. I grin when I realize it's filled with the missing pictures and letters. Nice try, Aunt Grace.

I take the bag out and start to search through it, but then I notice a large leather book in the trunk with Dad's name, Nathaniel, embossed on the front in gold letters. The spine makes a crackling noise as I open it. The yellowed pages are full of newspaper clippings, pictures, and other mementoes from my dad's past. I smile when I come across some awards from when he was in high school. He had the highest average in history for several years. I definitely didn't inherit that from him.

More newspaper clippings are near the back. Dad's baseball team came in third at the state championship during his junior year of high school, and his cross country team won several awards. The last picture on the page shows him standing next to another guy. They're both holding trophies. I lean closer to study the other guy's face and check out his name from the caption: John Miller. He looks familiar. Where have I seen him? Then it hits me—he's the same guy standing next to Dad in the picture I stole from Aunt Grace's bedroom.

I nearly drop the scrapbook when the attic door creaks open and footsteps pound up the stairs, followed by Aunt Grace calling, "Alora Walker, you better not be up here."

No! She can't be back already. My body goes on autopilot. Pocket the picture of Dad and John Miller. Put everything back in the trunk. Then my head snaps back and forth, searching for someplace to hide. There's an old chair across the room. I barely squeeze in the narrow space behind the chair before Aunt Grace tops the stairs.

I hold my breath and peer around the side. Aunt Grace stops in front of the trunk. I hope she can't tell I was snooping through it. She opens it and examines the contents. Seconds stretch to minutes. My chest feels like it's about to explode. When I think I can't take much more, she shuts the lid. I stay still until I hear the attic door shutting again. Then I let out a sigh.

That was too close.

I'll have to come up with a lie about where I've been. Aunt Grace will have already checked my bedroom, but I'll deal with that when I'm out of here. I hurry to the trunk and remove the scrapbook again. I want to keep it in my room.

A faint light slivers through the cracks around the door at the bottom of the stairs. All I want to do is slip out unnoticed, get to my room, and examine the scrapbook some more. Hopefully Aunt Grace will be occupied with Bridger for a while and won't look for me anymore.

I twist the doorknob, expecting it to turn, but it won't budge.

"No way," I mutter as I twist it again.

It still won't open.

I sink onto the step and rub my hand across my forehead. If I bang on the door and yell, Aunt Grace will know that I was hiding from her and snooping. That's out of the question if I ever want to search through Dad's trunk again.

I allow myself a minute of self-pity before I trudge back up the stairs. I'm not getting out of here by sitting on my behind. I head to the nearest window, which overlooks the front of the inn. The long gravel driveway stretches toward the road, and a few trees are spaced out across the wide lawn. I trail my fingers over the glass. As much as I hate it, this is my only way out.

I hurry to the other end of the attic and peer out the window over-looking the right side of the inn. A magnolia is growing maybe twelve feet away. It's not very old—the top of the tree barely peeks over the roof. But I could jump over to it and climb down.

Just thinking of crossing the roof, my heart slams painfully in my chest. The roof of a three-story building. And actually leaping from said roof to the tree.

I step back and lean against a dusty box, my legs suddenly weak. Maybe I should suck it up and call for help. That would be the smart thing to do. The safe thing to do. But my only chance of finding out the truth will disappear.

I'm on my own.

Before I can change my mind, I set the scrapbook down on the floor and go back to the window. My hands shake as I unlock the latch and push the heavy glass up. For a moment, it refuses to move. I almost give up. Almost. Gritting my teeth, I push harder. The window creeps upward with a groan. I step back as a warm breeze blows against my face. My skin erupts in goose bumps.

I consider leaving the scrapbook behind, but I don't know if I'll be able to get back up here right away. Hopefully dropping it in the shrubs will keep it from being damaged. I just hope *I* can make it down the tree in one piece.

This window is near the edge of the roof. After propping the scrapbook on the shingles, I crawl out and sit on the ledge, trying to get my nerve up to move. From inside the attic, the view wasn't too threatening. Now I feel like I'm sitting on the edge of a bottomless chasm, waiting to fall into for-ever. I can't make myself move. I can't catch my breath. Even if I wanted to, I know I couldn't scream or yell. Inside my head though, that's another story.

As I stare at the ground, wishing I was already down there, I hear myself shouting *somebody please help me.*

I scoot back against the side of the dormer window and pick up the scrapbook. Since my parents aren't in my life and I have no idea if they're still alive, I've sometimes imagined how I'd die. And obviously that day has come because I don't think I'll ever move from this spot. I'm probably having a heart attack. If I don't die by heart attack, I'll probably fall off the roof and break my neck. Or I could stay up here and starve to death.

My breathing becomes more labored, but I hold on to the scrapbook like it could keep me safe. Blackness settles over me. I close my eyes, praying that my death doesn't hurt too much.

16

BRIDGER
APRIL 10, 2013

"I can't find Alora," Grace says as she enters the room. A panicky expression is on her face.

When she returned from her errand earlier, she seemed upset because Alora wasn't with me. Then she went looking for her. It irritated me because I'd *finally* connected my DataLink to the antiquated Internet and was searching for more info about Alora. I had to sever the connection.

"Are you sure she said she was going to do her homework?" she asks.

"Yes. And she said she had some other things to do."

Grace sits across from me and heaves a sigh. "Yeah, I bet she's got things to do. I don't know what's gotten into that girl lately."

Interesting. So Alora has been doing something out of the ordinary. I wonder if that something will cause her death. I want to ask Grace what she means. Before I can, she launches into a mini-interrogation.

Ten minutes later she finishes. Now Grace thinks I'm a nineteen-year-old newly enlisted navy cadet who won't have to report until August, but has a thing for wearing the uniform.

Zed and Elijah would laugh their asses off if they were here.

Grace checks her phone, looking worried. "I texted Alora a little while ago and she still hasn't answered."

As long as I'm lying, I might as well give her another. Anything so she'll leave me alone. "I heard a noise in the back of the house a while ago. It sounded like a door closing."

"That wouldn't surprise me. Alora likes to run." Grace's face lights up in a radiant grin. She stands and takes a few steps toward the doorway. "I'm fixing to start supper now. Can I get you anything?"

"No, thanks."

"Well, just holler if you need anything."

After Grace leaves, I activate the DataLink again and wait as it locks on to a wireless signal. I search for any mention of Alora, but like before, I can't come up with anything. Just like I couldn't back in my time. That's beyond odd. Over the years, a lot of info was lost during the conversion of the old Internet to the DataNet, but I still should be able to locate any public data on Alora from this time period. It's like she doesn't exist, but that's crazy. She's here. I guess she just doesn't participate in anything.

I deactivate the DataLink and rub my fist in the other hand. How can I find out what's so special about Alora if I don't know anything about her? I could always ask but I'm a stranger to her. Somehow, I've got to gain her trust. That means interacting with her even more. Which I shouldn't do.

I slam my fist against the cushion. What was my dad thinking? Why did he want me to save Alora? Something isn't adding up, but I can't figure out what it is. A fog clouds my thoughts, keeping me from thinking clearly.

A familiar heavy sensation begins building in me. It starts in my chest and rapidly spreads through my body. Before I go into a full-blown panic attack, I pull a dose of Calmer out of my portacase. As soon as it's in my system, I lie back against the pillow and blow out a few quick puffs of air.

When the fog lifts, I sit up and swing my legs off the couch. My knee twinges, but the pain isn't as bad as before. If I keep it elevated longer, I might be able to clear out in another hour with almost no pain. That would be the smart thing to do. But I need to find Alora now. The sooner I can figure out what's going on with her, the sooner I can figure out why Dad wanted to save her. Then I can go home.

I pick up my portacase and limp out of the room. Grace is humming an off-key tune, then something loud clanks. I jump at the noise and hurry to the front door. I need to get outside so I can use the tracker on my DataLink to see if Alora is nearby. I could use it inside, but the last thing I need is for Grace to pop in while a holographic representation of her house hovers over my arm. I'm sure she'd wild out, and I don't have a Mind Redeemer, which I could use to erase her memories.

My knee is throbbing again by the time I'm on the front porch. I sink down on the nearest rocking chair and stretch my leg. Things are going from bad to worse. Even if I find Alora on the tracker, how can I get to her with my knee messed up? A pain patch would help, but I didn't bring one. At least I remembered the Calmer. I can push through pain if necessary. I wouldn't be able to function without my Calmer.

I activate the DataLink and open the tracker. A holographic globe appears over my arm. I enter my coordinates, and the globe is replaced with a holographic representation of the inn. I extend the search parameters to include up to a half mile around the inn. Then I program it to only display human life signs. Three red blips appear before me. Grace in the house, me on the porch, and another on the roof. I frown. That can't be right. Damn tracker must have a malfunction. The blip has to be Alora, but what would she be doing on the roof? It's more likely she's in the attic. That would explain why Grace couldn't find her earlier.

I deactivate the tracker. I could head to the attic and try to get Alora to talk to me. But what would I say?

And that's when I see Alora. One second I'm alone, then the next she's on the ground under a tree. I blink a few times, thinking I'm hallucinating again. But no, she's still there.

And she's not moving.

I ignore the pain pulsing in my knee as I rush to her side. She's clutching a large book, and she's so still. Like she's dead. Bile rises in my throat. It's like looking back in time, when Vika was the one stretched before me. Unmoving.

But this isn't Vika.

Alora's chest rises slowly, as if she's just taking a nap. I stare at her, then look at the roof. If Alora fell from up there, she wouldn't be laying here so peaceful. And I know what I saw. Alora didn't fall. She materialized before me. I shake my head in disbelief.

She's a Space Bender.

During my first year at the Academy, I learned that natural-born Talents existed throughout our history. But they're extremely rare. One of the tasks of the DTA is to identify them. Obviously Alora is one, but it still doesn't explain why my dad wanted to save her life. It doesn't make sense.

I also wonder if she even knows. She's passed out, which indicates her abilities are emerging. If she knows what's happening, that's fine. If not, I have to pretend I don't suspect anything. I can't change what's already happened.

Alora moans and relaxes her grip on the book. It slides to the ground, and her eyes suddenly fly open. She fixates on me and says, "Oh my God." Her fingers fly to her face as she sits up, now looking up at the roof. "Oh. My. God."

Yeah, she definitely doesn't know she's a Space Bender.

Alora's face grows even paler than it already is. She keeps her eyes—eyes that look so much like Vika's—trained on the roof. "What happened?"

It surprises me how much I want to tell her the truth. Anything to wipe the fear off her face. But I can't. "I don't know. I just came outside and I found you."

"But I . . . I don't understand."

She's in shock. I know that feeling. I had a hard time processing things the first time I shifted, and I knew what was happening to me. I can't imagine what it's like for her, realizing something is going on and yet not knowing what it is. She has to be wilding out. No wonder Grace suspects something is going on with her.

But it doesn't answer my questions. Yeah, she's a natural-born Space Bender. But I need to figure out what ties her to my dad.

Alora eases herself up and leans back over to pick up her book.

"Where are you going?" I ask.

She strides toward the front porch and answers without looking back. "I . . . I've really got to study. I'll see you at supper."

I wait for her to enter the house before limping back to the porch. I start to sit again, but I change my mind. I can't stay here tonight or any night. Accepting Grace's offer was stupid. What I need to do is try to shift closer to Alora's death date. Even if I'm a few days, or even a week or two off-target, it's better than being stuck in April. A part of me doesn't want to try it—there's a definite risk of ending up in my time. But I can't lose three months of my life staying here.

After I grab my portacase, I head for the woods next to the house and stop just inside the tree line. I close my eyes and clear my mind. I will my body to relax and picture July 4, 2013 in my head.

The air rushes away from me as I enter the Void.

I'm alone. I'm Nowhere.

My body grows tense. This has to work. I have to arrive on July fourth.

The sun is low in the sky when I reappear. Whatever the date is, the time is earlier than what I just left. I breathe deeply, savoring the oxygen rushing in my lungs.

The first thing I notice is there are no autos. The second thing I notice is a worried-looking man standing on the front porch of the inn, talking with someone dressed in a navy blue uniform. I stifle a groan. It's the man who was conducting the tour guide from my own time and a DTA military official.

Then I hear a voice behind me say, "Put your hands in the air."

17

The dismissal bell rings, covering a loud roar from my stomach. Thanks to Trevor, I had to skip lunch today and hide out in the library. From the moment I stepped on campus, it seems like he's been everywhere. And I have no desire to talk to him. Ever. I just wish he'd get the message.

I deposit my books in my locker and hurry outside. All I want to do is get home so I can search for a way to contact John Miller. I couldn't concentrate on anything last night after blacking out. How could I? I mean, how on earth did I get down from the roof without killing myself?

I thought that guy, Bridger, might have seen how I did it. But when I went downstairs and Aunt Grace realized Bridger had left without even telling us, she freaked out. We spent an hour combing the house to make sure he didn't steal anything. Which he didn't.

The tension I'd been feeling evaporates the moment I step outside. Trevor must have finally realized I don't want to be around him. I'm almost cheerful as I join everyone heading to the parking lot. Sela's last class is on the other side of campus, so it'll take her a few more minutes to get to her car.

I round the main building and stop suddenly when I see who's just in front of me—Trevor and Naomi. And like an idiot, I stand there, frozen.

Naomi's face is flushed as she talks to him. I can't understand what she's saying, but I can just make out the words "followed" and "need you." She wipes her eyes, not caring that she's crying in full view of everyone, and says in a louder voice, "Please listen to me." She then places her hand on Trevor's chest. He just brushes it off.

I wonder for a moment why she's acting so desperate and why she feels the need to follow Trevor around. Naomi is gorgeous and could have any guy she wants. But it's really none of my concern. What I have to do is get out of there before Trevor sees me. The last thing I need is to get involved in whatever drama is going on with them, but suddenly he looks up and locks eyes with me. He says something to Naomi and walks away. In my direction.

Goodbye, cheerful mood.

I make myself move before he can get to me. If there weren't so many kids around, I'd be tempted to run, but then I'd look ridiculous. Besides, it's not like I can hide in Sela's car. She has the keys.

I almost make it to the parking lot when I hear Trevor right behind me. "Alora, wait!"

Oh, this should be fun. I stop and slowly face him.

"Didn't you hear me?"

"Nope," I lie, keeping my eyes straight ahead. I'm going to kill Sela if she doesn't show up soon.

"I'm sorry about yesterday. I've been trying to apologize, but for some reason you've been avoiding me." He flashes a grin that would probably make any other girl throw herself at him.

I turn around and resume walking.

"Hey," Trevor says, stepping in front of me. "Can't you talk to me for a minute?"

I think about sidestepping, but there's no point. Obviously he's going to aggravate the crap out of me until I stop. "Fine. What do you want?"

Trevor runs his hand through his hair. "I can't believe you're mad because I went outside to talk to Naomi. I didn't think it was that big of a deal."

"You must think I'm the stupidest person on the planet."

"What're you talking about? She was trying to mess with you so I took care of it." His brow furrows. "Did you want to handle her yourself?"

Okay, so he's going to lie. I better stop this conversation before it goes any further. "I heard what you said to Naomi."

Trevor cocks his head to the side. "Heard what?"

"I heard you tell her that meeting me was a joke." My voice rises on the last word. Two girls walking by stare at us. When they're out of earshot, I continue, "After that I left. Simple as that."

I try to move around him, but he holds out a hand to stop me. "Whoa, I think you heard wrong."

Some people say their blood boils when they're angry. Now I understand what they mean. "Excuse me? I most certainly did *not* hear wrong."

Trevor rubs the back of his neck. "I'm screwing this up. What I meant is you must've misunderstood what I said. I didn't tell Naomi the meeting was a joke."

"I know what you said."

"Alora, I said it was *not* a joke. Naomi thought I was meeting with you to piss her off, but that wasn't what I was doing." He smiles again, reaching out to touch my arm. I jerk back. His smile melts away and he murmurs, "I'm really sorry. I wish you would've told me. It sounds like a big misunderstanding."

Seriously? Does he really think I'm that naive? I start to tell him exactly what he can do with his smiles and excuses when a shrill voice interrupts.

"What the hell are you doing?" Kate comes up behind Trevor, glaring at him.

"What're you talking about?" he asks, returning her glare.

"You're really going after her?" Kate gestures to me with a flick of her wrist.

"That's none of your, or anybody else's, business."

"I'm sure Mama wouldn't agree. She's gonna die when she finds out you're messing around with Grace's trash niece."

My mouth drops open as I try to formulate a withering comeback, but Trevor says in a low voice, "And who's gonna tell Mama? I know plenty of dirt on you, so you better keep your mouth shut if you know what's good for you."

"Whatever. Have your fun. And when you end up with a nasty disease, don't come crying to me." She spins around, her dark hair fanning out behind her, and storms back toward the school.

Trevor shakes his head. "Sorry about that. Kate and Naomi have been up each other's asses for as long as I can remember."

"Good for them." I turn around again. Maybe I can make it to the parking lot this time.

Trevor falls in step beside me. "Look, don't worry about Naomi. I'll take care of that problem." I glance up at him. He's staring straight ahead, his jaw clenched.

"What's that supposed to mean?"

"It means she won't bother us anymore."

"There's another problem," I say, frowning. "There's no us."

"Not yet."

Jeez, how cocky can he be? I will never fall for his tricks and worship at the Altar of Trevor. Not. A. Chance.

"What can I do to convince you to go out with me? And not just a study date, I want a real date."

My eyes want to roll so badly. He thinks he can charm me, but I know what I heard yesterday. He did tell Naomi meeting me yesterday was a joke. I may have had a few blackouts, but my hearing is fine. "No, Trevor. There's nothing you can say that'll make me want to go out with you. So why don't you do us both a favor and find somebody else."

Trevor pretends to think, scratching his chin. His eyes drift to somewhere over my shoulder and he grins. "How about this? We make it a double date: the two of us, your friend, and one of my buds."

"You know what I think? You need to clean your ears out. I said no, and I'm not going to change my mind. So please quit bothering me." I try to walk away, but Trevor grabs me, his fingers biting into my upper arm. I stare at the vise-like grip. "Let. Me. Go."

Trevor holds on a second longer before releasing me. He steps back, his eyes widening, his mouth parting slightly. "I'm sorry. I didn't mean anything. I just really want to go out with you, and you won't listen to me."

He looks like he wants to say something else. Instead he clamps his lips tightly together and walks away. I watch until he gets to his truck before checking out the red mark on my arm. It hurts a little, enough to remind me of what he did. Yeah, I definitely don't want anything to do with a guy who loses his cool when he can't get his way.

Sela arrives soon after I get to her car with a scowl on her face. "Girl, what was going on with Trevor? I saw y'all talking and him grabbing your arm. Are you okay?"

"Yeah," I say as I open the car door. "I am now."

Just as long as he stays away from me.

After Sela drops me off at home, I go straight to the kitchen to finally get something to eat. I glance through the window over the sink and spot Aunt Grace and Mr. Palmer in the rose garden, sitting on one of the white wrought iron benches. Mr. Palmer says something and Aunt Grace laughs and places a hand on his arm. I let out a snort. I can't believe she is flirting with him.

Aunt Grace is always friendly to guests when they stay, but it seems like every time Mr. Palmer is around, she goes looking for him. I know her husband has been dead for a long time and she's lonely, but it never occurred to me she might want to date someone, especially Mr. Palmer. He's nice enough, but not the type I'd expect Aunt Grace to crush on.

It's none of my business. I grab something to eat and head upstairs to search for John Miller's contact information.

An hour later, I still haven't found anything. From what little Aunt Grace has told me, she and Dad originally lived somewhere around Atlanta. There are thirty-three John Millers living there. I've already called half of them without finding the right one.

I close my laptop and stare at the wall. My head is pounding from looking at the screen for so long. And I can't get that confrontation with Trevor out of my head. I look at where he grabbed me, noticing the faint bruise. My muscles are tense and twitchy, like rubber bands ready to be launched across a room.

I need to get out of here.

After I change into a pair of running shorts, I tiptoe downstairs. I don't want to talk to Aunt Grace if I can help it.

But before I reach the back door, it opens and Aunt Grace steps in, followed by Mr. Palmer. She's got this ridiculously happy look on her face. As soon as she sees me, she changes into Concerned Aunt.

"Where do you think you're going, missy?"

"Out for a run."

"Have you finished your homework?"

"Yes, ma'am." I look away, hating how much I've lied to her lately, but I sure can't tell her what I've really been doing. And I'm going to go insane if I stay in my room any longer.

"Well, okay, but don't stay out all afternoon." She glances at Mr. Palmer and smiles. "Dave has never tried chicken and dumplings, so I'm going to make some for supper."

Mr. Palmer's eyes follow me as I move past him. "See you in a little while, Alora."

I jog to the path that takes me to the river. I stop when I reach the forest so I can slide my iPod out of the small pocket inside my shorts. Once the music is blaring, I really take off.

It feels good, my legs pumping and my heart racing. It's weird how this forest, with its tangled trees and gnarled bushes, unsettles and soothes me at the same time. I come here when I need to think, when I need to unwind, when I need to be alone.

So it's odd when a strange feeling creeps over me like a spider crawling on my skin. I feel like I'm not alone. I stop and take the earbuds out. A bird chirps overhead. Something scurries in the branches above me, probably a squirrel.

It's nothing. I tell myself to get a freaking grip and start running again. Soon I emerge on the riverbank. I sit on the dock, pulling my legs close to my chest, and stare at the flowing water. I wish I had my sketchbook with me. A lot of times, when I'm not in the mood to run, I'll come out here anyway and work on my drawings. Something about the water lapping gently in the background is soothing and makes it easier for me to concentrate on getting every line and detail just right.

Behind me, something steps on a stick. The snapping sound is soft, but seems magnified against the quiet. I scramble to my feet and stare hard at the trees. I don't see anything. That figures. It's probably an animal.

I guess it's because of what's happened to me this week, but I'm extra paranoid. I know that's crazy. Why would anybody want to follow me?

Oh well, I need to get back to the house. John Miller's info isn't going to magically appear in my inbox, no matter how much I wish that would happen. And the history stuff I need to study won't miraculously imprint itself in my brain.

Any more than the weird feeling that I'm not alone won't go away.

I head back to the path, but before I can start running, Trevor emerges from behind a large oak tree. I take a step back. "What are you doing here?"

"I didn't realize I was gonna end up here," he says with a shrug. "I felt like shit after I left you at school today. I went home, but I felt like I was suffocating there. I had to get out and walk. And the next thing I know, I saw someone running ahead of me. I got closer and found . . . you." He takes a few steps toward me. I force myself to stay still even though all I want to do is flee. "I guess it was fate."

Or not. The Monroes' house is on a huge tract of land several miles down the road from here. It's possible to walk from there to here, but the thing is, I've never seen Trevor in the forest before today.

I don't know what his game is. I just know I need to get away. How to do that without making him mad again? If he grabbed my arm in front of everyone at school, what would he do to me when we're alone? "I need to get back to the house," I say, edging away from him. "Aunt Grace told me I couldn't stay out here long."

"See, there you go again," he says, running his hand through his hair. "You're trying to avoid me. I don't get it."

He probably doesn't get it. From what I've heard, no girl has ever rejected Trevor. I decide to try a different tactic. "Why don't you call me later? I really do need to get back to the house."

I take a few more steps away from Trevor, but this time he moves to block me. My already racing heart goes into overdrive. I try to keep my voice steady as I say, "I'm not kidding. I have to go home."

"And I just want to talk to you for a few minutes."

"What's going on here?"

Mr. Palmer is standing a few feet behind Trevor, holding his camera. I let out a shuddering breath. I'm so glad to see him. "Nothing. I was just leaving."

Still eying Trevor, Mr. Palmer says, "Grace will have supper done soon."

"I was just telling Trevor I need to go," I say.

Trevor glares at Mr. Palmer, who's nearly as tall as him, then suddenly his face smooths out into a neutral, almost bored expression. "I guess I'll head home, too." He backs away from us and says, "See you at school, Alora."

When he's out of sight, Mr. Palmer asks, "Are you okay?"

"I'm fine." I take a few backwards steps as I say this. While I'm glad Mr. Palmer showed up when he did, I just want to get out of here. "I'm gonna run back to the house. I need to get my exercise in for the day."

He looks in the direction Trevor went, then smiles at me. "No problem. I would join you, but I want to take a few more pictures." He holds up his camera. "I'm really enjoying the scenery out here."

I start running again but can't shake the uneasy feeling that's descended over me. Like Trevor is still out there in the woods, watching my every step.

18

BRIDGER
MARCH 17, 2146

My hurt knee twinges as I whirl around. A military Space Bender is standing a few feet away, aiming a stunner at my chest.

"Get those hands up now," she commands.

The Academy requires cadets to receive a half-stun during the first year, to get an idea of what it's like to break the rules. I swore I'd never be on the receiving end of a stunner after that. I raise my hands high over my head.

"Good boy," she says. Her dark eyes narrow as she takes in every inch of me. I always thought it would be sexy to have a woman check me out like that, but this pisses me off. "Don't you dare try to shift, Creed. I've been authorized to use whatever force is necessary to take you into custody."

As I stare at the Space Bender, with that self-satisfied smirk on her face, I truly realize how completely screwed I am. I knew there was a high possibility I'd revert to my own time since I don't have a Chronoband. I should have taken precautions. Like shifting well out of the tracking parameters the DTA obviously set up around this area. But no, I had to hurry and shift without considering every option. Now the DTA will haul me before another tribunal. My only defense then will be to plea insanity.

Or I could go back again and finish what I started.

Two choices.

Both with bad consequences.

I close my eyes but realize I shouldn't have done that when the Space Bender yells, "Stop!"

Her stunner crackles a split second before I'm hit. Fire blazes through my body. This is so much worse than a half-stun. I feel like I'm dying. My muscles freeze, and I crash to the ground.

All I can do is glare at the Space Bender as she activates her DataLink. "I've got Creed. He was attempting to shift again, so I immobilized him."

She walks a few paces away, whispering into her DataLink. She doesn't have to worry about me going anywhere—I won't be able to move for at least ten minutes. And shifting is impossible until the effects of the stun wear off. It's just me and the ground. I grit my teeth so hard that my jaw starts to hurt.

The smell of dirt and grass fills my nostrils as I concentrate on calming myself. I try to think soothing thoughts. Like grabbing her stunner and shooting her so she can see how it feels.

Footsteps crunch across the ground behind me. "Well, look at what the cat dragged in," a man says in a nasally voice. He walks around me, followed by another man. It's the DTA official and the overweight museum tour guide.

The tour guide glares at me. "This is the fugitive?"

"Yes," the Space Bender says.

"Good. Now will you leave? I'm losing credits," he says while mopping his sweaty brow with a handkerchief.

Talk about disgusting.

The DTA official gives him a contemptuous look before saying, "We appreciate your understanding in this situation, but this is a matter of national security. I have to ask you to leave us now."

The tour guide's face reddens. "National security? Why don't you say what it really is—a cover up? Well, I'll tell you why. The government doesn't want the public to know that one of their precious Time Benders has gone crazy. That's what you get for messing with genetics!"

The DTA official sighs heavily before taking the tour guide by the arm. "Sir, I need you to come with me."

The tour guide continues to rant as the official leads him back to the museum. Even though he's a Purist, I almost feel sorry for him. They'll probably use a Mind Redeemer on him.

The minutes tick by. So slowly. My mouth has completely lost all moisture.

"Get up," the Space Bender says, just when I think I'm about to completely wild out.

I test my fingers first to see if they can move. They wiggle without any trouble. I slowly sit up. The lingering effect of the stunner is obvious. I wobble as I climb back to my feet.

The Space Bender points toward a shuttle behind the museum with her stunner. "Move."

"What are you going to do to me?" I ask in a hoarse whisper.

"No questions, Creed. Just walk."

My feet move as if they're made of steel. A guard waits outside the shuttle, looking like she'd rather be somewhere else. Another DTA official exits when we reach it.

He nods at my captor. "We're to keep Creed here until the general arrives."

"Understood," she replies.

I look back and forth between them. "Excuse me? What's going on?"

The DTA official says, "The general will arrive soon."

My stomach twists as I wonder what's going on. I expected to be taken into custody and transported back to New Denver. Not to have a big shot from the DTA travel out here. This is really bad.

A few minutes later a thin whining sounds in the distance. Soon a shuttle appears in the sky and lands. Two burly soldiers exit first and take up post on either side of the opening. The next person out makes my stomach twist even more than I thought possible.

It's General Anderson.

He fixes me in a stony stare, only looking away when he reaches us. "Excellent job, Lieutenant," he says to the Space Bender.

"Thank you, sir," she chirps.

"You are dismissed. Report back to headquarters immediately."

"Yes, sir," she says moments before vanishing.

General Anderson's gaze falls on the DTA official next. "You're also dismissed. Please assist with the memory erasure of anyone who witnessed Mr. Creed's appearance earlier."

The official gives a curt nod and stiffly walks toward the museum.

General Anderson's eyes swing back to me. Seconds stretch into eternity before he says, "Don't you have anything to say for yourself?"

"Probably not. He should have known better than to come out here and stick his nose in something that doesn't concern him." Another familiar voice floats from somewhere behind General Anderson. A low groan escapes me before I can stifle it. It's Professor March. This day keeps getting better and better. If my mother comes out next, I'm going to ask them to go ahead and shoot me. Professor March stops next to General Anderson. "Care to tell us what kind of havoc you've created?"

Despite being in this mess, I'm relieved. I didn't do any permanent damage in 2013 if he's asking me that. But from the looks of those two huge soldiers standing by General Anderson's shuttle, I've stirred up something big. I decide to play dumb. "I don't know what you're talking about, sir."

"Right. So you lied to your mother for no reason and come all the way to Georgia for fun? Try again," Professor March says, folding his arms over his chest.

The way Professor March looks makes me pause. He cocks his head to the side and raises his eyebrows. What is he trying to tell me?

"Enough of the games," General Anderson snaps. He marches up to me and stands so close I can smell stale coffee on his breath. "We used a Mind Bender to extract information from your friends. I don't know how it's possible, but we know somehow your father made contact with you on the Foster Assassination time trip. We know he left you a message. What we don't know is *why* he did that or what year you shifted to. I'm sure you can appreciate the seriousness of your situation, so don't lie to me."

My mouth falls open. I'd give anything to find out how Dad kept them from witnessing him at the Foster Assassination. But that's not even the most important thing. The fact that they're asking me all these questions tells me that the DTA wouldn't send another investigative team back to follow Dad while he was still alive. Meaning this isn't considered an immediate threat to our present.

So the only way General Anderson can get answers is by questioning me. If he sent a team back without authorization, the Chronobands would record the trip and alert the DTA.

Very interesting.

Professor March adds, "Think carefully. Your future depends on it."

A strange sensation startles me. It starts deep in my skull, a slow pressure that gradually increases. My eyes grow wider with the realization of what's happening. A Mind Bender is trying to hack my memories. I glance around the area, but nobody else is in sight. Whoever it is has to be in the shuttle. General Anderson or Professor March must have sent a signal to the Mind Bender to search my thoughts.

Hell no. That's not going to work.

Without closing my eyes, I concentrate on one thing—my father. He taught me to build a mental block to keep Mind Benders from extracting information. During our practice exercises, I always focused on the sound of his voice as he walked me through the steps.

Son, you've got to think of a mental block like it's a real wall. Think of yourself putting up a barrier between you and the Mind Bender. Layer by layer, brick by brick.

Picture the brick wall as an impenetrable fortress, one that can't be cracked, no matter how tough the assault may be. You've got to be stronger than that. And you are *strong. Just believe in yourself.*

I'm not sure if it'll work. Still I cling to the memory as if it's the only source of light in a dark room. Gradually the pressure fades to a dull ache.

My eyes flick to Professor March. He gives the smallest shake of his head. I almost stop breathing. The Mind Bender will sharpen the next attempt to extract my memories.

But nothing happens.

My gaze shifts back to General Anderson and I force myself to hold his stare. "I don't have anything to say, sir."

His jaw clenches. "I'm giving you the chance to help yourself. Don't make the same mistake your father did. What was Leithan doing? What year did you shift to? Why did he want you to go?"

General Anderson might as well have punched me in the stomach with those words. If I'm not mistaken, *he* didn't know what my father was doing in 2013.

My mind is reeling. My father—Mr. Always-Follow-the-Rules—really had gone rogue. My hands tighten to fists.

"I see you're not going to cooperate." General Anderson spins on his heel and zeroes in on Professor March. "I thought you said he would cooperate if you came."

Professor March shrugs. "I guess I was wrong."

The general stomps toward his shuttle, barking at the soldiers, "Escort Mr. Creed to the shuttle. Now!"

As the soldiers advance toward us, Professor March looks at his hand. His fingers uncurl, and something falls to the ground. It's a stunner. "Your father would be proud of you," he whispers.

Time seems to have slowed to a crawl. I watch him turn and head back to the shuttle. I glance from the soldiers to the stunner. For a moment, I consider leaving it. I'm already in so much trouble. If I pick up the stunner and use it, I could be nulled if they catch me. Or even executed. I'm not sure it's worth it.

But the game has changed. Dad wasn't on an assignment with the DTA. He was working for someone else. Probably whoever wrote the message I found on the hidden DataDisk. General Anderson wants to know.

I want to know.

I lunge for the stunner. The soldiers look shocked for a moment, but quickly swing their stunners at me.

"Stop him!" General Anderson shouts.

My fingers close around the weapon and I swing my arm toward the soldiers. I fire repeatedly while rolling to the side. Shots whiz past me, then the soldiers slump to the ground. I scramble to my feet and aim at General Anderson.

"You're making a big mistake," he says, his face a bright shade of red.

I hesitate, my hand shaking again. So much for the Calmer working.

"If you do this, I will find you. And I *will* bury you."

This time I fire. General Anderson joins the soldiers on the ground.

Professor March blows out a puff of air and runs a hand across his neck.

"Professor," I begin, but he shakes his head at me. He mouths, *shoot me*.

My heart feels like it's about to explode out of my body. I want to tell him I can't, that I don't want to hurt him. I don't want to do any more damage. But he's right. General Anderson will suspect something if I don't shoot him. I raise the stunner again and fire.

For a few moments, I stay frozen in place. Professor March lays there, muscles jerking. Guilt floods through me. I can't believe I shot him. I know he'll be okay. But still, I've never shot anyone before today.

I lean over and dry heave, thinking I'm now a walking dead man. I'm so furing screwed.

"Hey!" I look toward the back porch of the museum. A DTA official is standing there. "Stop!"

Time for me to shift. I close my eyes and concentrate on Alora's death date again, this time welcoming the nothingness that devours me.

19

My stomach churns as I wait for Sela in the parking lot. Trevor hasn't tried to talk to me once, not even in history, but he could still try to trap me out here.

I shield my eyes from the bright sun and search through the students. When I finally spot Sela racing toward me, doing an awkward speed walk, I allow myself to relax.

When she sees me, she gets a very large, manic-looking grin. "You'll never guess what just happened."

"You won the lottery."

"No, although that would be nice." Once we're in the car, Sela's grin manages to grow even bigger. I can't help but smile back. "Levi invited us to a party at his house tomorrow night."

And just like that, my smile vanishes as if someone flipped a light switch. Levi Banks is the only child of parents who have more money than sense, as Aunt Grace says, and rarely stay home. As a result, Levi likes to throw parties whenever they're out of town, but you can only go if you're invited.

He's also one of Trevor's best friends.

Sela pulls out of the parking lot. "I was talking to Jess at my locker when he stopped. He was so nice. He said he couldn't believe he'd never thought to invite me before. He even said I could ask anyone I wanted. So of course Jess and Miranda are going. But you have to go, too."

It's strange Levi decided to invite all of us just when Trevor has decided to make me his latest conquest. Really strange. I glance back to Sela. I hate to spoil her excitement, but she's forgotten my situation. "Well, I would go, but I'm still grounded. Remember?"

Sela's smile falters. "Seriously? I thought your aunt would've let you off the hook by now."

I shake my head. "No. She said I'm free after the weekend."

"That's so not fair." Sela drums her fingers on the steering wheel. "You know, maybe I can talk her into letting you go anyway."

"It won't work. When Aunt Grace makes up her mind about something, she sticks with it."

"Maybe," Sela drawls, "but she loves me to death. I bet you ten bucks that I can sweet-talk her into letting you go."

"You're wasting your time. Besides, she'd never let me go to one of Levi's parties. She's heard about them."

"Girl, do you think I'd tell her the truth? I'm not even telling my parents. We're officially going out to eat and to see a movie." Sela uses air quotes when she says officially.

There's no point in arguing with Sela. She's high from the invite and nothing will put her in a bad mood. Well, I'm sure she'll be in a less happy mood once Aunt Grace shoots her down, but it won't last long. Sela will go to the party anyway, along with the Brainless Twins. That thought sends a twinge of jealousy shooting through me. I don't want to go. Really. But Sela already spends a lot of time with Jess and Miranda when I'm not around. The three of them going to the party together will just further set me apart.

By the time Sela parks on the inn's circle driveway, she's decided how we'll fix our hair and planned a shopping trip to get new clothes.

While I climb out of the car like an old lady, Sela bounces out with the energy of a small kid. "Hurry up, slowpoke," she calls over her shoulder.

She's nowhere to be seen by the time I lug my books inside, but voices chime from the kitchen. The smell of something freshly baked saturates the air. I drop my books on the table by the stairs and hurry to the kitchen, where I find Aunt Grace spreading the last bits of strawberry frosting on a pink cake. From the bewildered expression on her face, I can tell Sela has filled her in on our fake plans.

"I'm sorry, hon, but Alora can't go out this weekend. Maybe y'all can wait until next week. Provided that she stays out of trouble."

I flash an I-told-you-so look at Sela. She ignores me. "But Mrs. Evans, I've already bought the tickets for the movie and everything. I've been planning this for ages." Sela proceeds to spin an elaborate story about how she wanted to take her three best friends out to show us how much she appreciates us and for making her feel so welcome since she moved to Willow Creek. From anyone else, it would sound like complete bull, but I have to admit Sela makes it sound real.

By the time Sela finishes, Aunt Grace is chewing on her bottom lip. "Sugar, I didn't know you had such a hard time. I guess I can let Alora off the hook early." She puts the spatula in the frosting bowl and folds Sela into a hug.

Sela grins over Aunt Grace's shoulder and flashes two thumbs up at me. I have to choke back a snort. I didn't believe she'd be able to pull it off. Then a sinking feeling settles in my chest.

Now I'll have to go to that stupid party with Sela. Wonderful.

As Sela extracts herself form Aunt Grace's hug, we hear a muffled shriek. We scramble over to the sink and peer out the window. An older-looking couple is in the backyard, halfway to the garden, carrying on about something. It looks like they're talking or arguing with someone else, but I can't make out who it is.

"Who are they?" I ask Aunt Grace.

"That's Mr. and Mrs. Jamison. They dropped in today and are staying for the weekend. Nice couple, but a little odd."

Sela lets out a low whistle. "Who's the hottie with them?"

I glance back out the window. Mr. Jamison has moved out of the way, revealing the third person. "No way," I whisper, feeling a tingle in my stomach.

It's the guy who was here a few days ago.

"I wonder what he wants," Aunt Grace mutters as she heads for the back door. Sela and I follow.

"Hello? You never told me who the guy is," Sela says as we descend the back porch steps.

"I'll tell you later."

Ahead of us, Mrs. Jamison is waving her arms wildly, gesturing toward Bridger, while Mr. Jamison snaps a picture of him. In return, Bridger holds his hands up like he doesn't want to have his picture taken. I'm surprised he's still wearing the same uniform he had on the other day. And he looks like he recently took a dirt bath.

"Will you stop that?" He asks in an exasperated voice.

"What's going on?" Aunt Grace asks when we join them.

Mrs. Jamison turns to me, her face a kaleidoscope of excitement. "Can you see him?"

"See who?" I ask.

"The ghost!" she yells, pointing to Bridger.

"I'm not a ghost!" he shouts, looking at me. "Tell her."

"Charles, she can see him! Oh, this is marvelous!" Mrs. Jamison fans herself. "Lordy, I'm light-headed."

"Calm down, dear," her husband says, patting her on the shoulder. "Remember your blood pressure."

Sela giggles. I scowl at her before repeating Aunt Grace's question.

Bridger points to Mrs. Jamison. "This woman thinks I'm a ghost. Obviously, I'm not."

"Yes, he is. He appeared out of thin air. Charles and I saw him. Didn't we?"

"We sure did," Mr. Jamison replies, snapping another picture.

I close my eyes. Great, we have ghost hunters staying with us. We get those from time to time, since the inn is a former plantation house. They're always convinced that spirits of Civil War–era people haunt places like this. "He's not a ghost. I know him."

Instantly, the Jamisons' excited expressions disappear like someone erased them. "You know him?" Mrs. Jamison asks in a disbelieving voice.

"Yeah. I met him a few days ago. His name is Bridger . . ." I raise my eyebrows at him.

He looks stunned for a moment before answering. "Creed. Bridger Creed. And I am *not* a ghost. I promise."

"But we saw you appear out of nowhere."

Aunt Grace sighs. "Mrs. Jamison, it is hot outside. Maybe your eyes are playing tricks on you."

"But—"

"My niece and I met him two days ago. He's new in town and he's most definitely alive."

The Jamisons cast a wistful glance at Bridger. I can practically see their dreams of finding a real spirit slip away.

"Dear, I guess we need to go get ready for supper," Mr. Jamison says, taking his wife by the arm. "Sorry to bother you, young man. It was an honest mistake." He escorts his wife back to the inn.

"Wow, talk about crazy." Sela breaks the silence, twirling a finger next to her temple. She smiles at Bridger and offers her hand. "Since Alora has forgotten her manners, I'll intro myself. I'm Sela Perkins."

"Nice to meet you," he says. From the tone of his voice, he doesn't mean it. He toys with the bag strap hanging over his shoulder and flicks his eyes back toward the forest.

"So, what brings you back?" I ask. "We didn't expect to see you again after your disappearing act."

"I wasn't expecting to be here again so soon, either."

Aunt Grace props her hands on her hips. "That was rude of you to up and leave without saying goodbye."

Bridger's mouth opens and shuts several times before he says, "I'm sorry about that. It's just that I got an urgent call from . . . my mother. She needed me back home and I had to leave right then. I didn't want to bother you anymore."

"But everything's okay now?" Aunt Grace asks. "How about your knee?"

"Everything's fine, so I came back to look for my father again."

Aunt Grace's face softens. She glances to me, then back to Bridger. "Well, my offer still stands. You're welcome to stay here."

Bridger doesn't say anything for a few seconds. It's like he's trying to figure out the pieces to an invisible puzzle. Finally he says, "Okay, I'll do it."

"Well, come on inside and I'll show you to your room."

A slow smile spreads across Sela's face as we watch Bridger and Aunt Grace walk to the house. "So he's new in town, huh?"

"Yes."

"Sah-weet." Before I know it, Sela calls out, "Hey, Bridger, wait up."

I stare openmouthed as Bridger faces us. Aunt Grace tilts her head to the side. I don't have any choice but to follow Sela and see what she's scheming.

"Are you gonna be in town long?" she asks.

He nods. "I think so."

"Oh, good. Then you'll need someone to show you around."

Bridger now has a deer-caught-in-the-headlights look. I probably look the same because I know what Sela is about to ask.

"I was thinking," Sela continues, twirling a strand of hair around her finger, "you could go out with me and Alora and some of our friends tomorrow night. We could show you around."

I know I'm looking at Sela like she's sprouted a second head. I want to ask her what she thinks she's doing, asking a guy we don't even know to go to a party with us. It's insane, even if he is cute.

Apparently Bridger doesn't think so. He hesitates for a moment, then says, "Sure, why not?"

20

BRIDGER
APRIL 12, 2013

After Grace deposits me in my room, I collapse on the bed. The fact that I'm an idiot keeps racing through my mind. It's like I'm trying to see how many stupid things I can do today. Travel illegally to the past? Check. Shoot my professor and a high-ranking DTA official? Check. Agree to socialize with some ghosts? Check.

Everything would be fine if I could shift to moments before I arrived back in 2146. I could warn myself to get out of there before the Space Bender could catch me. I wouldn't be a prime candidate for nulling right now. But you're not supposed to change what's already happened.

This is why I'm having such a hard time wrapping my mind around the fact that Dad wanted to prevent Alora's death. How it that possible without destroying the timeline?

I throw my hand over my eyes. My head could burst into flames and I'm sure I wouldn't feel any worse.

Then I remember something Alora said when I was dealing with that psycho couple. She told them she met me a few days ago. My hands fist, and I slam them against the blue comforter.

I'm still three months away from Alora's death date.

So basically I'm stuck here because I can't risk shifting back to my own time. General Anderson must be wilding out right now. He'll have the search parameters extended to encompass way outside of Willow Creek. And if I'm caught, he'll make damn sure I won't escape again. Not even with Professor March's help. And *why* did he help me escape? Nothing makes sense anymore.

I stare up at the ceiling, trying to come up with a way to get closer to Alora's death date. But of course I can't. Not without a Chronoband.

I blink back at the heaviness clouding my thoughts. I don't know how long I've been awake. It feels like forever. Time travel requires tons of energy, and I've already shifted three times today. I roll off the bed and strip to my Skivvies. The sour tang of sweat is even worse now that I'm undressed. I think about taking a shower, but it can wait. Instead, I fall back on the bed and close my eyes.

It's not like I'm going anywhere soon.

A loud rapping at the door jolts me awake. I blink several times, taking in the antique furniture. And then I groan.

Before I can say anything, the door opens and Alora peeks in. "Hey, Aunt Grace wants . . ." She stops when she notices I'm stretched out across the bed in my Skivvies. Her eyes seem to double in size. "I'm so sorry!"

She jerks the door shut.

"Alora, wait a minute," I say as I scramble off the bed. I grab my pants and pull them on as I half hop, half walk to the door.

In the hallway, Alora is leaning against the wall, taking deep breaths. Her hair is pressed behind her, but one strand is stuck against her cheek. My fingers itch to reach over and brush it away. Something I would've done with Vika.

"I'm so sorry. I shouldn't have barged in like that," she says.

"It's fine."

"No, it's not. Aunt Grace would have a fit if she knew I . . ." Alora trails off as she glances at me. She focuses on my bare chest for a second before looking down.

I feel sorry for Alora. If possible, her face is even redder than it was when she first saw me on the bed. So what if she saw me undressed? She's acting like she's never seen a guy in his Skivvies.

Before I can stop myself, I reach out to lift her chin. "Hey, it's not a big deal."

I start to tell her something else, but all thought evaporates when she fixates on me with those blue eyes. It's almost like I'm shifting through time. I can't breathe. I don't know what I'm feeling, but it's not good. I shake my head and drop my hand.

Alora takes a quick step back. "I've got to go. Aunt Grace almost has supper ready."

I don't know why, but I feel empty as Alora turns to walk away, then I remember she wanted something. "Hey, what did you want to ask me?"

"Oh, yeah." Alora pivots around and runs her hand across her forehead. "I forgot. Aunt Grace wanted to know if you'd like to join us for supper."

"I thought I'd have to eat somewhere else," I say. Am I wrong? These old-style bed-and-breakfast-type places only served food in the morning.

"Usually you would, but Aunt Grace thought you'd like to eat with us tonight. But you don't have to if you've got other plans." She finishes the last sentence in a rush.

The uncomfortable feeling from moments before disappears. This is perfect. If I'm stuck here for three months, I might as well start trying to figure out why my dad wanted to save Alora from dying. "No, I'd like that. And if it's okay, could I get you to show me around later?"

Alora bites her lower lip and glances past me. I turn to see what she's looking at, but there are only more closed doors. "There's something I need to do, but I guess I could show you around first."

"Great. I can't wait."

Alora's face glows as she smiles back. "I'll see you downstairs."

"Okay. I'll be down as soon as I shower."

I watch Alora walk away for a few moments before ducking back in my room. Weird, but I find myself feeling lighter and grinning.

I tell myself it's because this is the first step toward finding the truth.

Not because I want to spend time with Alora.

"Are you sure you don't want more?" Grace asks as I finish a huge slice of her strawberry cake.

I glance at the cake sitting on the kitchen counter before declining. I wouldn't mind having another. But the entire time we were eating supper, Grace asked one question after another. And I had to lie. She's definitely a nosy ghost.

Alora grabs our empty plates and sets them by the sink. "I'm going to show Bridger around for a little while before it gets too dark."

"Oh really? And where are y'all going?" Grace asks.

"What's up with all the questions?" Alora asks.

Grace's gaze slides over to me. "It's my responsibility to know what my niece is doing. Wouldn't you agree, Bridger?"

I know that look. My mom does something similar when she's in my business. The difference is that I can tell Grace is concerned for Alora's safety, not because she's a control freak. So I nod yes.

Grace's face relaxes. "Well, then, you two go on. I'll take cleaning duty."

Alora doesn't waste any time hurrying outside. I follow before Grace can think of something else to quiz me about. When we're on the back porch, she says, "Sorry about all that."

"Why?"

"Because of Aunt Grace. She likes to know everything."

"Don't worry about it. She's just concerned. There's nothing wrong with that."

"Yeah," Alora says with a shrug. "But she was starting to get on my nerves. I can imagine how you felt."

"Well, she is letting me stay here for a while and she doesn't know me," I say, smiling.

"Oh, please." Alora rolls her eyes. "That's not it. We have strangers here all the time." She then waves her hand around the general area of the backyard. "So, what would you like to see?"

I scan the yard. It looks the same and yet different from the museum setup in 2146. The grassy expanse stretching toward the forest is the same, with a dirt path bisecting it. But in this time there is a large garden full of brightly colored roses. There is also a small, paved area to the left of the porch where Grace and the other guests park their autos.

I remember the article on Dad's DataDisk. Alora's body is supposed to be found in an old, abandoned house on the property. I gesture toward a path parting the forest. "What's that way?"

Alora's mouth presses to a thin line. "It leads to the river."

"Can we go there?"

Alora focuses on the path for a few seconds, then says, "I suppose so."

I watch her as she bounds down the steps, her hair bouncing over her shoulders. The late afternoon sun makes it shine like it's lit from within, kind of sexy-like. I shake my head, disgusted. I don't know what's wrong with me.

Alora doesn't say anything once we're on the path. She walks fast, like she doesn't want to be here. I match her pace and check out the forest. Sun streaks through the trees, mixing dark with light. It gives the place a creepy atmosphere. I try to locate the abandoned house, but I don't see it anywhere.

The silence is getting to me. "So, have you lived here your whole life?"

Her jaw tenses before she says, "No."

"Okay then," I say slowly. "So how long have you lived here?"

"Ten years. Why?"

"No particular reason. Just trying to get to know you better."

"Right." She folds her arms across her chest and speeds up. "The river's just up ahead."

Wondering why she seemed so evasive when I asked a simple question, I decide to leave it alone for now.

The sound of flowing water reaches us before we get to the river. Alora visibly relaxes the closer we get. When we emerge from the forest, she smiles. A genuine smile that makes my pulse speed up. I stop and close my eyes. This is ridiculous. I've got to be having this kind of reaction because of her resemblance to Vika. Still, that's messed up.

Alora runs to a pier jutting out over the river. She sinks on the wooden planks and hugs her legs close to her body. I sit next to her, waiting for her to say something. Dad always told me if a girl doesn't want to talk, pushing her won't work.

"This is my favorite place to go," Alora finally says. "It's really peaceful out here."

I nod. "I know what you mean."

Alora looks at me. "Do you have somewhere you like to go back home?"

"Yes." I think of the mountains. I remember all the times Dad used to take me and Shan camping. All the times I went with Zed and Elijah. If I hadn't been so determined to find out what Dad wanted me to do, I'd be there right now. My throat tightens.

"I can tell you miss it."

A sense of loss hits me. I hadn't thought about it, being so obsessed with my dad, but that's a part of my life I'll never get back. I swallow past the lump in my throat and whisper, "Yeah, I do."

A muffled sound shatters the moment. Alora reaches into her pocket and withdraws her phone. She peers at the screen and lets out a little yelp. "I've got to take this. I'll be right back."

She strides off the pier and walks in a crazy pattern, going in one direction and then another. She finally stops near the woods. Her words drift back to me, soft, yet urgent.

While Alora talks, I try to figure out what's wrong with her. Obviously, she's not comfortable talking about her past. It has to be the key to why Dad wanted to save her. But what could be so important? I've got to somehow draw the info out of her.

But how without sounding like a nosy creeper?

Alora ends the call and walks back to the pier. Maybe I can get something out of her now. I scratch the back of my neck and try to act bored. "Important call?" I ask all smooth-like.

"I thought it was," she says in a quiet voice.

"Anything you want to share?" I hope I'm not pushing it with that line.

She grows serious, narrowing her eyes at me. "Why do you care?"

Think, Bridger. Dig yourself out of this before she clams up completely. "You seemed a little stressed earlier. And then you were all excited about that call, but now you seem kind of sad again. I'm concerned, that's all."

Her expression softens. "I'm sorry. I've just had a lot on my mind lately."

"I know what you mean."

I leave it at that and hope like hell that Alora will decide to trust me. She just looks at me, then back at the river. My mind screams for me to do something.

Finally, she sighs. "I can't believe I'm going to do this, but I need to tell somebody." She takes a deep breath. "That was a guy named John Miller, but not the one I'm looking for. I've been trying to contact the one who was my father's friend. I've searched a lot of phone numbers belonging to guys with that name, and I've been calling them, trying to figure out which one is the right number." Alora looks down at her phone like it's the most important thing in the world. "I'm still looking."

"Why do you need to talk to him?"

Alora seems unsure if she wants to continue.

"It's okay," I say. "If you don't want to tell me, I get it."

She closes her eyes for a moment, and then looks up at the sky. "My dad left me with Aunt Grace when I was six, and I don't know why. I can't remember much of anything before that. Hell, I don't even know if my parents are still alive."

"Why did he do that?"

"I don't know, and Aunt Grace won't tell me. She says he never told her, but I think she's lying."

"Why would she lie to you?"

"She thinks the truth could damage me," Alora says with a scowl.

My mind reels. Alora is having a hard time remembering anything from her childhood. And my father wanted to save her. Somehow I think the two are tied together. I wonder if it's possible that someone used a Mind Redeemer on her. Or maybe it's just because she was so young.

"So, that's why I'm looking for answers on my own." Alora stops and lets out a heavy sigh. "You have no idea what it's like, going every day not being able to remember my own parents. I mean, I knew them once, but in a way it's like I never did. And I kind of feel cheated, you know?" Her eyes fill with tears.

Fure, I'm in uncharted territory here. I have no clue how to deal with an emotional female. "Um, well, you could . . ." I begin, but something over Alora's shoulder catches my attention.

Just inside the tree line, the air in one spot is rippling. Like the air over a flame. I blink, thinking it's just my imagination. But the ripple is still there each time I open my eyes.

It's a cloaked person in the forest. And since that technology doesn't exist in this time, it has to be a Time Bender.

I spring to my feet and run toward whomever it is.

"What's the matter?" Alora asks.

I don't respond. What can I say? *Oh, it's nothing, just an invisible time traveler watching us.* Someone who could be reporting my location back to the DTA right now.

I get to the tree line, but whoever was there moments before is gone. I turn around, my head snapping from side to side. I don't see anything. What I'd give for a comm-set right now.

Alora comes up by me, her face pale. "Did you see someone?"

Even though I'm worried about who was spying on us, I can't help but notice how shaken she is. "I thought I did, but it's nothing."

"Are you sure?" She's peering into the forest, as if she expects someone to pop out at any moment.

I place a hand on her shoulder. Weird, but I feel all protective. "I'm positive. I guess my mind was playing tricks on me."

Alora's muscles relax under my fingers. "Oh, okay." She offers a thin smile. "You know, I need to get back to the house. I've got some things I need to do."

"That's probably a good idea."

We talk as we make our way back through the forest. Alora still seems on edge. I try to keep her mind off whatever scared her back there. I can't help but feel that something else happened to Alora recently in the forest. Something she doesn't want to tell me.

I don't know what that could be, but I do know one thing. From now on, I'm staying close to Alora. I'll try to figure out why her parents apparently abandoned her.

21

Sela turns in the long, paved driveway leading up to Levi's house. The closer we get, the harder my heart hammers and the more I wish I'd stayed home. What if Trevor tries to start something? I rub my arm where he grabbed me a few days ago. There's a small bruise on it.

Cars and trucks line the driveway. Sela parks and pulls her phone out of her purse. Her fingers fly over the screen.

"Who are you texting?" I ask

"Jess."

Oh, yes. We can't forget about the Brainless Twins.

After a moment, the phone chirps and Sela reads the message. "Jess says she and Miranda are waiting by the front door."

"Great," I mutter. As I climb out of the car, the hem of my dress rides up and two guys passing by notice. One leers at me. I tug it back down, wishing I had on a pair of jeans. I feel too slutty in this thing.

"Do I look okay?" Sela asks, coming up next to me. She smoothes the bottom of her dress and rearranges the top, making sure her cleavage is showing. She's blessed up there. Sela may have lost a lot of weight, but the boobs stayed.

"You're gorgeous." I try to grin, but I'm sure it looks more like a grimace. All I can focus on is Levi's house and the muffled music drifting from within. A few people are standing around outside, talking and laughing. I wonder where Trevor is.

Bridger climbs out of the back seat and joins us. "So, ladies, are you ready?"

No. And I swear, from the expression on his face, he's not either.

"Oh, yes," Sela says, grabbing Bridger's hand and mine. "Come on, you two. I'm ready to dance!"

My feet move forward, but my mind screams for me to stay at the car. I don't know if I can do this.

"It's okay. I'm here with you," Bridger whispers, his warm breath tickling my ear.

"Thanks." Funny, but it makes me feel a tiny bit better. I may not know Bridger very well, but I'd rather be with him than most anyone else here.

The Brainless Twins practically assault Sela when they see us. They hug her and gush about how much fun they're having. Of course, they ignore me, but flash dazzling, plastic smiles at Bridger.

After introducing them, Sela touches Bridger on the arm. "Promise you'll dance with me, okay?"

Bridger's cuts his eyes from Sela to me. "Um . . . sure."

Yeah, Sela is definitely not subtle.

Once we're inside, I can't hear anything, much less think. From where we're standing, it seems like every inch is packed with people, many of them holding plastic cups or beer bottles. Levi supposedly invites certain people to his parties, but it looks like the entire school came. And the smell . . . let's just say I imagine the boys' locker room smells something like this. I want to go back outside, but Miranda has other ideas—she leads us to a large den that's the source of the music.

Sela grabs my hand again. "Let's dance!"

I shake my head. I'm pretty sure I'll look like someone having a seizure.

Sela frowns. "Oh, come on!"

"You go ahead," Bridger says to her. "I'll stay with Alora." He puts a hand on my shoulder. My skin tingles under his touch.

Sela rolls her eyes. "Suit yourself, but you're gonna be miserable if you just stand around all night." Then she disappears into the crowd with the Brainless Twins trailing her, leaving me feeling abandoned.

My spine stiffens—all I want to do is get out of here. I almost decide to flee, but the warmth radiating from Bridger brings me back to reality. No. I'm not going to run away like a spoiled brat. I'm here and I'm going to make the best of it.

Somehow.

I start to speak to Bridger, but his expression makes me pause. His eyes dart from person to person, almost like he's searching for someone in particular. Probably someone who's not so lame to hang out with.

He suddenly looks over at me. "You know, you really look like you don't want to go out there."

"No, not really," I reply, turning my attention back to Sela. Now she's laughing with those twits.

"I don't believe you. And you know what? I think you don't want to go out there because you think you'll look too weird."

I glance sharply at him. It's almost like he can read my mind. "What would you know about that?"

"I get it. I used to be the same way when I started going to a dance club back home, but I got over it. I thought everyone would talk about how wild I looked out there. Then I realized nobody gave a shit. They just wanted to have a good time. I wanted to have a good time." He touches the tip of my nose. "And I think you want to have a good time."

My heart is full-on galloping. His eyes are so intense, it's like he can see my soul. But that's completely ridiculous and cliché. Still, he's right. I've never been invited to a party before. I've been content, but I don't remember being really happy.

I *want* to be happy.

I want to have a good time, even if it's for one night.

Bridger takes me by the hand. "Would you like to dance?"

I nod and his fingers tighten around mine. Before I know it I'm in the middle of the den, surrounded by dozens of writhing bodies.

I freeze, feeling stupid.

Bridger says, "Relax. Forget about everyone and focus on me."

He begins to move with the music. I hesitate, but he pulls me toward him, so close I can't help but move with him. I feel weird at first, but soon I just concentrate on Bridger as his body molds against mine, moving in perfect sync with me. As I loosen up, everything else melts away. It's just the two of us. I laugh, feeling more alive than I have in a long time.

We dance for two more songs until I see a familiar figure pushing his way through the crowd.

Trevor.

His eyes are fixed on me. And he doesn't look happy.

"Are you okay?" Bridger asks.

I don't have time to answer before Trevor reaches us. His eyes comb my entire body in a way that makes me want to shower in bleach.

"Hey, Alora. You wanna dance?" His words are slurred, and even with the mass consumption of alcohol going on all around us, the smell of beer on him is overpowering.

Bridger's mouth presses to a thin line as he faces Trevor. And he has to look up. Trevor's about three or four inches taller than Bridger, but he doesn't let that intimidate him. Bridger stands up straighter and squares his shoulders.

"She's dancing with me."

Trevor barely glances at him. "I didn't ask you."

"And I didn't hear her say yes." Bridger's hands curl into fists.

I refuse to let them fight in the middle of the party. It'll ruin everything. I jump between them and put my hands on their chests and push. "Stop it."

Bridger's eyes snap from Trevor to me. "I won't start anything."

Trevor points a finger at Bridger. "'Course you won't. Ain't nobody gonna mess with me."

Now I'm pissed. Trevor is so used to getting everything he wants, but it's time he realizes I'm not a prize for him to win. "Just leave me the hell alone. I don't want to dance with you."

By now the people dancing near us notice something is going on. They stop dancing and gape, but nobody does anything to help. Figures.

Trevor doesn't say anything at first. He takes a long swig of his beer and shrugs. "Whatever. You're nothing but a bitch anyway."

And then he leaves, heading toward the back of the house. With Trevor gone, everyone resumes dancing.

"What was that about?" Bridger asks.

I shake my head, feeling deflated. "It's a long story."

"Why don't we go outside and you tell me?"

That sounds perfect.

As we try to extract ourselves from the den, I search for Sela. She's on the far side of the room with the Brainless Twins, talking with a group of girls, including, of all people, Kate. Jealousy cuts through me.

Outside, the night air is cooler, but it feels nice after the stuffiness inside.

There's nowhere to sit in the front yard, so Bridger leads me around back. A large outdoor light illuminates the entire area. A patio set and lounge chairs line the inground pool. All but one are taken. Bridger goes straight to it.

Once we're perched on the lounge chair, I tell Bridger about everything Trevor has done, even following me in the forest.

Bridger rubs one of his fists with his other hand. "Somebody needs to kick his ass."

"No," I say. That's the last thing I want. I mean, Bridger just got here and he's got his own problems to deal with. He doesn't need to worry about my issues. "The best thing to do is ignore him. He'll get the hint and find someone else to chase soon enough."

The words sound good. I wish I believed them.

Bridger glances toward the house. "Looks like we've got company."

Sela stands outside the French doors on the patio, scoping out the backyard. I wave until she sees me.

"Hey," she says when she gets to us. She plops down between Bridger and me, forcing us to make room. "I've been looking everywhere for y'all."

I'm sure she has.

"It was too hot inside," Bridger says.

"Tell me about it," Sela says, fanning herself. "It's like a freaking oven in there."

"Where are Jess and Miranda?" I ask. It's not like them to be far from Sela when she's around.

Sela heaves a dramatic sigh. "They're dancing with two guys we just met. And I didn't want to stay in there all by myself."

"Okay," I drawl. So Sela's new besties ditched her. Somehow, I can't make myself feel sorry for her.

Sela babbles about this and that for a few minutes. Bridger and I answer when she asks a question, but otherwise just let her talk. Then out of nowhere, she says, "Oh, I almost forgot! Did you hear about Naomi?"

"No. Why?" I ask.

"Get this. Kate told us that Naomi's been boohooing nonstop since Trevor broke up with her. And when she tried to talk to him again yesterday after school they got in a huge fight. Anyway, she didn't bother going home last night, and nobody has seen her all day, either."

A chill crawls over my skin. It's probably nothing. I'm no fan of Naomi, but I wonder why she'd go all drama queen, especially over a jerk like Trevor. It's even weirder for her not to tell Kate where she went.

"Have her parents called the police?" I ask.

"Kate didn't say, but I imagine they have by now. I'm sure she's holed up in some hotel, drowning her sorrows in ice cream." Sela does this exaggerated shiver like the thought of eating ice cream is too horrible to imagine. "The whole thing is ridiculous. Guys are so not worth it. No offense, Bridger."

"None taken," he replies.

Sela gazes at the house like it's one of those fruit smoothies she's always drooling over. "I'm bored." She jumps up and faces Bridger. "And *you* promised you'd dance with me. Remember?" She extends her hands toward him.

Bridger's mouth forms a perfect O and he looks at me like I can get him out of it, but I know Sela. She won't shut up until he dances with her.

"Go ahead. I'll be fine out here."

"I don't know," he says slowly.

"You can come, too," Sela says to me. "Nobody said you had to stay out here by yourself."

I shake my head. The last thing I want to do is go back in that house. Trevor adores being the center of attention, meaning he'll most likely stay inside with everyone else.

"Oh, good lord," Sela says. She grabs Bridger's hand and pulls. "Alora's a big girl. She can take care of herself for a few minutes."

I smile up at them. "That's right. I don't need a babysitter."

Bridger keeps looking back over his shoulder at me as Sela leads him back to the house. I can't help but grin. It's weird, him being so protective. He doesn't even know me.

But I think I'd like to get to know him better.

That thought surprises me. I must be losing my mind. I shouldn't be thinking about Bridger in any way other than friendship.

A group of guys suddenly spill out of the house. They're loud, laughing at something that's probably lame.

Trevor is with them.

My muscles tense and I quickly scan the yard, trying to find someplace to hide. If I try to circle back around front, he'll see me. If I stay put, he'll see me. The only other option is to head to the small pool house behind me.

I force myself to walk. *Try to look casual,* I tell myself. Nobody will notice me if I stay calm. I've done a good job of staying invisible at school most of the year. Maybe that'll be true here.

I'm shaking by the time I reach the building. I press my back against the brick wall and hug my arms close to my chest, telling myself to calm down. Trevor was with his friends. Surely he didn't see me sitting by the pool.

"What are you doing?" a slurred voice asks.

My eyes snap to my left, where Trevor is standing at the corner of the pool house. I push off the wall and take a few steps backward. "I told you to leave me alone."

"Why do you have to act like this?" he asks, advancing toward me. "All I wanted to do was dance with you." His face is hard and ugly. Angry. "But no, you throw yourself at the first guy who comes along. Kate's right. You ain't nothing but a skank."

I should run away, but I can't move. I'm still shaking, but not just in fear. From somewhere deep inside, a hot flame fans anger through me. "And you're nothing but a self-centered asshole. You think you can just decide you want to go out with me and I'll fall at your feet? Think again. I'll never go out with you."

The satisfaction of saying how I really feel doesn't last. He rushes toward me, getting in my personal space. It takes every nerve I have to make myself stay still.

The smell of beer hits me as Trevor brushes past, knocking my shoulder. "You'll be sorry you said that."

22

Yesterday at breakfast Alora cleared her plate and went back for seconds. This morning, she's pushing her food around with a fork.

Something happened to her last night. She won't say what, and that's irritating the hell out of me.

I close my eyes and think back to the party. The sea of faces swimming before me began to blur together after a while. Any one of them could be Alora's future killer. But if I had to bet on it, I'd pick Trevor. And I bet he's the reason she's so quiet now. I just wish there was something I could do to make her feel better.

Grace sweeps into the dining room with a pitcher of orange juice. As she refills glasses, she frowns at Alora. "Sweetie, do you feel all right?"

"I'm fine," Alora says in a flat voice. "I just didn't get much sleep."

She does look tired. But I know a leave-me-alone excuse when I hear one.

"Maybe you should try meditating," the crazy woman, Mrs. Jamison, says. "That works wonders, doesn't it, Charles?"

"Oh, yes. It relaxes the body and the mind." Charles checks his watch and pats his wife's hand. "Are you finished, dear? If we're going to leave on time this afternoon, we should get started."

By "get started," they mean scour the property again for ghosts. That's what they did all day yesterday and late into the night, according to Grace. I want to roll my eyes so bad.

Grace keeps her face blank as she says, "Good luck with that."

"Thank you. The spirits are restless today. I can feel it in my bones," Mrs. Jamison says.

After they depart, Mr. Palmer says, "I should be going too."

"I thought you were staying until the end of the day." Grace puts the orange juice pitcher down and props one hand on her hip.

"I need to head out earlier than I thought I would." He rakes his fingers through his hair as he stands. "Although I do hate leaving such wonderful company."

"You're more than welcome to stay longer. Especially since I barely saw you yesterday," Grace says.

"No, I really need to get going."

"Do you need help with your luggage?"

"No." Mr. Palmer's voice is sharp and reverberates throughout the room. Then he smiles. "I'm sorry. I mean I can handle it."

"Oh, okay. At least let me walk you out."

Mr. Palmer seems uncomfortable, his smile forced. He nods at me before heading to the foyer. Grace follows.

When they're out of earshot, Alora lets out a sigh. "I'm glad he's leaving."

"Why?" While Mr. Palmer does have an oddness about him, he doesn't appear overly strange. I've barely seen him around since I got here.

"I don't know," she says with a shrug. "Maybe it's because I'm sick of seeing Aunt Grace acting like a teenager around him."

"Or maybe you just don't like his glasses." I try to make the comment sound like a joke, but I'm serious. People in the past relied on glasses. In my time they're practically unheard of, except for those idiotic Purists.

For the first time since last night, Alora cracks a grin. "Yeah, maybe that's it. They're the dorkiest things I've ever seen."

Now that Alora has stopped looking like the world is about to end, I want her to stay that way. Even though I'm dying to find out what upset her in the first place. "So, what are you going to do today?"

"I really need to study for this test I have to make up tomorrow," she says, her eyebrows raising.

"Okay, so why do I get the feeling you have something else in mind?"

Alora glances at the foyer, where Grace is still talking to Mr. Palmer. She whispers, "Because I do."

I whisper back, "And what would that be?"

"I've been calling the numbers for every John Miller around Atlanta I can find, but it would help if I knew exactly where he used to live."

I think for a moment and grin, realizing what she has in mind. "You want to go back to the attic."

"Yes, but Aunt Grace will be here all day and she won't let me up there."

"What do you want me to do?"

Alora bites her lip. "Can you distract her for a while? Maybe fifteen or twenty minutes so I can sneak up there again."

A half hour later, I'm still sitting in the dining room with Grace and the ghost hunters.

Alora went upstairs right after Mr. Palmer left. Her excuse was that she wanted to take a nap. When Grace came back to clean up the dining room, I asked her if she had time to tell me about the history of the inn. Grace was surprised, but she agreed. The Jamisons came through soon after and joined us.

Grace is in the middle of a tale about a Civil War soldier who was supposedly buried on the property when I spot Alora on the stairs. She waves for me to join her.

"I'm sorry," I say, interrupting Grace. "I forgot that I'm supposed to . . . call someone right now."

"Really?" Grace asks.

Standing, I say, "Yes. It's about my father."

"Well, okay." Grace looks at the Jamisons. "Do y'all want to hear the rest?"

At their enthusiastic encouragement, Grace continues with the story while I slip out. "That was smooth," Alora says when I get to the top of the stairs.

"Hey, it worked."

From the way Alora is beaming, I can tell she found something. "What did you get?"

"Come on, I'll show you."

She leads me to her bedroom and locks the door behind us. I inhale the scent of something floral. It's the same smell that always lingers on Alora. And I can't stop staring at everything. It's so purple.

Vika would have hated it.

I close my eyes and tell myself to get a grip. Alora and Vika are two different people who live, or lived, in two different centuries. Of course they're different.

Alora grabs a blue book off her desk and takes it to her bed. I hurry over and sit next to her.

We study the cover first. It's a marbleized blue with a silver eagle and the words THESE ARE THE DAYS . . . 1988 stamped on the front. The spine crackles as Alora opens it, and a musty smell filters out as she flips through the pages.

"This is Dad's senior yearbook." She flips back to the front. The first pages are covered with notes and signatures of students who went to school with her father. She finds what she's looking for on the first printed page—the name of her father's hometown.

Larkspring, Georgia.

The place her aunt wouldn't even tell her about.

Alora hands the book to me. She then goes to her desk and activates the laptop.

After a minute, she types something. "That's all I needed. I keep getting too many hits for John Miller, but this will help me narrow it down."

I could probably find the information way faster than she will with her computer, but I can't exactly whip out my DataLink in front of her. I join her at the desk.

When Alora gets a hit, she lets out a triumphant whoop and takes out her phone. "He lives in Covington now, just outside of Atlanta," she says as she dials the number displayed on the laptop screen. The transformation from gloomy Alora is nice. I find myself smiling with her and my pulse races.

I tell myself it's because we're closer to finding answers.

Her eyes grow wide after a few seconds. "Hi, is this John Miller?"

I listen as she asks questions and answers some in return, growing more excited. While she's talking, I wonder if she has something in here that could help me figure out her past. I take in everything. The neatly made bed, dresser with girl stuff sprinkled across the top, her desk. The desk has the laptop and the stack of yearbooks. There's also something else, a deep purple book. It's blank on the front. I wonder if it's a journal.

"Wow," Alora says in a breathy voice. I turn back around. She's still holding her phone. Her cheeks are pink.

"I take it that was the right guy?"

"Yep. Oh my God, I can't believe I found him."

Without warning, she jumps up and throws her arms around me. I can't move. All I can concentrate on is her body pressed against mine. I'm aware of every curve and every contour. Vika was the last person to touch me like this.

Alora pulls away, looking up at me. "Is something wrong?"

Yes. Everything.

"No," I whisper.

Neither one of us can look away. I'm caught up in searching the details of her face. The concerned look in her eyes. The tilt of her nose. The curve of her lips. I can't stop staring at those lips.

A pounding sound shatters the moment.

We break apart, our heads snapping toward the door.

"Alora, what's going on?" Grace asks in a sharp tone.

Alora's eyes slide to the yearbook. "Hide it," she hisses while closing the laptop. I grab the yearbook and shove it under her bed while she pulls a large textbook out of a bag and places it on the desk.

"Ready?" she whispers.

I nod.

Grace's brows are drawn together when Alora opens the door. Her face rapidly evolves from concern to confusion to anger. "What are you two doing in here?"

"Bridger was helping me study."

Grace turns her attention on me. "I thought you said you had to call someone about your father."

I feel myself blushing. This is going from bad to worse. It's like I'm getting interrogated by my mother. But I can't blame Grace. A guy who's new in town caught alone in her niece's locked bedroom doesn't look good.

Alora interrupts before I have to tell another lie. "He was finished and I needed someone to quiz me. He told me you were busy with the Jamisons downstairs. And you know I need to pass this test. So . . ."

Grace's face relaxes some, but she still doesn't look convinced. "Fine. But I don't know why y'all locked the door. *That*'s not necessary for studying."

23

I wipe my palms on my jeans as the bus creeps closer to the school. I can't get Trevor's threat out of my head. What if he tries to start something else with me? I just don't want to deal with his crap anymore.

And I also have to figure out how to get to Covington to talk to Mr. Miller. The only thing I can think of is to ask Sela to take me, which means coming up with yet another lie.

I hate how I'm telling so many lies lately.

Bridger didn't understand why I couldn't borrow Aunt Grace's truck, but he doesn't know her like I do. Aunt Grace rarely lets me drive it, and when she does, she has to know exactly where I'm going and what time I'll get back. If she thinks I'm hanging out with Sela all day Saturday, she won't interrogate me.

Everyone files off the bus, lost in a sleepy haze. I stop by my locker without talking to anyone and head to class. Throughout first period I'm invisible. Everybody is buzzing because Naomi's parents notified the police of her disappearing act. By the time I get to second period, things change. A few kids stare at me like they've just noticed my existence for the first time. Third period is even worse. I duck into girls' restroom between classes to check if I've got food stuck in my teeth or something.

With every hushed word and every quick glance coming more frequently as the morning passes, I'm certain a rumor is going around about me. I'm also certain it has to do with Trevor, but I don't know what it is. Nobody will tell me a thing.

At lunch, all it takes is one look at Sela's horrified face to know it's bad.

"Have you heard what Trevor's telling everyone?" she asks as I plunk in the seat next to her.

The heavy weight on my chest doubles. "No," I say slowly, dreading what she's about to tell me.

She whispers, "He said that you two hooked up at Levi's party."

"What?"

"Girl, the stuff he said you did is nasty." Her lip curls like she's sucked on a lemon.

"But he's lying!" My face feels like it's on fire. "Oh my God . . . and everybody believes him?"

"I guess," she says with a frown as she glances toward Trevor's table. His friends are listening to him talk about something, probably getting off on whatever lies he's telling them now. He flashes a completely obnoxious smirk in my direction.

I bury my face in my hands. I never thought I could hate someone as much as I hate Trevor. And to make things worse, the Brainless Twins show up and proceed to spew very specific details about what I supposedly did with Trevor.

"Knock it off, y'all," Sela says. "Alora would never do those things."

"Yeah, but a bunch of the guys said they saw Trevor come out from behind the pool house and Alora came out right after," Jess says.

Sela waves her hand in a dismissive gesture. "Like Alora would go back there with him in the first place."

Miranda says, "Lisa in my business class said she saw them too."

My stomach is churning so much I'm afraid I might puke. "It makes me sick that you'd sit here and tell me that stuff like it's the truth," I say in a low voice. "You want to know what happened? I went back there because I was alone outside while all of you were in the house dancing." Sela flinches like I slapped her. "When Trevor came outside, I hid behind the pool house because he'd started some crap with me earlier. But he saw me and followed. I told him to leave me alone and that I'd never go out with him, then he said I'd be sorry. End of story."

I glare the Brainless Twins before I stalk out of the cafeteria, ignoring the stares burning into my back.

Sela catches up with me in the hallway. "Hey, I'm sorry, but I never said I believed any of that stuff. Besides," she says, placing her hands on her hips, "you never told me Trevor threatened you. Why didn't you say anything?"

"Because I was scared. I thought if I told you what Trevor said, then Bridger would get in a fight with him. And if that happened, you know all hell would've broken loose and somebody would've called the cops."

"Why didn't you say something yesterday?"

"I just wanted to forget about it." I look back toward the cafeteria. "I guess that's impossible now."

Sela hugs me. "I'm so sorry. Someone should de-nut that jerk." She releases me and says, "So, you want to go back and finish eating? I'm actually starving."

I shake my head. "No, I don't think I could keep anything down. And I've got to make up that history test today, so I guess I should study."

"If you must," she says with a grin. "I'll see you after school."

Before she leaves, I decide to ask her about taking me to Covington. Might as well get it over with. "Can you do a favor for me this Saturday?"

"Maybe," she drawls.

"I need you to take me somewhere," I say, rubbing the back of my neck. My mind races, trying to think of an excuse. Then the perfect lie crystallizes. "Well, me and Bridger actually. He has a lead on his father, but he needs to go to Covington."

Sela chews her bottom lip for a second. "I can't. I've already made plans."

"You did?"

"I was gonna tell you. Cheerleading tryouts are in two weeks, so I planned to practice all day Saturday and Sunday with Jess and Miranda. And I really want you to come, too. It would be so cool if we all made the squad."

I can't believe it. After everything that's happened to me today, all she wants to do is practice cheers? I shake my head. "No."

Sela blinks. "But you promised you'd go out for the squad with me."

"You were the one who wanted to make the team. I just went along because you wanted me to."

"Really, Alora? You were all for it last week, then boom . . . new guy shows up and you suddenly change your mind. How convenient."

Suddenly, I need to be alone. Away from her and everyone else. "You know what? Forget I asked for help. Go practice with your little friends. I don't care."

I turn and walk away.

By the end of the day, my head feels like someone is squeezing it. I'm positive I won't pass the makeup history test, I can't remember anything that my teachers talked about, I'm not speaking to my best friend, and everyone at school thinks I'm a slut.

Lovely.

Several guys ask me to do disgusting things to them while I'm on the way to my locker. By the time I get there, I have to blink back tears.

I barely get the door open when a voice behind me says, "So, have you enjoyed your day?"

I spin around and glare at Trevor. I'd love to slap the smirk off his face. "No thanks to you. Why did you tell those lies?"

His eyebrows shoot up. "What lies? I haven't told any lies."

Several kids around us snicker and someone says, "You two going somewhere?"

Trevor's smile widens.

"No," I snap.

This is ridiculous. He's feeding off the attention. I bet he'd love it even more if I start crying. Blinking rapidly, I pull out the books I need for homework and slam the door. But when I try to move past Trevor, he places both of his hands on the sides of my locker, blocking me from leaving.

"Where you going?" he asks. I get a whiff of cologne and sweat as he leans close and whispers, "Go ahead, run back to your new boyfriend. Have your fun. But keep in mind I'm just getting started."

As soon as he steps back, I rush past him. Clutching my books to my chest, I wipe my eyes and flee to the closest girls' restroom. It's bad enough everyone around my locker me saw me crying. I won't let the rest of the school see me too.

At least the room is empty. I lean against the door, still holding my books tight, and try to hold back the sobs. It isn't fair. Some stupid guy can make up a bunch of crap about me and everybody believes him without question.

I close my eyes as the pressure in my head builds. There's no way I'm riding with Sela this afternoon. I'll have to either take the bus or walk. I really wish I was home. For a second, I picture the inn as if I'm standing in the front yard.

My head feels light. I keep my eyes closed, hoping the faint feeling will pass.

When I open my eyes again, I'm standing in front of the inn. The sun is shining. Birds are chirping. My jaw drops and my books fall to the ground. I kneel down and run my fingers over the ground, feeling the spiky blades of grass. It's real.

I'm at the inn.

"Alora!"

My eyes snap up. Bridger is running down the front porch steps. He helps me stand when he reaches me.

My chest heaves as I look around. The last thing I remember was standing in the restroom at school. And now I'm home. "How did I get here?"

Bridger's eyes flick toward the ground. "I don't know."

"What? You were on the porch. You didn't see anything?"

He swallows and looks back up at me, his face blank. "I was . . . reading. I didn't notice you until just now."

24

A warm breeze blows as I wait across the street from Alora's school. I left the inn a few hours ago. I told Grace I was going to check around town for news about my father. Instead I came here.

It's been two days since Alora shifted. Two days in which she hasn't said much to Grace or me. Two days in which I've let her suffer in silence. It's killed me, watching her in so much pain. And that pisses me off. Her feelings shouldn't matter to me.

But they do.

I can't stop thinking about the way she looked right after she shifted. Her face was so pale. She had to have been close to wilding out, yet I didn't tell her the truth. I couldn't. Not when I don't know how that would affect the timeline. So I let her think something was wrong with her. Now I feel like a furing jerk.

A loud bell shrills from the school—my cue to get moving. I cross the street and make my way to where the buses are parked. Grace told me Sela usually takes her home, but Alora admitted yesterday that they got into a fight on Monday. That didn't surprise me. I've been here less than a week, and I've already picked up on a wedge between them—namely those two girls who met us at the party.

Students spill from the main building. As I search for Alora, I overhear some of them whispering about a missing girl. The fear in their voices is unmistakable. That makes me wonder if Alora's future killer is here with her. My gut still tells me it's got to be Trevor. But I could be wrong. It could be anyone. I just wish I knew for sure.

I have to look away for a moment when I finally see Alora. The sadness clinging to her makes me want to do something to make her smile again. I shake my head to cast the thought away. Alora is the object of my mission. Her happiness should be irrelevant.

But when she spots me and a hint of a smile touches her lips, I find myself grinning.

"What are you doing here?" she asks when she reaches me.

"I thought you'd like to walk home today."

She glances at the gray sky. "No, thanks. It looks like it's going to rain."

"It could, but then again it might not," I say with a shrug. "You can always play it safe and ride the bus, but where's the fun in that?"

"Seriously, Bridger?" she asks, her lips twitching.

"Seriously. Live a little, walk with me."

Alora pretends to think for a moment. "Well, if you insist."

It's strange how I feel almost weightless as we walk across the campus. But the feeling evaporates when a guy approaches us. His mouth is curled in a malicious sneer. I hear a sharp intake of breath from Alora.

"Hey, Alora, do you think you can fit me in your schedule this week?" he says, glancing at me. "Looks like you're in demand now."

Alora's face turns scarlet.

"What the hell," I say as I turn around, wanting to choke him.

Alora grabs my arm and hisses, "Stay out of it."

I gape at her. "Why? He insulted you."

"It's nothing," she says, her voice strained.

"No, it's not. Why did he say that?"

"Please, leave it alone."

Two voices scream in my head. One tells me to kick that guy's ass. What if he's the one who is supposed to kill her? The other says I have to let it go because I can't change the timeline. No more than I've already done. "Fine. But you owe me an explanation."

Alora's brow crinkles. "Excuse me? I *owe* you an explanation? I don't remember asking you to come here today."

The argument I'd already formed fades away. She's right—I just showed up. She never asked me to walk her home. Still, it's not right for her to let that idiot insult her and not stick up for herself.

The silence between us is thick and uncomfortable for several blocks. Finally I can't take it. "I'm sorry. I shouldn't have tried anything back there."

"It's fine," she says, staring straight ahead.

"No, it's not. It's just . . ." I stop walking and place a hand on her arm. She freezes and I swear she shudders underneath my touch. "Something is wrong with you. Grace thinks it's because you and Sela got in a fight, but there's more to it. Like whatever is going on with you at school. And how you got home on Monday."

Alora shakes her head. "I really don't want to go there."

"Keeping secrets could make things worse. Maybe you should tell someone what's been going on."

Her mouth opens and shuts several times before she can speak. "I was at school Monday afternoon . . . in the restroom. I felt dizzy. I remember I wanted to go home. And then . . . I was."

"Has that happened to you before?" I knew when she materialized in front of me last week her shifting abilities were emerging. What I don't know is how long it's been happening.

"Yes. The first time was last Monday. That's why I had to make up the history test. I blacked out at school and woke up in my bedroom." She blows out a puff of air. "This Monday was the fourth time."

If Alora slapped me, I wouldn't be more surprised. She's shifted four times in a week? That can't be right. A natural-born Talent like Alora will probably develop in a different way. But when Talents manifest in my time, they start slow. Maybe one incident a week for a few months while the Talent intensifies. I wonder why her shifting abilities are emerging so fast. How she's kept it from her aunt.

"Have you told Grace?"

"No. She'd drag me to the doctor, which she really can't afford. And now I'm developing a side of crazy. Nice, huh?" She lets out a harsh laugh and starts walking again.

I fall in step beside her, processing everything I know. I probably shouldn't keep pushing her, but she's talking to me again and I can't pass up the chance. "Look, something's going on between you and Sela, so if you still want to talk to your dad's friend, you'll have to either find another ride or call him."

"I already told you I want to talk to him in person."

"Yeah, but you could always do a . . ." I trail off, trying to remember what the tech was called in this time. "A video chat."

Alora huffs in annoyance. "Yeah, I could, but I don't *want* to. It's not the same as looking someone in the eye. I'll get more out of Mr. Miller if we meet face to face."

I think for a moment. "Okay. But you're going to have to borrow Grace's truck unless you have any other ideas."

"She won't let me. She's freaky possessive of that truck," she says as fat drops of rain begin to fall. "Oh, great," she mutters.

"What? It's just water," I say, smiling. "You won't melt."

"Well, you stay out here if you want. I'm not waiting for it to get worse."

She breaks into a run, and I follow. We barely make it two blocks before it starts to pour. By the time we reach the inn, we're soaked and shivering. Alora cracks the front door and calls for Grace.

A minute later, Grace steps out on the porch and hands us two fluffy towels. "Good heavens, you better hurry up and dry yourselves off or you're gonna catch a cold."

I smother a smile. That's such an archaic statement.

Once we're no longer dripping water, Grace shoos us inside. She orders us to change clothes then meet her in the kitchen. I don't argue. Grace always has something fresh from the oven in the afternoons. No way I'm going to turn it down. I'll never get this kind of treatment again once I return to my century.

Grace has three cups of hot cocoa and thick slices of homemade bread sitting on the small kitchen table. I wrap my fingers around a warm mug and take a sip.

Grace sits across from me. "How did you two get caught in the rain?"

"I was on my way back here and happened to pass by Alora's school as the bell rang. I thought she'd want to walk today instead of riding the bus." At least that's not a lie. I've never ridden in one of those autos before, but I imagine it's similar to riding in one of the Academy's shuttles—crowded, loud, and smelling like someone's armpit.

"Uh huh. And did you find any more information about your father?"

"Not exactly."

"What's that mean?"

Damn, she's not going to leave me alone. Possible answers I can feed Grace flit through my mind. I'm saved when Alora walks into the kitchen.

"What are you talking about?" she asks

"I was asking Bridger a few questions," Grace says, keeping her eyes on me.

Alora sits between us and attacks her bread. I stare at her, fascinated, as she practically inhales the first piece and slices another.

"Didn't you eat lunch?" Grace asks.

"No," Alora says, her gaze locked on her plate. "I had to study."

"Don't lie to me. Did you skip lunch just to avoid Sela?"

"No, I really did need to study."

Grace's eyes harden as she looks between us. "Really? So why do I have the feeling y'all are keeping something from me?"

Alora stays silent. I picture the prick who insulted Alora and my fists tighten under the table. What is she hiding from us?

A loud rapping wrecks the moment. Grace's head whips toward the front of the house. "I wonder who that is."

Alora and I stay at the table while she goes to check.

Alora pushes her plate away and says, "There goes my appetite."

"Is she always like that?"

Alora sighs. "Always. I love her to death, but she is so overprotective sometimes. It's never really bothered me before, but now I feel so . . . smothered."

I know exactly what she means.

Grace's voice floats from the front of the house, sounding irritated. "What the hell does she want?"

Alora's brows shoot up and she quickly stands.

"What's wrong?" I ask, following her out of the kitchen.

"Aunt Grace only cusses when Celeste is here."

I start to ask who Celeste is, but now we're standing just outside the foyer, where a gorgeous woman with dark hair has started screaming at Grace. Grace says something back to her, but then the woman notices us.

My stance tightens as she shoulders past Grace, pointing her finger at Alora. "I don't know what kind of game you're playing, but you better stay away from my son. I won't have a white trash tramp ruining him!"

Alora stumbles back as if the woman's words physically hurt her. My hands curl to fists. I'm sick of people treating her like scum today.

Grace steps between Alora and the woman. "Celeste, you can't just barge in here flinging wild accusations."

Celeste pinches the bridge of her nose and loudly exhales through her mouth. "If you'd answer your damn phone, then I wouldn't have to barge in here."

"I've been busy," Grace says.

"I'm sure you have," Celeste huffs.

Grace's nostrils flare. "Bridger and Alora, will you please give us some privacy?"

Gladly. Wishing I could do more to shelter Alora from this crazy woman, I entwine my fingers with hers. Then we retreat to the kitchen. When we're in there, Alora pulls free from me.

I don't say anything at first. We listen as Grace and Celeste talk in hushed, urgent tones. Finally I ask, "What did that woman mean? Who is her son?"

Alora lets out a shaky breath. "That's Trevor's mother."

Crossing my arms, I ask, "Why would she accuse you of going after him?"

"I don't know," she says, her eyes filling with tears. "Maybe because he's been spreading rumors about me at school."

By the time Alora is finished filling me in on what Trevor's been telling everybody, I would gladly make sure he'll never be able to procreate. White hot anger washes over me. It's all I can do to keep from marching back in the foyer, but I know it'll be for nothing. Celeste is obviously one of those idiotic parents who can't see the truth about their children.

So I do the only thing I can do. I cross the short distance to Alora and wrap my arms around her. She instantly melts against me. Her shoulders shake as she cries against my chest.

A heavy, familiar knot forms in my chest. I need a dose of Calmer. But I can't leave Alora like this. Instead, I focus on holding her and how her body fits perfectly against mine. How she smells of lavender and rain. The heaviness in my chest begins to lessen.

I don't know how long we stand like that—maybe seconds, maybe minutes—but I don't care. A part of me knows I'm so drawn to her because she looks so much like Vika. But Vika is dead. And technically Alora is dead too. She's a ghost. But I'm with her right now and she's hurting and I want to make it stop.

If I could just tell her the truth about her abilities. That might help some.

But I can't. I just can't.

Alora severs our connection when the front door slams and mumbles an apology.

Moments later, Grace storms in the kitchen. "I can't believe what that woman just told me."

"What did she say?" Alora asks.

Grace sinks on the closest chair. She shares how Celeste learned from her beautician what's been going around the school. The beautician's daughter told her what Trevor had been saying. And of course, Celeste's twisted mind put the blame on Alora.

Grace looks like she's aged a decade by the time she finishes, graphic details and all. "Please tell me none of it is true."

"It's not. I'd never do anything like that."

"I didn't think so," Grace says with a weak smile. "But sometimes the truth doesn't matter in this town. It's what everyone *thinks* is the truth that matters. That's probably why Sela isn't speaking to you, isn't it?"

That's interesting. Grace doesn't know what the fight was about, either. I wish Alora would tell us, but she just looks down at her lap.

Grace makes a *tsk*-ing sound. "I may not get out much, but I've heard Sela's mom has been brownnosing with all those big shots in town." Grace snorts. "I never thought Sela would act like her. I guess I was wrong. I'm so sorry you've had to put up with all this, sweetie. It's not fair."

Alora tears up again, and Grace gathers her into a hug. "If there's anything you need, just tell me. I know you relied on Sela for a lot of things, but I'll do my best to help you out."

Alora's eyes were closed, but when she hears the part about needing anything, they pop open. I know what she's thinking.

Should she ask Grace to borrow the truck now or wait and risk losing this moment?

Alora's brows rise as if she wants me to tell her what to do.

I don't hesitate.

Ask her for the truck, I mouth to her.

25

I feel sick," I say as I take the exit leading to the Starbucks where I'll finally meet John Miller. My hands are sweating, so I rub them one at a time on my jeans.

"I'd suggest you pull over, but I don't think that's a good idea under the circumstances," Bridger says, peering out the passenger window. He's right. The Saturday morning traffic in Covington is worse than I thought it would be. Plus, I'm not used to driving in heavy traffic period. In fact, I'm not even supposed to be here.

Aunt Grace thinks I'm taking Bridger to Athens to track down a lead on his father. It was the first thing I could think of when I asked her to borrow the truck and, thankfully, it worked. She agreed under the conditions that we get back by three o'clock and check in with her every hour. So far she's called twice.

By the time I find the coffee shop and park, my hands are shaking. "I don't know if I can do this."

Bridger places a warm hand on my shoulder. I nearly jump as an electric surge shoots through my body.

"It's just your nerves. As soon as you talk to Mr. Miller, you'll be fine."

"But what if I'm not? What if I make a complete ass of myself?"

"You've got to quit worrying. This is what you wanted. Now you've either got to go in there and talk to Mr. Miller or go back home and stay clueless. The choice is yours."

As Bridger holds my gaze, waiting for me to decide, it hits me that I'm at one of those crossroads you always hear people talking about. Take one path and your life goes one way, take another path and your life will be totally different. I'm almost tempted to stay in the truck and keep living my life as it is now. It's safe and comfortable, like a soft blanket. Or it was until I started having those blackouts.

Squaring my shoulders, I open the door. "Let's do this."

We go inside and immediately I spot Mr. Miller. He told me he'd be the guy with glasses and an Atlanta Braves cap. He's sitting at a booth, checking something on his phone.

"Do you want me to go with you?" Bridger asks.

"No, I need to do this alone."

Bridger offers a small smile. "Okay. I'll be over there if you need me," he says, nodding at an empty booth close enough to Mr. Miller that I will be able to see him, yet far enough away to allow privacy. "Do you want something to drink?"

"No," I say as my stomach flips again. "It probably wouldn't stay down."

A part of me wishes I could go with Bridger as he leaves to place an order. But I can't chicken out. I force myself to go over to Mr. Miller's booth.

"Hello," I squeak. Nice . . . I sound like a five-year-old.

Mr. Miller glances up from his phone. He smiles, but then it slides into a look of confusion. "You're Alora?"

"Um, yeah." Wow, I sound so brilliant.

He stands, towering over me, and extends his hand. "I'm John Miller."

I shake it and slide into the seat opposite him. My tongue feels heavy and thick. I try to lick my lips, wishing I'd told Bridger to bring me a frappé. I glance longingly at the front of the store, where he's still standing in line.

"So, you're Nate's daughter. How can I help you?" His voice seems guarded.

"I guess I better begin by telling you I don't remember anything about him or my mother. I've lived with Aunt Grace since I was six, but for some reason she doesn't want to tell me what happened to them."

Mr. Miller steeples his fingers together, wearing a slight frown. "And I suppose you think I can give you some answers, correct?"

"Yes."

"Do you have any pictures of your father?"

"Yes. Let me get them." I fumble through my purse until I find them.

My hand trembles as I hold the pictures out to Mr. Miller. As he studies them, his brows arch. "Yep, that's Nate and me all right. Talk about a blast from the past."

I begin to relax. "Can you tell me what he was like? Or when was the last time you talked to him?"

Mr. Miller's lips press together in a thin line, and he slides the pictures back to me. He stays silent, which unnerves me.

"What is it?" I ask.

"I'm trying to figure out what's going on. You definitely resemble Nate and Grace. But . . ." He stops and cocks his head to the side. "I told you before, Nate never said anything about having a child."

My skin crawls with the certainty that whatever he has to say next won't be good.

"And you know what else I'm having a hard time believing? That you're really Nate's daughter."

"But you said I look like him."

"True, but you look like Grace, too. Maybe you're her daughter."

Heat rushes to my face. "If that's true, why would she tell me I'm Nate's daughter?"

Mr. Miller shrugs. "I don't know. You need to ask her."

I want to scream. "Haven't you heard me? Aunt Grace won't tell me anything about my past. She thinks it'll damage me."

"Like I said, I don't know. Maybe you are Nate's kid and he didn't know about you."

"No, that's not right," I say. "Aunt Grace said he's the one who brought me to her house. He left me there ten years ago and told Aunt Grace he'd come back for me, but he never did."

Suddenly, Mr. Miller stands and snatches up his coffee. "I don't know what kind of stunt you're trying to pull, but I'm not amused."

I stare at him in confusion. "I don't understand. I'm not trying to pull anything. I just want to know about my father, that's all."

"You just told me a lie, so now I know Nathaniel Walker can't be your father."

"What do you mean? He *is* my father."

"That's impossible. The Nate Walker I knew died in 1994."

I stay seated, too stunned to move, and watch as Mr. Miller storms out of the shop. His last words ring in my ears, along with another thought.

How could Nate Walker be my father if he died in 1994?

I was born in 1997.

26

Aunt Grace is standing on the back porch before I even park the truck, hands on hips and features contorted into a murderous glare.

"Are you ready for this?" Bridger asks, keeping his eyes on her.

"Yes," I reply.

Normally the sight of an angry Aunt Grace would make my pulse spike, but right now I don't care. I've had the whole trip back from Covington to digest what I discovered from Mr. Miller.

And I'm pretty pissed myself.

My mind has been full of questions, mainly centering on the fact Aunt Grace has been lying about more than I thought. On the drive back to Willow Creek, Bridger argued that Mr. Miller could've been the one lying, but I don't believe that. Bridger didn't see his shocked expression when I said Dad left me with Aunt Grace. Bridger didn't hear the anguish in his voice when he said my father died in 1994.

As soon as I park the truck, I say, "Okay, this is probably going to get ugly before I get anything out of her, so I'd rather talk to her alone."

"Are you sure? I'll stay with you if you want me to."

I want to say yes. Confrontation of any kind isn't my thing and I'd usually avoid it at all costs, but I can't today, not when it involves something I've wanted to know for so long. "I'm sure. As soon as I'm done, I'll tell you everything."

He rubs the back of his neck. "If you need me, I'll be in my room."

Aunt Grace is now waiting next to the truck. As soon as I open the door, she hollers, "Where have you been and why haven't you answered my calls?"

"We're only a half hour late."

"When I give you a time to have *my* truck back, I expect it to be back at that time. Just like I expect you to answer your phone when I call."

Bridger is still standing next to the truck. I give him what I hope is a reassuring smile and say, "I'll be fine."

He seems like he wants to say something, but presses his lips together and trudges toward the back porch.

Grace watches Bridger as he walks away. "That's it? I let y'all borrow *my* truck to track down a lead for his father and he can't even say thank you?" When he's inside the house, Grace swivels around and glares at me again. "What do you have to say for yourself, missy? I didn't know if you'd had an accident or if someone kidnapped y'all. Have you forgotten that Naomi Burton is still missing?"

My stomach is all knots and butterflies. A moment ago, I was set to confront her, but now the familiar feeling of wanting to flee takes over.

"Well, don't just stand there and pretend you're innocent. Answer me!"

The uncertainty vanishes when she says that. Ever since I've lived with Aunt Grace, I've tried to do what she told me to do. I'm grateful she's been here to raise me. I've always trusted her. But that trust was destroyed today.

I grab my purse out of the truck and slam the door. "You want to know where I've been? I visited an old friend of Dad's today. Remember John Miller?"

For a moment, Aunt Grace continues to glare at me, but then my question sinks in. Her jaw drops and she lets out a small gasp. "How did you find out about him?"

"I saw him in those pictures of *my* father that you hid from me."

Understanding dawns on her face. "You were in the attic last week." She closes her eyes while trying to steady her breathing. When she opens her eyes again, she asks, "And where did you go to meet John?"

My heart is doing a wild dance in my chest. How I hate this. Hate. It. I have to make myself say, "Bridger and I went to Covington. That's where Mr. Miller lives now."

"You went where?" Aunt Grace asks, each word climbing in pitch. "Good grief! I can't believe you two did this to me. I trusted both of you and this is the thanks I get."

"Don't blame Bridger. He felt sorry for me because he knows what it's like to not have your father there for you. I asked him to help me."

"It doesn't change the fact that both of you lied to me," she snaps.

"Like you've been lying?"

Aunt Grace crosses the short distance between us, getting all in my personal space. I step back and bump against the truck.

"What have you done?" she whispers.

"What's that supposed to mean?"

"Think of the consequences. What if this does something to you?"

"How can finding out about my past hurt me? It seems like you're the one who's afraid to find out. That or you don't want me to know."

"What exactly did John tell you?"

"He said my father died in 1994, which doesn't add up since I was born in '97."

She shakes her head. "John never really had it together. He must've mistaken Nate for someone else."

"Oh no, don't even try that. He was adamant. I showed him a few pictures I found, and he still said I couldn't be Nate Walker's daughter."

"That's crazy!"

"Is it? Or is there another reason you're lying? Did you kidnap me?"

"Alora, how can you say that?"

"Why don't we go to the police department? I bet they'll help me find the truth." The look on Aunt Grace's face makes me feel awful. It's shock, anger, and something else. I expected fear, but it's different. The look is so sad that I instantly regret everything I said.

"How did I let this happen?" Aunt Grace groans, covering her face with her hands. She doesn't speak for a while. I want to scream at her to say something, but then I realize she's crying. Her shoulders shake as muffled sniffles come from her. I've never seen her cry before, and I don't know what to do. Should I try to comfort her? Or should I just leave her alone?

I settle for taking her by the arm and leading her to the porch, where we sit on the steps. "I didn't lose my mind after talking to Mr. Miller. Don't you think I deserve to know the truth now?"

She wipes the tears away with the back of her hand. "I didn't want to say anything because I didn't know how you'd take it. Whatever happened to you must've been bad and I didn't want you to relive it again. And . . . Nate also asked me not to tell you."

Hearing her last sentence makes my insides grow cold. I swallow a few times and wait for her to continue. But Aunt Grace sits quietly and stares into the space ahead of her, like she's seeing what happened in the past.

Finally, she begins. "Nate enlisted in the army straight out of high school. At the time we thought it was the best thing he could've done since he used to get in lots of trouble. Skipping classes, staying out late doing God knows what. Anyway, when he was twenty-four, he was on an assignment in Iraq, and the truck he was riding in drove over a land mine." She draws a ragged breath. "John was riding in another truck behind Nate. He told me later that he saw Nate's truck explode. We were told that there were no survivors."

I remember Mr. Miller's reaction when he said that Dad had died in 1994. His face was twisted in anger, but his eyes told a different story. They held a haunted look, as if the memory was heartbreaking.

"So I was shocked when Nate showed up in 2002, on my birthday of all days. I was sitting on the river dock feeling sorry for myself. By that time Mama, Daddy, and Darrel were all dead. Nate scared the crap out of me because I didn't even see him walk up. I remember thinking that I'd finally lost my mind." She gives a harsh laugh. "But he was real. Of course, I wanted to know what happened, but he said it was classified. All he would say was that he had new life and that he just needed to see me for a little while. We ended up talking for hours like he'd never even left. When he said he had to go, it nearly broke my heart. He promised me he'd be back next year, on my birthday. And sure enough, he kept his word."

She falls into silence again, this time not saying anything for a long time. I begin to get impatient and figure I'd better prompt her before she decides to end her story there.

"I don't understand. If he had this whole new life and everything was classified, why did he leave me with you?"

Aunt Grace stares at her hands, clenching and unclenching them on her lap. "That's the weird part. He didn't even mention you when he visited that first time, but when he came the next year, he was so excited. He said he'd finally gotten away from whoever was holding him to that mission, and he was gonna bring his family to live close by. I was so happy for him. Darrel and I never had any kids, so imagine how I felt when I found out I had a niece."

"He didn't tell you he was going to bring me?"

"No, and what's really weird is he came twice that day. The first time was in the afternoon, when he told me about you and his plans. Then that night he showed up again at the house. You were unconscious. And he looked like he'd been through hell. He said you and your mom had been attacked and he only had time to get you away. He said he was gonna leave you with me so he could get back and find out what happened to her."

"So he came back later?"

She frowns. "No. He just told me to take care of you. And before he left, he gave me a key. He said it was to a safety deposit box and to only open it if he didn't come back. I begged him to tell me what happened, but he wouldn't. He made me promise I'd never tell you what little I knew. That's the last time I saw him."

I try to swallow, but my mouth is bone dry.

"So, that's everything," Aunt Grace says. She stands and holds out her hand to me. I grasp it and let her pull me up. "I'm sorry I kept the truth from you, but I did it because that's what Nate wanted. Whatever happened to you and your mama must've been horrible. Horrible enough that you buried that memory deep in your mind. And knowing my brother, he'd rather you not remember." She takes my other hand and folds them into her own. "Sweetie, I'd never do anything to intentionally hurt you. You're the only family I have left. I'd do anything to protect you."

I can't form words. I stare back at Aunt Grace, unsure of what I'm feeling. For the first time, I understand why she lied to me. And as much as I hate it, I don't blame her.

I don't even know how to begin to process what she told me. My life could be the plot of a movie. The only thing missing is an evil madman and then it would be perfect.

"Are you okay?" Aunt Grace asks in a quiet voice.

"I think so," I say, remembering something else she said. "You mentioned a safety deposit box. Where was it?"

"It was in Atlanta."

"What was in it?"

A thick pause follows. "It didn't reveal any more information about what Nate had been doing for all those years. It just had papers I'd need to take care of you. Your birth certificate, social security card, things like that."

"That's all?"

"That's all."

"Can I see them?"

Aunt Grace lets my hands go and sighs. "Really, they're just legal documents, nothing you'd need to examine for yourself. I have them stored for safekeeping."

"Can you at least tell me my mother's name?"

"Sure," she says softly. "It's Addie. But don't bother trying to find any information on her. I've already searched and I couldn't find anything."

I wonder if she's lying again. Probably. But instead of accusing her, I paste on a smile and hug her. "I'm so sorry for lying to you and sneaking off today."

"I'm sorry for not telling you what I knew." Aunt Grace gives me a squeeze then pulls back. "I guess we're even, huh?"

"Yeah, I suppose so."

"Are you okay?"

"Yes, ma'am. I have a part of my life back."

"I'm sorry I don't know more. I still hope Nate will come back one day."

"Me too."

"Well, let's try to put all this behind us for the time being. We can't sit around waiting for him or your mom to show up. We've got to live our lives or we'll drive ourselves crazy."

I follow Aunt Grace inside, thinking she's right. Already I feel better, like the pieces of my past are clicking into place. But I'm still not completely satisfied, and I won't be until I have the whole picture.

My parents wouldn't want me to mope around, mourning the loss of the life I should've led, but that doesn't mean I have to stop looking for more answers. Because I know Aunt Grace, and there's no good reason for her to keep those papers from me if they're really just legal documents.

She's hiding something else.

27

silver stream of moonlight illuminates my bedroom. The clock reads 12:03. Alora should be here soon. She wants to make sure Grace is asleep before we sneak downstairs. She's positive Grace is keeping something else from her. And she's sure whatever it is will be in the safe hidden in the study.

After Alora told me what Grace admitted, I thought I'd wild out. What if the military in this time had discovered people with Talents exist? Could that have been what Alora's father was doing with them? But that doesn't make sense. From everything I learned at the Academy, the governments of the world didn't even know about Talents until scientists began genetically modifying people. In the past, natural-borns kept their abilities a secret.

A soft tapping tears me out of my thoughts. I jump off the bed and open the door.

Alora is dressed in a robe and slippers. It's hard to see any color in the dim hallway, but the robe is definitely something pale. She appears almost angelic in the surrounding darkness.

I've got to quit thinking like that.

"Are you okay?" she asks, cocking her head to the side.

"I'm fine," I say quickly. "It's just . . . I didn't realize you'd be dressed like that."

Alora seems startled, glancing down at her robe, then smirks. "Oh, you think what I'm wearing is silly? What about you, Mr. Military? If Aunt Grace catches us downstairs, I'm sure she'll wonder why you're dressed like that."

She's right. I'm wearing my uniform. I figured if I needed to hide, the best way would be to use the cloaking device. But I can't tell Alora that. Instead, I grin and say, "Well, it's better than wearing what I usually sleep in."

Alora's eyes flick to my chest. I wonder if she's blushing because she's remembering me in my Skivvies. And that makes me grin.

"Well, wear whatever you want. Just stay quiet." She marches away from me, using her phone to light the area ahead of her. I close my door and hurry to catch up to her.

Downstairs, Alora stops at the closed study door in the hallway across from the kitchen. She pulls a small bobby pin out of her robe pocket and holds her phone out to me. "Keep the light on the handle, okay?"

My fingertips barely brush against her skin as I take the phone from her. But it's like a jolt from a stunner, minus the pain. I jerk my hand back, thinking I'm seriously going to wild out if I stay in this time much longer. I can't do this. I can't develop any feelings for Alora. She's not Vika, she's a ghost. Nothing more.

Alora rubs her hand before inserting the pin in the doorknob. "Can you hold the light steady? This isn't easy."

"I thought you were good at picking locks."

"I've only done this twice, and both times were during the day. So excuse me if I'm not fast enough for you."

For a moment I'm worried she's irritated with me, but then a corner of her mouth curves up. I concentrate on her lips while she works. As soon as she stops smiling, she bites the bottom lip. Then she licks it.

I have to look away.

Finally, I hear a small click and a triumphant, "Yes."

Alora locks the study door once we're inside and flips the light switch. The room is painted a smoky shade of blue. It's doesn't have much room for furniture. Just an antique desk in front of the lone window, two narrow bookcases stuffed with books on either side of a fireplace, and a comfortable-looking chair in the corner.

"Over here." Alora crosses over to the closest bookshelf and glides one hand along the side of the dark wood. "Last year Aunt Grace decided to tell me where she keeps her important paperwork in case something ever happened to her. She'd been to the doctor because of chest pains. Turns out it was caused from anxiety." She lowers her gaze, as if the memory is painful. "Anyway, she said there's a wall safe back here."

"Do you know the combination?"

"Yeah, it's her wedding anniversary. So all we have to do is move this."

I eye the bookshelf. "Did she show you exactly how to get in there?"

"No, she just said I'd have to punch in the numbers on a keypad."

Seems easy enough. But if there's one thing I've learned, things that should be easy rarely are. I position myself next to Alora and grasp the side of the bookshelf above her. "You move from the bottom while I get the top. Ready?"

"Yes," she says in a breathy voice. I nearly let go of the shelf. She sounded so much like Vika.

I swear I'm losing it.

But I push on. Even with Alora helping, the shelf doesn't want to move. It takes a few minutes, inching it slowly, before we have it out far enough to expose the safe.

"I can't believe I'm nervous," Alora says as she kneels in front of the safe. She trails her fingers over the keypad and looks back up at me. "What if there's something really bad in here? I mean, she said my dad wouldn't want me to know."

I kneel next to her and place my hand on her shoulder. I understand what she's feeling. It's mixture of excitement and dread when you realize what you're about to learn could change everything. That's how I felt just before I read the info on Dad's DataDisk. "It's okay," I whisper. "It's normal to feel like that. But you know what? If you back off and don't open that safe, you'll regret it. You'll wonder every day what's in there."

"I know," she says. "It's just . . . it's kind of surreal."

She looks away from me before I can answer and punches the code on the keypad. I hold my breath.

Nothing happens.

Alora frowns and punches the code again.

Still nothing.

"Come on!" She tries the code again.

"You said the code was Grace's anniversary, right?" I ask.

"Yeah. June 26, 1996 was the date she got married."

"So you're putting in 6, 26, 96?"

"Yeah, I tried that. Let me try zero six instead," she says. Her fingers fly over the keypad.

Nothing.

Alora bangs her fist on the side of the safe. "I don't understand. She said it was her anniversary. What if she changed the combination?" She leans her forehead against the wall and mutters, "Just freaking great."

I rub the back of my neck, thinking. That doesn't seem right for Grace to change the combination without telling Alora. Especially if she wanted

Alora to have access to it in case of an emergency. "What about trying the numbers in reverse order?"

Alora punches in the numbers again. This time the light next to the keypad glows green. Alora presses her palm against her chest and murmurs, "Yes."

I blow out the breath I didn't realize I'd been holding.

Then she opens the door.

My heart pounds as I peer over her shoulder. A tall stack of envelopes rests on top of some folders. But on the very top is a polished wooden box. Alora removes it first.

I move out of the way so she can scoot out from behind the bookshelf. She places the box on her lap and flips the lid open. I want to go over and nose through whatever's in there myself, but I make myself wait. This is stuff from her father.

Alora lifts out a paper and studies it. "This is my birth certificate," she says, glancing up. "My mom's name *is* Addie. At least Aunt Grace didn't lie about that. And I was born in Denver. Weird, huh? Wouldn't it be cool if my parents knew your parents?"

I just smile.

Alora sets her birth certificate on the floor and thumbs through the rest of the papers. "These are old medical records. I wonder why my dad wanted to keep them from me. It doesn't make sense." She lets out a heavy sigh, but then her eyes grow huge. I wonder if it's a pic of her family. She extracts the object of her attention.

And for a moment I forget to breathe again.

Alora is holding a delicate silver chain with a pendant featuring a smooth black stone. It's something I've seen before, when Professor March lectured about contraband tech in my time—a Jewel of Illusion.

How did Alora's father get his hands on something that doesn't exist yet?

I wonder if my dad gave it to him. Grace retrieved this stuff when Alora first arrived here. So why would Dad go back in time and give a Jewill to Alora's father, then attempt to save Alora's life this year?

No wonder Alora's father didn't want her to have access to this. Pressing the stone for ten seconds activates the cloak. I could imagine the chaos that would create if she did it in a public place.

"What's wrong?" Alora asks.

At the sound of her voice, my eyes snap to her. "I was just thinking that's a nice-looking . . . necklace."

Lame, Creed. Lame.

"It's beautiful. I wonder if it belonged to my mom." Alora holds up the Jewill. It sways slightly, glinting in the light. "You know what? I'm keeping this." She opens the clasp and fastens the chain around her neck. It takes all my willpower to keep from snatching it away.

Because there's one thing I'm certain about—Alora has no business with a Jewill.

I've got to get it from her. But how?

28

The second hand on the clock ticks as if it's coated with molasses. I'm so ready to get out of here. Not only does biology bore me, but the room smells like chemicals and something musty. I try to pay attention to the teacher, but my mind keeps going back to what Aunt Grace told me about my father.

I pull my necklace out of my shirt and cradle the pendant in the palm of my hand. It's comforting, having something that came from my parents. I like to think it's a gift from them. Maybe it was the last thing they ever gave me.

But why did my dad want to keep it from me?

The intercom buzzes overhead, and the secretary summons Kate to the office for dismissal. As she gathers her things, I take in her appearance. Her hair isn't carefully styled, she's not wearing any makeup, and she looks exhausted. I guess Naomi's disappearance is taking a toll on her. Kate hurries out without looking at anyone.

The teacher resumes his lecture, but ten minutes later another student is called to leave, this time one of Kate and Naomi's best friends. She doesn't look any better than Kate. Nobody can concentrate on class after that. A few students keep sneaking glances at the one desk that was already empty— Naomi's.

That first week after Naomi disappeared, everyone thought she just took off because she was upset over the breakup with Trevor, but not now. Not after being gone so long without contacting her parents or her friends.

It's been three weeks since she disappeared.

After class dismisses, I hurry to my locker. Most everybody is talking about Naomi. Some even cast suspicious glances my way when I pass, as if I'm responsible for her disappearance. Near my locker, I overhear a girl saying that her parents won't let her go anywhere alone right now. I can relate. Aunt Grace has been on edge too.

When I get to history class, I steel myself to face Trevor, but he's not there. That's not surprising—he usually strolls in at the last minute.

But he never shows up. Maybe he was called for dismissal along with Kate. I don't know, and I don't care. I settle in and attempt to listen to the lecture, but soon the intercom buzzes.

This time I'm the one who's summoned.

Feeling every eye on me, I quickly collect my books and dart out, wondering what is happening. It can't be a coincidence Trevor wasn't in class, and before that both of Naomi's best friends were called out for dismissal.

By the time I get to the office, my skin is crawling with chill bumps. Aunt Grace is sitting in a black chair, clutching her purse with both hands. She jumps up when she spots me.

"Why are you here?" I ask.

"Not now," she hisses. Her eyes flick to the desk, where both secretaries are not even trying to hide the fact they're listening to us. Aunt Grace strides to the door and holds it open for me.

When we're in the truck, she slams her left hand on the steering wheel. "I can't believe this is happening."

"What's wrong?"

"I got a call a little while ago. The police chief wants to ask you some questions about Naomi Burton."

"Why does he want to talk to me?" I ask, even though I have a good idea. It all comes back to Trevor. Why did he have to get all freaky obsessive over me?

"I don't know, sweetie," she says. "He just said to get you down there pronto."

My stomach is a roiling mass of nerves by the time she parks at the police station. When we enter the lobby, I have to hold my breath so I won't puke—it smells like someone mopped the floor with a sour sponge. Aunt Grace wrinkles her nose before she greets the officer behind a bulletproof window. While we wait for him to alert the chief of our arrival, I check out the area.

I'm surprised and relieved Trevor and Kate aren't here. It's bad enough the chief wants to question me, but having to be here with the Monroes would be like having someone poke my eyes with white hot needles.

"Y'all can go on back to the chief's office," the officer says when he returns. He buzzes us through a door to our left. We enter the room with the officer and he escorts us to the chief's office.

Chief Lloyd, a tall man in his early fifties, is seated at his desk. His eyes are heavily smudged and his gray hair looks like he's run his hands through it quite a few times. He stands and offers his hand to Aunt Grace.

She doesn't take it.

His eyes harden. "Please, sit," he says and waits for us to do so. "I guess you're wondering why I asked y'all to come down here."

Aunt Grace leans back in her chair and crosses her arms. "Oh yes, that's definitely crossed my mind." I swear her voice could cut steel. She told me that he had the nerve to hit on her a few weeks after Darrel's funeral, then he got angry because she rejected him.

So yeah, the chief is a douchebag, or at least used to be one.

"Well, let's get started." He turns his attention to me. "Now, Alora, when was the last time you saw Naomi Burton?"

And here it goes. I rub the side of my neck. "About three weeks ago. Friday after school, on the eleventh of April." I remember the date because it was the day before Levi's party. "I saw her going to the parking lot."

"Did you talk to her?"

"No, sir. I was with . . . Sela. Sela Perkins." A lump forms in my throat. I almost said my friend Sela.

Funny how so much can change in a few weeks.

"How did Naomi appear to you?"

"She was upset."

"Upset? Like angry or sad?" He leans forward and props an arm on the edge of his desk.

I picture how Naomi looked that day. How she was crying. And I think about the day before that, when I heard her say something about following Trevor and needing him.

"She was definitely sad," I say. "Her boyfriend broke up with her."

"And you're sure you didn't have any direct contact with Naomi?"

Aunt Grace huffs. "Oh, for heaven's sake, she just told you she didn't talk to the girl."

Chief Lloyd shoots a stony look at her. "I'm going to ask you to step outside if you don't remain quiet."

If Aunt Grace could shoot laser beams out of her eyes, the chief would be scorched right now. I answer his question and several more, all pertaining to Naomi's whereabouts during the week before she disappeared. Even how she and Kate interrupted my so-called study session with Trevor.

"And you're sure you and Miss Burton didn't have a major altercation during that week? Something about fighting over Trevor Monroe."

"No, I've already told you what happened." My whole body tenses. I wish he'd let me go.

The chief raises an eyebrow as he studies me and he says, "That's . . . interesting."

"What is?" I ask.

"That's not what Mr. Monroe said."

"Whatever that little bastard said is a lie," Aunt Grace says, gripping the armrests of her chair.

"I'm beginning to wonder that myself," he replies.

To say I'm stunned is the understatement of the year.

Aunt Grace lets go of the chair. "Well, I'm glad you have enough sense to realize that."

I give her a withering glare, wishing she'd tone down the bitter act, and then ask the chief, "What has he done?"

"I'm not at liberty to discuss Mr. Monroe's actions." He checks something on his computer before asking, "Do you have anything else to add before I let you go?"

I'm about to tell him no so I can leave, but I remember what Trevor said to me, just before he grabbed my arm at school.

Look, don't worry about Naomi. I'll take care of that problem.

The words are on the verge of spilling from my mouth, but I swallow them back. I'm afraid. I mean, look at the hell Trevor put me through when I didn't want to go out with him. I don't want to do anything to set him on me again. So that's why I say, "No, sir. That's all."

"If you're sure, I believe that'll be all for now." He stands and says to Aunt Grace, "Thank you for bringing her in. If I have any more questions, I'll call you."

"It was my pleasure," she says, sarcasm dripping from her words as she snatches her purse off the floor. "By the way, have y'all had any luck finding Naomi?"

The chief's jaw clenches. "We have."

"That's good news," I say, casting a curious look at Aunt Grace.

She asks what I'm thinking. "So why did you want me to drag Alora down here if she's been found?"

Suddenly, I know why. My heart slams in my chest before I even hear the chief's words.

"Because Naomi's body was discovered this morning. This is now officially a murder investigation and we have to follow up on every new lead."

Oh my God.

Naomi's dead.

Naomi's dead.

Naomi's dead.

The words flash like a neon sign in my head. I'm no fan of Naomi's, but the news is still hard to take. I slump back in my seat, feeling nauseated.

"Oh no, sweetie. Are you okay?" Aunt Grace asks, her face pinched with worry.

I want to tell her I'm not. I can't believe this is real. I want to curl up somewhere and cry.

Chief Lloyd clears his throat. "Can I get you something?" He seems like he'd rather be anywhere than here with me.

"No . . . I'll be fine," I lie. My tongue feels sluggish in my mouth. Water would be nice, but I'd rather get out of here, fast.

"Are you sure?" Aunt Grace asks. "I don't want you passing out before we get back to the truck."

"I'm fine. Really." I make my voice sound stronger, more sure.

Aunt Grace helps me stand and I force my legs to stiffen, wishing my stomach would stop doing crazy flips. I can't believe it. A girl is dead. What if Trevor is the killer? Sure, I don't have any proof except those words he said to me about Naomi.

A few minutes ago, they didn't seem so important. Now, they make all the difference in the world.

"Well, then, let's go. You need some rest," Aunt Grace says.

"Thanks for coming in," the chief says, following us to the doorway. "And remember, if you think of anything else, call me."

I want to tell him right then what Trevor said. I know I should tell him. But I hesitate. If Trevor really did kill Naomi, what would he do to me if he found out what I said? Do I want to take that risk?

Or do I let a possible murderer get away?

We make it out of the chief's office and it hits me that I'm running away. Like I'd been running away from my fears for so many years. I listened to Aunt Grace and ignored searching for answers to my past because deep down I was afraid of what I'd find out.

I'm sick of being afraid.

Before I can change my mind, I pull my arm away and stride back to the chief's office. Aunt Grace calls my name, but I ignore her.

The chief looks up from some papers he was sorting through, startled. "Did you forget something?"

My voice trembles as I say, "Yes, sir."

29

flop back on my bed and rub my eyes. I've just wasted two hours searching the Internet. I don't know why I keep looking for more info about Alora's parents. But I keep trying, anything to keep myself busy.

I try to figure out something else I can do, but I can't focus. My skin starts to feel clammy. I close my eyes and think about Alora and everything I know about her. And suddenly I start to feel a little better. But no matter how many times I go through the facts, I can't work out why my dad wanted to save her. What would tie a man from 2146 to a ghost from 2013?

What am I missing?

I've got to get out of this room before I wild out. I step into the hallway, thinking I should go downstairs, but an idea creeps into my mind. It's something I thought about doing before—sneak into Alora's room.

She could have something in there that would help me. Something she may not know about. Or I could see if she left the Jewill home today. She shouldn't have future tech in her possession. But she's worn it every day since we opened Grace's safe. It's a miracle she hasn't activated the cloak.

If I'm going to do it, I need to go now while Grace is still gone. She received an urgent phone call a few hours ago and had to leave in a hurry. Before I change my mind, I stride down the hallway to Alora's door and turn the handle. "Fure," I mutter, slamming the palm of my hand against the door. It's locked.

I rush into Grace and Alora's bathroom and rummage through the drawers. They're full of girl stuff. Makeup, goop to fix hair, and things I don't even recognize. Why do they need so much stuff? Finally, in the very bottom drawer, I find a few bobby pins.

It doesn't take long to pick the lock. Still, I have this twitchy feeling all over by the time I enter her room. Alora's lavender scent is everywhere, and I get an overwhelming urge to just leave. I don't understand that. I've made hundreds of trips to the past. I've gone through personal belongings of other ghosts. I've listened in on private conversations and recorded them. And it's never bothered me until today. Now I feel like a perv.

I push the feeling aside. It's stupid of me to even feel like that. Not when I have a mission to complete.

I study the room. Everything is still neat, just like it was when I was here before. I remember how it felt when she hugged me. The memory of her body pressed against mine sends a jolt of longing through me.

Fure! I've got to stop doing that.

I decide to start with her desk. I spend a few minutes searching through the drawers. They're full of normal things. In the bottom drawer, there's a small wooden box. I open it, and lying on a velvet surface are the pictures of Alora's dad. I study them, thinking how much Alora resembles him. She has the same dark blond hair. Same shaped face. Same eye color.

And I can't get over how much Alora and her father look so similar to Vika. I close my eyes for a moment. I've got to stop comparing Vika and Alora.

I check the box for hidden compartments before slipping it back into the desk. I start to search her dresser next, but then I spot a small backpack propped against the desk. The dark purple book I saw before on Alora's desk sticks out of the top. Alora was sketching in it last week. She never offered to let me look in it.

So I have to shut out the stab of guilt as I flip through the pages. It's full of drawings. The sketches at the front of the book are really good. They're dated from a little over a year ago in small, neat numbers.

The later pictures are even better. There are a lot of scenes of the river and the dock. Even some of Grace and Sela. I also recognize Alora's father.

Two in particular catch my attention. Drawings of two women. My jaw drops. The dark-haired woman looks familiar.

But the other woman—the blonde—is the one that stuns me. If I didn't know better, I'd swear Alora sketched Vika's mother, Colonel Fairbanks.

30

Aunt Grace parks the truck behind the inn and I slide out, staring at the puffy white clouds dotting the sky. They've always reminded me of cotton candy, so light and carefree. But standing here, watching them float by while a breeze blows, I can't help but think how wrong they look. There should be thunder and lightning and darkness.

"Come on, sweetie," Aunt Grace says. She's holding the back door open for me. "Maybe you should lie down for a while. You've had a shock."

I slip past her, relieved she's relaxed since we left the police station. She was horrified when she realized I almost walked out without telling Chief Lloyd what Trevor had said to me, but after I confessed that Trevor followed me to the river, she understood. And she was furious. She talked to the chief about possibly taking out a restraining order against Trevor, which made me feel better and worse at the same time. There's no telling how he'll react when he finds out what I've told them.

I walk in a daze down the hallway, not sure of what I want to do. It's like I'm in a bad dream. I hope things don't get any worse.

"Do you want something to eat?" Aunt Grace asks. I turn around and find her standing in the kitchen doorway, with a too-bright smile on her face. That's how she copes with bad stuff—paint a pretty picture for everyone and hope real life will follow suit. It's what I've done too.

And I'm sick of it.

Don't get me wrong, I appreciate the life she's given me. But now it feels so false. I don't want to pretend anymore.

"No, I'm going to my room. I want to be alone for a while."

"Well, okay," she says, her smile faltering. "I'll be here if you need me."

It's a relief to get away from her. Then I find Bridger waiting for me in the hallway upstairs. Normally my pulse would speed up from seeing him.

For the past few weeks, I've grown to depend on his friendship, especially since I'm so alone in that department now.

But even the sight of him doesn't help. I'm hollow. "Hey, is everything okay?" he asks, falling into step beside me.

For a moment, the old instinct flares and I almost say yes. "No."

"What's wrong?"

The thought of talking about Naomi again nauseates me. "I just got back from the police station. The girl who's been missing for the past few weeks was found dead this morning. A jogger found her body in some woods down in Walton County."

"That's the girl Trevor broke up with before he started harassing you, right?" I nod, and Bridger runs his hands through his hair. "Why did the police want to see you?"

My voice sounds flat as I explain what Trevor said to me.

We stop in front of my bedroom, and Bridger places his hand on my shoulder. His touch sends a wave of warmth through my body. "Listen, I know you're blaming yourself, but you can't do that."

"But what if I'd said something sooner?" I ask, putting voice to another fear that crossed my mind on the way home. "Trevor told me he was going to take care of the problem with Naomi on Thursday, before she disappeared. She might still be alive if I'd told somebody."

Bridger shakes his head. "I don't think so. Maybe it was her time to go."

I give him an incredulous look. "How can you say that? She was murdered. I could've prevented her death if I hadn't been so stupid."

"Nobody can predict the future."

"Yeah, but—"

"Please, try to stop worrying. There's nothing you can do about it," he whispers.

His gaze is so intense, almost anguished. I can't look him in the eye anymore. I don't understand why he's being so nice, especially since I'm partially to blame.

"Alora, look at me," he says.

I have to pry my gaze from my feet to meet his steady stare. He seems to be searching for some kind of answer, one that I'm sure I don't have.

"It's not your fault."

I want to protest, but he places a single finger over my lips. They tingle under his touch.

"Just hear me out. Do you know for certain that Trevor killed Naomi?" he asks.

"No, but the chief indicated whatever Trevor said to him isn't adding up. And what about the things he said to me?"

"That's not proof. Until you hear for sure he's been charged, don't assume anything. You never know, someone else could've killed Naomi."

That thought never occurred to me. It just seemed so obvious Trevor was the one. What if the real murderer is still out there? That's not exactly reassuring, but for some reason it makes me feel a bit better. Because if that's true, it would let me off the guilty hook. But I doubt that's the case.

"Look, I'm going to go lie down for a while." I start to enter my room, but the expression on Bridger's face stops me. "Did you want something?"

He rubs the back of his neck. "It can wait."

"Are you sure?"

He gives me the smile that shows his dimples. "Yeah. You've had a rough day. I'll talk to you when you get up."

"Okay, give me an hour and I'm all yours."

As he walks way, he casts a wistful glance back over his shoulder at me. I almost call out for him to come back.

When I'm in my room, it dawns on me that Bridger might have found something important, but he kept it from me because he knew I was too upset. Yet another reason to feel guilty. I sit on the bed and try to clear my mind, but I can't. An image has been stuck in my head since I left the police station—that of Naomi's decomposing body lying out in the open. Of course, the chief couldn't show us pictures of the crime scene, but my mind's been doing its worst.

After a half hour of trying to sleep, I give up. I'd thought being alone would help, but something about my room is too suffocating. I need air. I need to run. I change into some shorts and running shoes and go downstairs.

Aunt Grace is in the kitchen, pressing a glob of ground beef into a thick patty. "Hey, sweetie. Do you feel better?"

"Sort of. I wanted to let you know that I'm gonna run for a while."

"Are you sure that's a good idea? I'm not crazy about you going off too far, at least until this mess with Trevor is sorted out."

She's thinking the same thing I am—how going to the river alone isn't safe for me anymore.

"I'll stay close to the house, or I might run by the highway."

She thinks for a moment then heaves a sigh. "Fine. But don't stay gone long. Supper will be ready soon."

"Yes, ma'am. I'll be back in a half hour, tops."

Outside, I cast a longing look toward the path to the river. Chances are Trevor won't ever follow me out there again. But I don't want to go there by myself, not anytime soon. And that makes me so angry. The jackass has taken away the one place I've always been able to go to feel better.

I jog down the driveway. I almost turn back when I reach the road, thinking Trevor or someone else in his family could drive by at any time, but they'd be stupid to stop and confront me. And I'm really not ready to go back home yet. I turn right and run toward town. The inn is about a half mile past the city limit. It won't take long to get there.

By the time I reach the WELCOME TO WILLOW CREEK sign, sweat beads across my forehead and down my back. But I feel a lot better. My head is clearer and the sluggish feeling that's been strangling me since I found out about Naomi is gone. I'm almost to my driveway again when I see a familiar truck racing toward me.

Trevor's truck.

"Oh no," I whisper. I look around wildly, but there's nowhere I can go, nowhere to hide. Maybe he won't recognize me.

But apparently I don't have any luck.

His tires squeal as he hits the brakes. I'm frozen in place. I hope someone drives by soon.

My pulse is racing by the time Trevor gets out of the truck. He stalks toward me, pointing his finger. "You bitch! What did you tell the police?"

"I don't know what you're talking about."

"Liar," he hisses. "Don't even think about trying to get out of this. You're gonna fix things. Now." He's less than a foot from me, his face contorted in rage.

The roar of an approaching car draws our attention. A flicker of hope surges through me. I'll do something to catch their attention so Trevor will have to leave me alone.

A small, black car comes into view. Immediately the hopeful feeling evaporates—it's Kate. She slows as she nears us, but when she realizes Trevor is talking to me, she shoots off again.

When she's gone, Trevor says, "Get in the truck."

"No!" Has he lost his mind? That's the last thing I'd ever do.

But he doesn't give me a choice. He checks to make sure no other cars are coming and then grabs me by the arm, his fingers digging in my flesh, and drags me toward his truck.

"Let me go!"

He yanks the door open and shoves me inside. I try to get out, but he fixes me with a frigid glare. "If you move a muscle, you'll regret it."

My body is shaking as Trevor climbs in. He floors the accelerator and the truck fishtails before lurching forward.

"Where are you taking me?" I ask, my voice sounding hoarse.

"I don't know what lies you told the chief, but I did *not* kill Naomi. Hell, she begged me to protect her. She claimed somebody was following her, but I didn't believe it. I just figured it was a trick to get me back." His voice cracks on the last word.

I stare at him, shocked. Naomi thought somebody was following her? I think back to that day I saw her arguing with Trevor at school. I definitely heard the word "followed," but I'd just assumed she was talking about following Trevor to Java Jive that day he met me there. What if I was wrong? Could there have really been someone else following her? Someone who murdered her?

I turn away from Trevor and try to force down the panicky feeling rising in me. And that's when I notice how fast he's going. The scenery passes by in a blur of greens and browns. All I can think about is what will happen to us if he loses control. I want to scream at him to slow down. As if that'll do a lot of good. There's no reasoning with someone who's as upset as he is.

"You know, I really did like you for a while," he finally says.

I just hug my arms tightly against my chest.

"And I can't believe you, sitting there all stuck-up like you don't give a shit about anybody. I thought you might've been shy or whatever, but I was wrong. You're just happy throwing wild accusations out there when you don't even know what you're talking about." He looks at me with eyes that are cold. Dead. "I should've listened to Kate. Hell, I should've listened to Naomi."

That hurts. I've had enough to put up with in my life and he's twisting things around to make me sound like the worst person alive. But I'm not sure how he'd react if I stand up for myself. I need to get him to calm down.

"I'm sorry," I whisper.

"You're sorry! You go and tell a bunch of lies to the cops and that's all you have to say for yourself?" He jerks the wheel to turn at the intersection by the school, then yells, "I was doing you a favor by asking you out. You should've thanked me, and then you had to act all high-and-mighty. Or was it because of that new boyfriend of yours? He must be really good if you'd pick a scrawny nothing like him over me."

His words make it clear he thinks something not so innocent is going on between Bridger and me. That pisses me off. But still, I remain silent.

I blink back tears as I stare ahead. The light at the approaching intersection turns yellow.

My eyes are drawn to the accelerator. Trevor still has it floored. He's not letting up. My mouth opens to ask him to slow down. And then I see it.

A car speeding toward the intersection from the right.

I snap my gaze back up at the now red light. I squeeze my eyes shut, wishing I was home. Anywhere but here. I just want to be safe.

I don't want to die.

31

"Have you seen Alora?" I ask Grace when I get downstairs. I checked her room first, but it was empty.

Grace looks up from her phone. "She went for a run. I was just texting her because she's late. She was supposed to be back ten minutes ago." Grace tries to keep her voice light, but worry is etched across her face.

A nervous flutter fills my stomach. "Did she take the river trail?"

"No, she said she was going to run along the highway."

"I'll look for her," I say. It's all I can do to keep from tearing out of the house.

As I run down the driveway, I wish I could just shift to the highway already. Horrible thoughts race through my mind. All pertaining to that dickhead and his obsession with Alora. I tried to make Alora feel better by reminding her that someone else could've murdered that ghost. But my gut was telling me the whole time that it had to be Trevor. Yet one more mistake I made back in my time. I should have studied every homicide around here in the months prior to Alora's death date to see if there was a pattern.

I'm a failure. Dad wouldn't have made that kind of mistake.

I don't see Alora when I get to the end of the driveway. I activate my DataLink tracker. Red dots blink on the holographic image, but they're all concentrated in housing units. A dot is speeding toward me from town. I look up to find an auto heading my way.

I study the dots again. Alora wouldn't visit one of her neighbors. She's never done that in the time I've been here. She doesn't have any other friends. But it doesn't make sense for her to not be around here.

Unless someone took her.

I walk a short way along the side of the road toward Willow Creek. Then I freeze. Skid marks streak the side of the road, along with torn grass where someone sped away.

I run back the inn to let Grace know what I've found. And I swear, if Trevor has Alora, I don't know if I can stop myself from hurting him.

"I'm gonna kill him," Grace says again as we hit the city limits.

We're heading to the police station. Even though we don't have proof, we're both positive Trevor took Alora. He must have seen Alora on the side of the road and forced her to get in his auto. But where did he take her?

We pass Alora's school, but soon reach a stalled line of autos snaking up the road ahead of us.

Grace frowns. "Good grief, I should've taken one of the side streets." She stretches her neck forward and then peers over her shoulder. "There's no way I can turn around."

I roll my window down and lean out. The air smells of smoke and gasoline. I can barely make it out, but it looks like a pile of twisted metal is sitting under the traffic light. Flames lick at the sides. Several firefighters hose it with jets of water. People in the other autos are gawking out their window. A few are standing at a barricade that's been set up.

Grace rolls down her window and gestures to an older woman coming back from the barricade. I recognize her from the bakery Alora took me to a few times. "Hey, Mrs. Randolph," she says.

"Oh, hello, Grace."

"What's going on up there?"

Mrs. Randolph shakes her head. "It's terrible. A truck ran the red light and was broadsided by a car. So sad."

"Do you know who they were?"

"Well," Mrs. Randolph says, looking back at the wreckage. "The man who was in the car died on impact. He was just passing through town. But the other was the Monroe boy."

I've experienced moments twice before when it feels like time has stopped. Both times I couldn't breathe. The first was when I found out Dad was dead. The second was when I found out Vika had died.

And now.

Grace's voice is shrill as she asks, "You mean Trevor Monroe?"

"Yes. He ran the red light."

A red hovercraft-type vehicle appears overhead. Its blades roar and pulse the air. It lands in the parking lot just ahead of us.

Grace tears out of the truck and runs toward the barricade. I follow close behind, my heart feeling like it could explode from my chest. Grace tries to push through, but an officer blocks her.

"You don't understand," Grace says, tears running down her cheeks. "I think my niece is in there."

"Ma'am, if you'll calm down, I'll see what I can find out. But I can't let you go up there. Do you understand?"

She nods and turns to me when the officer walks away, talking into an antiquated handheld communication device. "I should've made her stay at the house. This is all my fault."

"Don't jump to conclusions. We don't know for sure she was in there," I say, hoping that's true. But I can't suppress the feeling of dread that's gripped me.

This can't be happening. If Alora is dead, that means I've changed history. I've screwed up the timeline. I want to die. I run my hands through my hair and try to force myself to calm down. To breathe slowly. Grace and I, along with the other nosy ghosts, watch as the medics push a stretcher covered with a white sheet and load it onto the ambulance. Another stretcher is loaded on the red aircraft.

But if Alora wasn't in there, where is she?

The officer strides back to us, his face hardened in irritation. "Ma'am, I don't know where your niece could be, but she was not in the truck."

Grace blinks a few times. "What? I'm positive she was with Trevor."

Tires squeal somewhere behind us. Everyone turns around, trying to locate the source of the noise. A white auto has just parked behind us and three people spill out.

The rest of the Monroes.

They run up to the barricade, looking frantic.

The man yells, "Where's my son?"

I recognize the woman and girl with him as Trevor's mom and sister. Both are sobbing uncontrollably and don't even glance our way. Officers usher them to a group of medics huddled near the ambulance.

After the red aircraft lifts off, a few people head back to their own autos. Most stay. Grace is still as a statue. She's fixated on what's left of the autos lying in the intersection. It's a miracle Trevor survived.

The Monroe family staggers from the ambulance shortly after the red aircraft departs. The man has one arm wrapped tightly around Celeste and the other around Kate. It's so strange seeing Celeste like that. I think back to a few weeks ago. When she wilded out and accused Alora of trying to ruin her son. And yet I feel sorry for her. For all of them. I know what they're going through.

Grace must think the same thing. She steps forward and says, "Celeste, Rob, I'm sorry about what happened. If there's anything I can do for you, please let me know."

They stop and look at Grace as if she's something that should be scraped off the bottom of their shoes. Rob says, "I'll tell you what you can do. If I find out your niece is responsible for this, you better get yourself a lawyer."

"Wait, what? How could she be responsible? I was on the way to the police station because she never came back from her run and we found skid marks by the side of the road. I figured your son must've forced her in his truck."

"That's funny," Rob says, his eyes slitting together. "Because the paramedic told us the first thing Trevor said when they pulled him out was it was Alora's fault."

I swear, I'd punch this jerk if I could. Now I see where Trevor gets his arrogance. But before I can say anything, he leads Celeste and Kate back to their auto.

Grace stares after them. "I don't understand. If they claim this is Alora's fault, then where is she?"

"I don't know." At least I'm not lying, because I'm positive Alora shifted if she was in the truck.

But where did she go?

32

crack open my eyes, scared of what I'll see. I'm stunned to find it's night. The moon is a thin sliver, a smile mocking me.

I've had another blackout.

My skin crawls. I try to sit up, but my body doesn't cooperate. Then the events from this afternoon invade my thoughts. Learning of Naomi's death. Trevor forcing me into his truck. The car hurtling toward us at the intersection.

"Oh no," I whisper, taking in where I'm at. Even in the moonlight, I realize I'm near the pier at the river.

A crushing weight constricts my chest. The suffocating air closes around me, choking me. I roll to my side and curl up, gasping and fighting back tears. My hand finds my necklace and I clasp it, feeling the smooth stone pressing into my palms

What is wrong with me?

I don't understand any of this. I don't know how I got out of the truck, how I'm not in a hospital right now—or worse, how I'm not dead. It's like the rules for reality have changed. You're not supposed to escape a wreck without getting hurt. I force myself to sit up and check for injuries. There's no blood. Not even a single scratch. Only my arm hurts where Trevor grabbed me.

And I'm even worried about Trevor, despite what he did to me. I wonder if he's okay.

Aunt Grace has to be flipping out. It takes a lot of effort for me to stand, and I have to stay still for a while before I'm steady enough to walk. The other times I blacked out, I woke feeling dizzy, but nothing like this.

As I half walk, half stumble through the forest, an owl hoots somewhere above me. Leaves and twigs crackle with each step I take, each one sounding like a gunshot, but I don't care. It's not like anyone would be out here wanting to hurt me at this time of night.

I make a noise that sounds like a cross between a strangled laugh and a snort. And then I cry. I lean against a tree until the tears stop.

Yeah, when I get back to the inn, Aunt Grace is probably going to drag me off to a psych ward. I'm a freak. A lucky freak, but still a freak.

Another thought surfaces. I don't have to tell Aunt Grace I blacked out. I could let her think Trevor released me or I escaped and hid from him. She might buy it. Then she won't have to take me to get my head examined. I could go on pretending everything's fine.

Even though it's not.

I rub at my face and push on.

At the edge of the forest, I stop. The inn is fully lit, illuminating Aunt Grace's truck and several cars. Crap, I don't need this. I guess it's to be expected since I was taken against my will, but I don't want to listen to a bunch of questions when I don't have the answers.

Before I know it, I'm almost at the back porch. I expect voices to blare from inside, but instead an eerie quiet blankets the house.

A lone figure sits on the top step. A sigh of relief escapes me when I realize it's Bridger. He's leaning forward with his arms propped on his legs, rubbing one of his hands. He doesn't notice me yet.

And I run toward him, calling his name. I didn't realize how much I wanted to see him until now.

His head snaps up and his eyes grow wide, then he leaps off the steps. When he reaches me, I throw my arms around his neck. His arms wrap around me and he holds me tight. I feel safe, like I belong in his arms.

Shocked, I pull away, my face and neck burning.

"Where have you been?" he asks.

I can't answer. I don't know what to say yet. Tell the truth, or go with the lie. It'll be easier if Aunt Grace thinks I found a way to escape Trevor. That would mean no trips to the doctor and no medical bills.

But there's one problem—I'd already decided earlier to stop pretending. Me going to the doctor will hurt Grace financially, but I can't ignore these blackouts anymore. I mean, what if I'm dying? It's not worth it to keep something like that to myself. Because back in Trevor's truck, as the car was racing toward us, all I wanted to do was live.

"I had another blackout. One minute I was in the truck with Trevor and then the next thing I knew, I was at the river." Funny, as I'm telling Bridger, lightness spreads through me. It feels wonderful and the words keep pouring out.

Bridger runs a hand over his mouth. "So you don't remember anything from the time you were in Trevor's truck until you woke up at the river?"

"Yes," I say, wondering what he's getting at.

"Do you realize you've been missing for about four hours?"

"No," I say, starting to get nervous. Four hours. What did I do during that time?

"People have been searching everywhere for you. They went through the woods, and Grace had them comb the area around the pier because that's your favorite place. They got back a half hour ago and you weren't there."

The light feeling evaporates, confirming I'm either insane or dying. Or both.

"Bridger, who are you talking to?" someone calls from the porch. It's Aunt Grace. From where she's standing, I know she can't see us while we're swallowed by the shadows.

I don't wait for him to answer. I rush toward the porch, calling her name.

"Oh dear God!" She flies off the steps and folds me into a tight embrace. It's hard to breathe, but I don't care. When she finally lets go, she takes me by both shoulders. "I thought I'd never see you again. Where have you been?"

My gaze flicks to Bridger and he gives me a tiny nod. So I let myself open up to her and tell her the truth. Even knowing she'll drag me to the head doctors.

I expect her to yell at me for keeping the blackouts from her, but she doesn't. She just pulls me close again. Her voice is thick with emotion as she says, "We'll worry about that later, sugar. I'm just glad you're safe."

"Me too. By the way, how is Trevor? The last thing I remember was that car heading toward the truck. I don't know how he kept us from getting hit."

Bridger looks away, but Aunt Grace gasps. "You mean you were still in the truck then?"

"Well, yeah. He must've sped up or something."

"But . . . how is that possible?" she asks.

"What do you mean?" My eyes flick from her to Bridger.

Aunt Grace's head snaps toward Bridger. "You didn't tell her?"

"No," he says.

"Tell me what?"

"The car hit Trevor's truck," Aunt Grace says in a quivering voice. "He's at Emory in Atlanta, in the ICU." She exchanges a look with Bridger before continuing. "And apparently before they flew him to the hospital, he blamed everything on you."

33

"So, how did the appointment go?" I ask Alora as soon as she enters the front parlor.

"It was fine." She sits in the chair across from me. Her eyes have a hollow look.

For the past two days, ever since Alora finally admitted to everyone that she's been having blackouts, I've been at war with myself. I wanted to tell her nothing is wrong. In fact, I almost did several times. Each time I made myself stop. And each time the guilt gnawed at me. I feel like I'm betraying Alora. But what choice do I have? I can't march up to her and say, *Hey, you're not sick and you're not crazy . . . you're a Space Bender.* I'm sure she'd think I was insane.

"Okay." I lean forward and steeple my fingers together. I don't want to seem like I'm prying into her business. Aw, screw that. "But what did the doc say?"

Alora's eyes snap up to me. It's like she forgot I'm in the room with her. "I'm sorry. I'm just out of it, I guess." She gives me a thin smile. "Anyway, he doesn't think I'm crazy, but he wants to send me to a neurologist."

She falls into silence. We both know what that means—more tests. Tests I know she doesn't need.

I focus on my clenched hands. "When is that appointment?"

"Next Monday." She sighs and then says, "At least school is almost out. If they find anything wrong with me, I can start treatments over the summer."

Alora thinks she has a brain tumor. I almost laughed when she told me yesterday, but she was serious. All I could do was tell her that she's overreacting. That didn't go over so well.

"Alora, where are you?" Grace calls out from the back of the house.

"In here," she replies.

Grace's footsteps echo through the hall, then she pokes her head in the doorway. "Hey, Bridger. I didn't know you were in here."

Yeah, where else would I be? I give her a half wave. "I was asking Alora about the appointment."

Grace's smile falters. "It was fine."

"Yeah, everything was just freaking great," Alora mutters.

An uncomfortable quiet follows. Alora fidgets with her fingers. Grace bites her lip. I scratch my neck, trying to think of something to say. Something to make Alora feel better.

Finally, Grace clears her throat. "You know, I thought I could fix some sandwiches for a picnic. It's too pretty outside to be cooped up in here." Her eyes flick back and forth between Alora and me. "How's that sound?"

Actually it sounds perfect. "I'm up for it," I say.

"Good. I'll get everything together. Be back in a jiffy."

After Grace leaves, I watch Alora for a few moments. Now I feel even worse than I have for the past two days. Dark circles ring her eyes and she's slumped in the chair, like there's a literal weight crushing her spirit.

Not only does Alora think she's sick, she's also been questioned by the police several times about what happened with Trevor. At least nothing came of that. Trevor doesn't remember how Alora got out, and she doesn't either. The police figured Trevor just let Alora out somewhere before he got to the red light.

But I know better.

And now I want to take that pain away. I wish I could.

She needs something to distract her. Something that she normally does that could take her mind off things.

Something like drawing.

I shift my eyes away from Alora, remembering how I found her sketchbook. Heat burns my face. It's like I've been stabbing her in the back. But I had to do it. I *had* to. And I still need to find out about the women she drew.

I run my hand through my hair. How can I ask her about drawing? "Since we're going on a picnic, why don't you get your sketchbook? You might want to work on something while we're out."

That was smooth. Elijah and Zed would laugh their asses off if they were here.

But Alora doesn't laugh. Her eyes come back into focus. "Yeah, that's a good idea. I haven't had time to work on anything lately." She stands and stretches and I can't help but notice how her light blue tank top slips up, exposing the skin above her shorts.

I look away, rubbing the back of my neck. I wonder if she saw me checking her out.

Not good, Bridger. Not good.

"I'll see if Grace needs any help while you get whatever you need," I quickly say. I can't get to the kitchen fast enough. If I didn't know better, I'd think I was developing feelings for Alora. But that's impossible. I wouldn't do something that stupid.

"Where's Alora?" Grace asks.

"She went upstairs to get her sketchbook."

"That's nice. I haven't seen her draw anything lately."

Grace busies herself with loading way more food into the picnic basket than Alora and I will be able to eat.

Alora joins us, the small backpack I found the sketchbook in slung over her shoulder. "Are you ready?" she asks me.

"Yes." I start to pick up the basket, but Grace grabs it first.

"Don't worry, I'll carry it."

"You're coming too?" I ask, trying to keep the disappointment out of my voice.

Grace grins. "Well, of course. I'm not gonna let you two have all the fun."

Alora's eyes widen.

Nice. How am I supposed to get Alora to talk about those sketches if Grace is there, poking her nose in everything?

After we're finished eating, I lay back on the blanket Grace spread out on the pier.

"I'm full as a tick," Grace says, interrupting the quiet. She stretches out her legs and sighs. "I need to come down here more. This used to be mine and Darrel's favorite place to go."

"Really?" Alora asks. She's sitting cross-legged next to Grace, drawing something. "I never knew that."

A pained expression crosses Grace's face. "Yeah, I didn't do such a good job of letting you know a lot of stuff."

I hope Grace doesn't decide to share her entire history with Darrel. I hate feeling so selfish. But ever since Alora slid the sketchbook out of her backpack, my fingers have itched to grab it.

"Don't worry about that. You were just looking out for me."

Grace lets out a snort. "Yeah, a lot of good I did."

Even though I'm irritated with Grace right now, I feel sorry for her. Everything she's done has been to protect Alora. If only my mom would act more like Grace.

"I've got to get back to the house," Grace says. She stands and grabs the picnic basket. "You never know, we might get a drop-in guest." From her tone, she doesn't believe it. Grace hasn't had any guests in over two weeks.

"I'm not finished yet," Alora says. "Are you ready to head back, Bridger?"

"No. I kind of like it out here."

"I was hoping y'all would keep me company, but if you want to be like that." Grace winks, but grows serious as she focuses on me. "Don't leave her alone, okay?"

"You know I won't," I say.

At the same time, Alora lets out an exasperated, "Really, Aunt Grace?"

"Sweetie, you can't be by yourself. Not under the circumstances."

After Grace leaves, Alora huffs and rolls her eyes. "I wish she'd stop treating me like a baby."

"She's just worried about you."

"Don't start that."

"Start what?" I ask, tilting my head to the side.

"Defending her. She's smothering me. Besides, didn't you tell me your mom does the same thing?"

"Yes, but the difference is my mother is only looking out for herself."

Alora sets the sketchbook on her lap. "How do you know that?"

"I just know." I stare at the ripples and small waves lapping against the shore. That's just how Mom is with me. Her criticisms come in short, steady streams, never stopping.

"Maybe that's true, but what if you're wrong? What if your mom's trying to protect you?"

I snort. "Yeah, right. If there's one thing I know about Morgan Creed, it's that she's only interested in protecting herself or my brother."

"I think you're overreacting," Alora says, arching an eyebrow.

"If you ever met my mother you wouldn't say that."

Alora gets this funny look on her face, all dreamy-like. "I'd like that."

"What?"

"Meeting your mom. She sounds interesting."

My mouth goes dry. Alora will never get to meet my mom. It's another reminder I'm not where I belong.

"Are you okay?"

"I'm fine," I say. I'm not sure how we got on the subject of my mother, but I have to change it. Now. I lean over and peer at Alora's book. "Can I see what you're drawing?"

She bites her lip. "I suppose so, but promise you won't laugh."

"I promise," I say, taking the book from her.

I'd figured she was drawing the river. So I'm surprised to find myself looking at a half-finished sketch of me. "Wow."

Her face turns pink. "I'm sorry. I should've asked first. Do you want me to stop?"

"No, it's okay. I like it," I say, grinning.

I know she wants to finish, but I need to pretend to see those sketches of the two women for the first time. So I act all smooth and skim through the pages. "Nice," I say. When I get to the ones I'm looking for, I stop. "These are really good. Who are they?"

Alora's expression grows somber. "I don't know."

"Wait . . . I thought you could only draw people you've seen before."

She crosses her arms against her chest. "What I meant is I *have* seen them. I dream about them sometimes. I figured one is my mom, but I don't have a clue which one."

And as if lightning has struck me, an answer materializes in my mind. Adrenaline rushes through my body. Of course! Vika doesn't look like her mother at all, yet she bears a strong resemblance to Alora and Alora's father. Plus, there is the fact that Alora is a Space Bender. What if Alora and Vika are sisters? Vika was always a little jealous of my relationship with Dad—she was the product of a sperm donation. What if the donor was Alora's father? What if Vika and Alora share the same mother? But how, and more importantly, why would Colonel Fairbanks want to have a child with some-one who lived in the past? With someone who was probably a natural-born Space Bender?

I'm missing something. But what?

"What's wrong?" Alora asks, jerking my attention back to her.

"Sorry, I was just thinking."

"Whatever it was, it must be good. You look happy."

"You have no idea." I grin. The surge of excitement shooting through my veins is intoxicating.

For the first time since that whole mess on Monday, Alora really smiles. It's beautiful, lighting up her whole face. I love it. I stare at her lips.

I want to kiss her more than anything.

Before I can stop myself, I cup her cheek and hold her gaze. I shouldn't do this. My mind's screaming at me to stop. I'm not supposed to mess around with a ghost. But I can't stop. My lips brush against hers, silencing the screams. This feels so right. So perfect.

Alora's body tenses before relaxing. She wraps her arms around my neck and presses her body closer to mine. And when her mouth parts . . . oh hell, I nearly lose it.

Then I remember what I'm doing. Who I'm kissing.

I can't do this.

I pull away from her. Instantly, I miss the warmth of her body against mine. From the startled look on her face, she's feeling the same way.

"What's wrong?" she asks in a breathless voice.

I can't speak for a moment. My heart is hammering too hard. When I'm able to think again, I say, "Maybe we should go back to the house."

Alora's brow crinkles, but she doesn't say anything. She picks up the forgotten sketchbook and shoves it back in her bag. When she stands, she glares at me. "You know, you can't kiss somebody then pull back and pretend nothing's wrong. Did I do something?"

I jump up and grab her hands. "I'm sorry. It's just . . . I felt bad. I thought I was taking advantage of you."

"You weren't," she snaps.

I've got to be smart about this. She thinks something is wrong with her and that's not it. "Alora, you've been through a lot in the past few days. And you're about to go to another doc and go through who knows how many tests." I take a deep breath as the guilt spikes. "So I don't feel right doing this. Not now."

She snatches her hands back. "You know what? I need a friend. I need someone who likes me and wants to be with me. Not another protector. Aunt Grace has that area covered."

She turns and stomps away, leaving me gaping at her.

I should follow Alora, but I stay put. I could kick myself for kissing her. I acted like Zed. No, I'm worse. He just leers at the hot ghosts and talks a lot of junk, but he's never acted on it. Me kissing Alora, now that was stupid.

And what if she doesn't want to talk to me anymore? Grace is putting all her faith in letting docs find the answers, but they won't. It's impossible for them to detect the space-bending gene. Alora is going to be subjected to test after test. It's going to torment her. I don't want her to go through that.

But what if she's supposed to go through those tests? I'm not supposed to change things.

This is so damn hard to figure out. Things would be so much simpler if I could flip a switch and make her memories of why her parents abandoned her all those years ago come back.

Something clicks with that thought. I'd already wondered if Alora's memories were deliberately erased. That could have been what happened, especially if Colonel Fairbanks is involved. Or Alora could have just forgotten because it happened so long ago. Either way, I can help her regain her memories. A Mind Redeemer can reverse the effects of a memory erasure or help suppressed memories resurface.

The problem is I'd have to shift back to 2146 to get one.

34

"You need to finish your lunch," Aunt Grace says, glancing at the half-eaten cheeseburger I wrapped and tossed on the truck's dashboard.

We're back in Willow Creek after spending most of the morning at the medical imaging center in Athens. It took forever for someone to call me to the back, and another hour to perform the scan. I wonder if they'll find a tumor. Then again, finding nothing won't be much comfort, either, but I won't know for a few more days. Just what I wanted, more waiting and wondering.

"Worrying won't help. You need to keep your strength up."

I ignore her. Arguing with Aunt Grace is pointless. She doesn't understand forcing food down my throat will probably make me puke. She's old school—eating always solves problems. Or at least lessens them.

I wish I could talk to Sela, but we're still on the outs. Despite everything that's happened to me, she walks right by me at school as if I'm invisible. Just like everyone else. Even though the police investigated and declared that I'm not to blame for Trevor's accident, everyone still thinks I'm responsible. They've been saying that it's really convenient that I can't remember Trevor supposedly stopping and letting me out somewhere, which is what the police chief concluded. If Trevor said I'm to blame, then that *must* be the truth.

I stare out the window and frown. It's too bright and cheerful for my mood. I bet if I rolled the window down, birds would be chirping a Disney tune.

Aunt Grace slows and pulls into the parking lot of The Gingerbread House.

"Why are you stopping here?" I ask.

Aunt Grace gives me one of her *are you serious* looks. "Because I'm tired of your moping."

"Aunt Grace, I don't . . ."

She holds up a hand. "Let me finish." She sighs and her face softens. "I know you don't want to go through all those tests, but if something's wrong, we need to know so we can get it fixed. You're all I've got left in the world and I'm gonna do what it takes to make sure you're all right."

"But what about the bills?"

"Don't worry about that. You're more important."

I open my mouth, ready to argue, but instead a choked sob slips out. She leans over and holds me close, stroking my hair. When I'm done crying, I look up, hiccuping.

"Now, don't you feel better?" she asks, smiling.

"I guess so."

"That's my girl. Keeping that stuff bottled inside is toxic. You could give yourself an ulcer, worrying about things all the time."

"That would be better than a brain tumor."

"Not funny," she answers in a flat voice. "Now come on. There's nothing some cupcakes won't fix."

When we walk in the store, Mrs. Randolph gasps. "Well, well, look who's decided to grace me with her presence."

Normally I'd have a retort, but my mind is blank, thanks to the tumor I more than likely have. "I know," is all I can think to say.

Aunt Grace goes straight to Mrs. Randolph and begins to chat with her. Aunt Grace is probably spilling my business while Mrs. Randolph shares the latest gossip. The joys of small-town life.

I wander around the shop, inspecting the spread. The smell of fresh bread, warm cookies, and cakes welcomes me like an old friend. My traitorous stomach doesn't care. It churns and protests. Sweat beads on my face.

Aunt Grace and Mrs. Randolph don't even notice as I slip away to the restroom. I close the door and prop my hands on the sink, taking in huge gulps of air. Then I splash my face with cold water. When I feel stronger, I straighten and lean back against the door.

My hand creeps up and cups my necklace. Now that I know most of the truth about my father, it's been a comfort, like a long lost gift from him. I hate that I have to hide it under my shirt. Squeezing it, I close my eyes. I wish everything was different.

Things began to fall apart when Trevor first hit on me. I wish there was some way I could go back in time and refuse to even meet with him that Wednesday. Then maybe he wouldn't be in ICU, near death, and Naomi would still be alive. And I wouldn't have this heavy guilt on top of the whole blackout business.

A too-familiar wave of dizziness washes over me. Crap, this had to happen again. I force myself to hold still and breathe slowly, but it doesn't work. Panicked, I crack open my eyes, but everything is going black.

When I come to, I'm still leaning against the door. Maybe I wasn't out too long this time. That would be nice for a change, instead of being unconscious for hours.

I check my appearance in the mirror. My face is colorless and dark smudges line my eyes. My hair is a mess. I try to quickly smooth down the flyaway strands and frown. It's funny how this light makes my skin look shimmery. Or I could be imagining it. That's possible if I have a brain tumor, right?

The air in the bakery is cooler than it was in the restroom. As I hurry to the front of the store, I expect to hear Aunt Grace and Mrs. Randolph still yapping, but all I can make out is the faint sounds of a television set.

The moment I get to the end of the hallway I freeze, unable to believe what I'm seeing.

It's *me*, standing on the other side of the room at the cash register.

When I'm able to catch my breath, I take a few hesitant steps forward, thinking the other me will disappear. It has to be a hallucination.

It *has* to be.

The other Alora finishes talking with Mrs. Randolph and heads toward the door. She's wearing a pink T-shirt and faded denim capris—the same outfit I wore when Trevor first asked me out right after detention.

Oh my God. What's happening to me?

I'm drawn to her like a magnet. I watch as she slows before reaching the door and studies the shop. I remember doing that, thinking someone was watching me. Then someone touched me. I'm standing so close I could touch *her*, but I'm afraid.

I look down at myself. I'm still here, but the other Alora can't see me. She has to be a hallucination or I'm here in spirit form. I almost laugh, thinking how some of Aunt Grace's guests would love that.

The other Alora's face pinches as she turns back to the door. Before I can change my mind, I reach out my hand. I'm not sure what I expect, but when my fingers brush against warm flesh, a chill shoots through my body.

She yells and Mrs. Randolph rushes around the counter, asking what's wrong. I don't hang around. I'm pretty certain I'm going to puke.

I make it back to the bathroom and lean over the toilet for a few moments, expecting to hurl. I never do. My stomach still churns, though.

How was that possible? I keep replaying the episode in my head. Maybe I imagined it. But I remember it happening weeks ago. How the touch seemed to sear into my skin. I thought I was going nuts then, but now it's worse. The other me felt so *real*.

Pressure settles over my chest and I gasp for air. Not again. I drop the lid to the toilet and sit, while lowering my head between my knees. Breathe in. Breathe out.

I close my eyes and clasp the necklace. I'd give anything to get back to where I was. Erase the last few minutes I witnessed.

Then blackness swallows me.

The first thing I do when I come to is puke. Footsteps run down the hallway, and the door bursts open. "Oh, sweet heavens!" Aunt Grace shrieks as she rushes to me, her face pale.

Mrs. Randolph hovers in the doorway, looking horrified. Her hand flutters to her chest and she asks, "Do you want me to call 9-1-1?"

"I don't know. Maybe I should take her to the hospital myself."

I jolt up when I hear those words. I want to tell her about the hallucination, but hearing the word hospital makes me realize I don't want to go there. If I am dying, I'll have to spend enough time there in the future. "I'm fine, Aunt Grace. I'm just nervous."

She makes a *tsk*-ing sound and helps me stand. "That cheeseburger probably didn't help. You need soup."

Mrs. Randolph chimes in, "Oh yes, that'll make everything better."

If only that were true.

Aunt Grace escorts me back to the truck like I'm an invalid. As I wait for her to climb in the driver's side, I can't help but wonder if I should have told her what I saw.

I wonder what I'll see next if the hallucinations continue.

35

t's almost three o'clock when I wake from my nap. I stretch on the soft covers, feeling a little better, but then the incident at the bakery ignites in my mind.

Instant bad mood.

The room seems to shrink. I grab the bag with my sketchbook and head out to the river. At least I don't have to worry about running into Trevor.

I'm almost done with a sketch of me and the other Alora when Bridger emerges from the woods. Heat rushes through me as I remember the kiss from last week. I don't know why, but he's been distant since it happened, and that hurts so much. I thought he was starting to like me in *that* way. I guess he changed his mind.

"Hey, I've been looking for you," he says when he reaches me. "Grace told me you weren't feeling well."

"I'm okay now. I just needed a nap."

"That's good."

"Yeah."

I wait for him to say something else, but he just clasps his hands behind his back and rocks on his heels. I don't like how awkward he acts around me now. Even though he's only been here for a month, it feels like we've been friends forever. But that amazing and awful kiss changed everything. I shift my gaze from him.

"What are you drawing?" he finally asks.

I snap the book shut and slip it into my bag. "It's nothing."

Bridger sits next to me and stares at his hands, which he's rubbing together. "I'm sorry."

"For what?" I ask, startled.

"For last week. I shouldn't have kissed you. I took advantage of you." He's still won't look at me.

And now I feel even worse. So he thinks he's to blame for my awful mood. Sure, the kiss unnerved me, but I did like it.

"Don't apologize," I say, drawing my legs to my chest. "The kiss was nice." Just great, that sounded super lame. Who says a kiss is nice? "No, it was more than nice. It was really sweet."

That didn't sound much better.

Bridger finally looks my way, offering a tentative smile. "I'm glad. I thought you hated me."

"I couldn't hate you for that. Not when I enjoyed it." Yeah, I wish I could take that last sentence back.

He gives a light laugh and stares at his hands again. "Me too."

More awkward silence. I want to go back to being comfortable around him, being myself. I need to make things right. "I'm sorry I didn't talk to you much at breakfast. I was worried about my appointment. And then I had another blackout."

His head snaps in my direction. "What? Did you wake up somewhere else again?"

I'm not sure I want to tell anyone about this latest incident. It's still burning in my mind, a reminder something is very wrong with me.

"No, I stayed in the same place."

"That's not so bad," he says, looking hopeful. "You must not have been out very long."

"Yeah, but . . ." I start and then stop. I want to kick myself for almost blurting out what happened next. It's one thing to black out and not remember how you get from one place to another. It's crazy territory when you think you can see yourself from several weeks in the past. I hope he didn't notice the slip.

"But what?" he asks, his expression full of concern. I feel my resolve starting to slip. Maybe he won't think I'm crazy. Maybe he'll still want to be my friend.

I swallow and take a deep breath. Bridger smiles encouragingly, so I tell him what happened.

But by the time I'm finished, he's not smiling anymore. He's still as a stone.

"What's wrong?" I ask.

"I . . . it's just," he begins, rubbing the back of his neck, "I wasn't expecting to hear that."

"Yeah, it freaked me out too."

"I can imagine. Look, I've got to go. There's something I need to do."

My stomach sinks as he hurries away. I feel so completely and utterly stupid for telling him the truth, so naive for trusting him. I wish I could take it all back.

As I watch him melt into the forest, anger punctures through the hurt. How could he act all concerned and then just leave? Running away with some lame excuse isn't going to cut it. I snatch up my backpack and sprint after him, shouting his name. He ignores me at first, but I keep at it, determined to make him stop.

"What's your problem?" I ask when I catch up to him. "Why did you want to know what's going on with me and then take off the minute I told you?"

"It's not like that. I remembered something I have to do." He can't look me in the eye again.

"Right, and I'm a fairy princess. I don't expect you to understand what I'm going through, but don't treat me like this. Whatever's wrong with me isn't contagious."

His face reddens. "I'm sorry. I didn't mean to upset you."

"Whatever," I mutter. "I know you think I'm nuts, but you could've at least had the decency to not run off. I mean, do you think I like having this happen to me? I didn't choose this."

Bridger's face is a flurry of emotion. "I know you can't help it. It's something you were born with."

My heart does this weird thud. "What's that supposed to mean?"

He doesn't say anything for several uncomfortable seconds. "What if you weren't hallucinating at the bakery?"

I snort. "Okay, and if I wasn't hallucinating, then what was it?"

"What if I said you traveled back in time?"

My mouth drops open.

He rushes on, "You said before you blacked out that you wished you could go back to before all this started, right?"

"Yeah, so?"

"So, that could've been the trigger to send you back in time." He steps back and raises his eyebrows at me, as if taunting me.

I'm not taking that bait. I jab him in the chest with my finger. "You must think I'm an idiot."

"No, I don't," he says, frowning.

"Yes, you do. I mean, really, *time travel?* That's the most ridiculous thing I've ever heard. If you think I'm crazy, then say it to my face. Don't make up a stupid story."

"But I'm not . . ."

I brush past him. "Save it," I hiss over my shoulder. "And don't worry about having to be around me anymore. I have no interest in continuing this so-called friendship."

36

t's a little after two in the morning when I make my move. I activate my uniform cloak and slip out of my room. The silence is suffocating as I creep down the hallway. My mind is still reeling from the knowledge that Alora is a Space Bender *and* a Time Bender. A Dual Talent.

They're not supposed to exist.

When I stop at Alora's door, my pulse spikes. Fure, I hate doing this. But if I'm going to shift to 2146 to get a Mind Redeemer, I'm not leaving without the Jewill. Future tech can't remain in this time. And if I can't return, at least I'll know the Jewill can't be used to alter the timeline.

Before I can change my mind, I twist the door handle. It's locked. Figures. I pull a pin out of my pocket and within seconds, the door is open. Careful to not make any noises, I slip in through the cracked door.

I survey the room before moving. It smells like Alora—full of that lavender sent that always clings to her. I shove aside the guilt for invading her room yet again. Then I stay still until my eyes adjust to the darkness.

I don't even bother searching the room. I only need two things.

The first is easy. I find Alora's small bag and ease the sketchbook out. I take the book to the moonlit window and rip out the first drawing of Colonel Fairbanks and the dark-haired woman that I find. The tear sounds thunderous, and my eyes flick to Alora. She doesn't move. Relieved, I slide the paper in my pocket and return the sketchbook. Then I turn my attention to Alora again. And the Jewill.

Alora is curled up, and her blankets are wrapped around her like a cocoon. This is not going to be easy. My hand trembles as it hovers over her.

Steady, steady, steady, I say to myself as I peel back the blanket. It feels like I'm moving in slow motion. Slowly, her neck is revealed. I let out a small sigh when I spot the Jewill around her neck. Now to get the thing off.

I try not to focus on her face as I brush her hair aside, but my eyes won't cooperate. I take in her profile, the way she's breathing softly. She frowns and makes a sad sound. She must be dreaming something bad.

I hope it's not because of me.

The thing is, I never meant to hurt Alora. What was I thinking? Blurting out that she's a Time Bender. No wonder she acted the way she did. Stuff like that is science fiction in this century. I wish she would've let me go when I walked away. But she couldn't leave it alone and, for once, sticking to the truth backfired.

Suddenly Alora turns. I have to jump away to keep from getting hit. She kicks at her blanket and then settles on her back. One arm is slung over her head, the other resting by her side. The chain trails down the side of her neck.

My fingers touch the smooth surface of the black stone pendant. I can't help but wonder again, how did her father get this? Did Colonel Fairbanks accidentally leave it behind?

Alora moans, and I release the pendant. She turns once again, facing away from me. This time I feel a sense of relief. I can see the clasp. I don't know how, but I manage to unfasten the chain and slide it out from under her neck. I barely get if off her neck when Alora jolts upright, her eyes wide. Her arms flail out and hit my chest.

She screams.

A piercing, blood-chilling scream that could probably shatter glass.

I lurch away from Alora and look down at my body. I'm terrified my cloak's gone, but it's still activated.

Footsteps pound across the hallway. Then Grace pushes the door to the bedroom open. Alora has stopped screaming. She's clutching the blanket to her chest.

"What's the matter, sweetie?" Grace asks.

"I thought someone was in here. I *felt* someone." Alora's eyes are huge.

Even though Alora can't see me, I look away from her. This isn't right. I shouldn't be in here.

"You must've been dreaming," Grace says in a soothing voice.

Then Alora feels around her throat. "My necklace," she breathes.

That's my cue to get out. But I stand in the doorway, watching Alora frantically search through her sheets for the Jewill. Grace asks her what she's talking about.

I'm certain the key to why my father wanted to save her is locked in her subconscious. I'm certain it's because she's a Dual Talent. I just don't know why that would be so important to people in my time. It's not like Alora could ever shift to the future. Time Benders can only travel to the past and back to their own present time. I have to get a Mind Redeemer to help her remember.

I drink in every part of her with my eyes. If I'm going to do this, I'm going tonight. And since Mind Redeemers are secured at the Department of Temporal Affairs and the Academy, along with Chronobands, I might not be able to get one.

I might not be able to make it back.

This could be the last time I see her. I want to tell her goodbye. I want to feel her again, maybe get one last kiss. But I can't do that when she hates me.

I have to content myself with a silent goodbye, and then I walk out of the room. Possibly forever.

37

A cool blast of air encases me as soon as I emerge from the Void. I'm in an abandoned sector of Old Denver. The day is bright and clear, like it was when I left 2013. The difference is that moments ago, the area was warm and alive with people. Now, it's like a graveyard.

I suck in several deep breaths. Then I deactivate my DataLink and the cloak. I feel exposed, but I can't risk getting tracked again. Government shuttles have sensors to detect them. If one happens to pass over me, it'll automatically cross-reference approved missions that require cloaks.

As I set off in the direction of New Denver, I reach into my pocket and clasp Alora's Jewill. How she must have hated me when she realized I took it. I think back to the minutes after I left her room. I stopped long enough to grab my portacase before leaving the house. Then I had to fight off more guilt when I stole Grace's truck. That was hard. They trusted me and look what I did to them.

I abandoned the truck once I got to Athens so I could take a bus to Denver. At least I left my remaining cash in the truck. I hope Grace accepts—accepted—it as an apology. Anyway, I figured it would be better to shift here. General Anderson will keep the Willow Creek area staked out until I'm captured.

Yeah, it seems like I'm piling on the regrets. But I can't worry about what I've done. I have to focus on getting a Mind Redeemer and restoring Alora's memories. I'll do everything I can to get back there. Because in the back of my mind, another idea hatched while I was on the never-ending bus ride to Denver. It teased me at first, gradually burning brighter and brighter.

If I can save Alora like Dad wanted, what's to say I can't save him too?

I reach New Denver at sunset. They sky is pink and orange. I wish I could see the mountains in the distance. It's hard to see them over the skyscrapers.

Everything is so different from Willow Creek. I try to imagine how Alora would react if she could see all of this. She might wild out at first, but I have a feeling she'd love it.

The city buzzes with noise. People talking. The steady whirring of shuttles as they zoom overhead. Announcements blasting over the Jumbotrons. Life going on even though mine's falling apart. I notice a nearby Jumbotron flashing pictures of people wanted by the Federation.

I'm on there.

My hands ball into fists. I'm in more trouble than I thought if they're plastering my face everywhere. There's also a ginormous reward—a million credits. Enough to live on for over a year. I glance around, trying to see if anyone has spotted me. It doesn't seem like I've been recognized, but I don't want to sit around and find out.

I end up at Dad's apartment. It's a risk, but I can't go to Mom's place. She'd drag me to the DTA herself. And I'm not sure Shan would help me. At least if I'm here, I can change clothes and use the TeleNet to contact Professor March.

After I clean up and dress in some regs, I stash Alora's Jewill in the hidden desk drawer. If I'm caught at least this will be safe.

In the living room, I activate the TeleNet. I almost give the command to call Professor March, but hold off. Maybe there is someone else Dad knew who could help me. I give the command to call up his contacts list and scan through those. There are dozens and dozens of avatars displayed, mostly people he used to work with. I'm just about to close out the contacts when I notice one avi of a dark-haired woman. I've seen her somewhere. I swipe it and then suck in my breath when it enlarges.

She looks almost identical to the woman Alora drew.

Holy fure.

The name flashing under it reads Adalyn Mason. I give the command to activate the file, and several digigraphs flash on the screen. I select the first one. A scene plays, showing the woman and Dad. It looks like they were in their late teens or early twenties. They're at a party and Dad tries to get Adalyn to dance with him. She reluctantly gets up from her seat, but I can tell she's happy. They join a few other couples already dancing. I smile as I realize Professor March is one of them.

The digigraph ends and loops back to the beginning. I watch a few more. They're all of Dad and Adalyn. And they're obviously in love. The last digigraph raises a lump in my throat. Dad and Adalyn are surrounded by a lot of people. Dad serenades her in an off-key voice. Then he drops down on one knee and proposes.

My legs feel weak. Watching these digigraphs surfaces a forgotten memory. The day Mom took me and Shan to Dad's apartment to try and talk him into giving their marriage a second chance. This woman is the same one we caught hugging Dad.

And at some point, she was with Alora.

Talking to Professor March can wait. I give the command to search for Adalyn Mason's address.

I need to talk to her. Tonight.

I hesitate outside Adalyn's door. It didn't take me long to get here—it turns out she lives in an apartment two blocks from Dad's building. I wonder how she'll react. She'll probably know who I am. But will she help me or turn me in to the DTA? I press my thumb over the sensor.

A few moments later, Adalyn answers, wearing a plain, light green suit. Her face is ashen. "It's you," she whispers.

"I need to talk to you," I say.

She peeks out in the hallway before waving me into the apartment. As I pass her, I notice a faint scar running from her hairline to her left cheek. I wonder what happened. The next thing I notice is the smell. Lavender. Just like Alora.

"I suppose you're here looking for answers," she says after we're seated in her living area. So the lady knows how to get to business. I like that.

"Yes. I was at Dad's apartment and I found some old digigraphs of the two of you."

"Yes. We were . . . friends." Her eyes take on a faraway look.

"It seemed like you were more than friends," I mutter. My mind jumps back to the day Mom and I saw them together. How he gazed at Adalyn as if she meant everything to him. I can't remember him looking at Mom like that. For a split second, I feel a stab of resentment. It doesn't last. Mom is impossible to get along with.

Adalyn clears her throat before speaking. "We were engaged, but that was a long time ago. Right after we graduated from the Academy."

I listen as she goes on to explain how Dad's insistence on joining the military sector of the DTA drove them apart. She didn't trust the military back then, and she doesn't trust them now.

"So you work for the civilian branch now?" I ask when she's done.

"In a way," she says. "I program Sim Games."

"Really? Aren't you a Time Bender?"

"I am, but I can't shift anymore." She points at the scar.

"What happened?"

Adalyn takes a deep breath. "The DTA tried to take my daughter away. I resisted."

"When did that happen?" I ask, feeling my skin grow cold.

"Ten years ago when my daughter was just six years old."

"What's her name?"

"Alora."

I get this weird dizzying sensation. Alora is this woman's daughter. I was so sure that her mother was Colonel Fairbanks. I feel like I'm watching myself as I say, "I've met her."

"What? You . . . how did you do that? Is she in this time again?"

"What do you mean?" I ask, leaning forward. "Or better yet, what do you know?"

Adalyn clasps her hands together and stares at them. "A few years after I broke up with Leithan, I met Alora's father, Nathaniel. We had this whirl-wind courtship and soon after applied for a marriage contract, but it was denied. We never knew why, but we kept seeing each other in secret. But then a few months later, things began to change. Nathaniel became volatile and paranoid. He said he was being followed. He also claimed that he discovered his whole life was a lie. He said he'd been cloned."

She pauses to let out a shaky breath. "And his temper, oh that was off the charts when I didn't go along with what he said. I ended the rela-tionship, but by then I was pregnant. Since I wasn't supposed to be with Nathaniel anymore, I said I used a donor. But Nathaniel knew the truth."

I rub my forehead. "Wait, you're telling me Alora's father lived in *this* time? That can't be right. I just spent the past month living in the same house with his sister in 2013. I saw pics of him."

"I know, but this happened seventeen years ago. I didn't know the truth back then."

Okay, time to shut up, I tell myself.

"After Alora's birth, Nathaniel came and went in our lives. He was good to her, but he still scared me. He'd go on and on about how he was really from the past. I did my best to shelter that part of him from Alora. She loved him so much." Adalyn rakes her hands over her hair. "There's another thing. When Alora was born, I found out she carried genes to bend space *and* time. That terrified me. I didn't know what the DTA would do if they found out."

"What did you do?"

"I have a friend who works in the labs, and she helped me cover up everything. But I lived in fear that the DTA would discover what we did."

"What about Nathaniel? Did he know?"

"Yes. When I found out I was pregnant, he confessed that he could bend space and time as well. He said he was born that way. I didn't believe him until he showed me. He also said the DTA would take Alora away if they found out, and we'd never see her again. He wanted us to flee, but I refused. The DTA would never let us just walk away."

Adalyn is right. That's one of the few bad parts of being a Time Bender. The government has to have access to our whereabouts at all times. And we're never allowed to abandon our time-bending responsibilities since there aren't many of us.

"So how did Alora end up in the past?"

"Several months after her sixth birthday, a military official showed up with two officers. They said there had been an audit of the genetics lab and they discovered something. She said Alora was special and that they needed to take her with them. I knew what she meant, but I played dumb. I just asked her why." Adalyn's nostrils flare and she closes her eyes for a moment. "She refused to tell me, so I tried to stop them. Then suddenly Nathaniel appeared behind me. The next thing I remember is lying on the floor and feeling nothing but pain. When I woke in the med center, they claimed Nathaniel took her."

I give her an incredulous stare as I think back to my own childhood, hearing about a young girl who was kidnapped. So that was Alora. And I remember Alora's sketch. I take it out of my pocket and hand it to Adalyn. "Is this the woman who tried to take Alora?"

Adalyn studies the drawing and nods. "Yes, that's her. I'll never forget her name. Halla Fairbanks." She glances back up at me. "I never liked that woman, but I actually feel sorry for her now. I heard her daughter passed away recently."

I look at the floor, my stomach clenching. "Yes. Vika was my girlfriend."

Adalyn leans over to touch my hand. "I'm sorry. I know you still must be hurting."

She's right. It still hurts, but the pain isn't sharp like when Vika first died. It's more of a dull ache now. I wonder if it's because of Alora. If spending time with her took the pain away. I feel traitorous. How could I develop feelings for someone else so soon after my girlfriend died? What does that say about me?

"Is there anything else you want to know?" Adalyn asks after a few seconds.

"About Vika . . . did you ever see pics of her?"

Adalyn nods. "I just have the pic from Alora's obituary, but the resemblance between the two of them is uncanny."

I hesitate. I've already asked so much, but I need to know for sure. "Are they sisters?"

Adalyn shrugs. "I don't know. Possibly. But if Nathaniel is Vika's father, I don't think he was aware of it. Halla is the one who would have the answers."

That's true. Vika was always under the impression that she was the product of a sperm donation. She could have been, but what are the odds of her looking so much like Alora and Nate?

I wonder what Colonel Fairbanks is up to. What did she want with Alora?

And another thing.

"How did my dad get involved with all of this?"

"Toward the end of our relationship, Nathaniel talked a lot of nonsense. Not only did he say he was a clone, he also said he was from the twentieth century. I thought he was just wilding out until the DTA tried to take Alora. I'm almost glad he got to her first, but he never told me where he was taking her. I figured they were hiding out overseas. But last year I decided to look into his claims, and I found an article about a Nathaniel Walker who was killed in 1994. And then I found this." Adalyn sweeps a finger over her DataLink and taps a few instructions. A hologram appears over it.

It's Alora's obituary.

Adalyn continues, "She's using Nathaniel's last name in the past, but in this time she went by mine. I think that's why the DTA never found her."

My stomach does this weird flip. "I saw that on the DataDisk Dad had at his apartment."

"I sent it to him. I know I hurt Leithan a long time ago when I ended our engagement, but we remained friends." Adalyn's eyes fill with tears. She quickly brushes them away. "When I found Alora's obituary and knew I couldn't go back myself, I needed someone I could trust to do it for me. The only person I could think of was Leithan. He promised he'd get my baby back. She doesn't belong in 2013. She's not supposed to be dead. She's supposed to be here."

She picks up a digigraph that's resting on a table next to us and hands it to me. It's of Alora. She looks like she's maybe three or four years old. She's running through a Green Zone. She lets out a peal of laughter as she jumps into a man's arms. He spins her around, holding her tight against his chest.

It's the same Nate Walker I saw in Grace's pics. Nate, whose death was supposedly faked in 1994, who abandoned his daughter to Grace in 2003. Nate in this time.

How is that possible? Time Benders can't shift to their own future. And cloning was outlawed in 2109.

Or was it?

As I sit there, numb to the core, I try to sort through everything I've learned. It seems impossible, but here it is in front of me. Alora and her father in this time. And my father was going to prevent her death because she was never supposed to be in 2013.

But why did he involve me? Is he really dead or is something else going on?

I'm too jacked to go back to Dad's apartment after I leave Adalyn. It's late, but I need to talk to Professor March. He has to know something. I mean, he helped me escape before.

I realize how careless I've been just before I reach his apartment. Someone points at me. Before I can flee, I hear a familiar voice behind me.

"Well, well, we meet again, Mr. Creed."

I whip around and find myself facing three Space Benders. They're pointing stunners at me. The one in the middle is the one who spoke. It's the same chick that caught me the last time in Willow Creek.

38

The pages of Dad's senior yearbook rustle as I flip through them, seeking one with his picture. I come to the attic at least once a day now and search through his trunk.

Since the end of May—when the scans revealed that nothing is wrong with me—Aunt Grace decided to drop the whole "remembering the past will make things worse" stance. Especially when the doctors said stress from not knowing what happened to my parents could have triggered my blackouts.

The attic door creaks, and Aunt Grace calls out, "Alora, I need you to run to town. I'm out of ketchup and brown sugar."

I groan. The annual Fourth of July Jamboree is tomorrow, and this year Aunt Grace is determined to win the barbecue cook-off. She's been on a tear trying to perfect a new sauce since she learned this year's grand prize is five hundred dollars.

"I'll be down in a minute."

"Okay," she replies. The door creaks like she's closing it, then she calls out again, "Why don't you see if Sela can spend the night? I haven't seen her around lately."

I wish Aunt Grace would stop dropping hints about me talking to Sela again. She made the cheer squad, and her new friends don't like me.

They, along with most everyone else in town, are still saying I'm to blame for Trevor's wreck. After the coroner announced Naomi had been sexually assaulted, and the DNA didn't match Trevor, people rallied to support the poor football star who won't get to play in the fall. They've been saying if I'd never pointed the finger at Trevor, he never would have been hurt. Never mind the fact that Naomi's killer is still out there somewhere.

The bad thing is a part of me believes them. If I'd just kept my mouth shut at the police station that day, none of this other stuff would have happened.

This whole situation is so messed up.

I trail a finger along a picture of Dad standing with the baseball team. I can't help but wonder how my life would be different if I was still with him and my mother. My vision swims with more stupid tears. I rub my eyes hard. I've cried enough this past month to fill an ocean, and I'm sick of it. But I still think about how things could be different—better.

It would be so nice if I could go back in time and change everything.

And that makes me think of Bridger. If it's possible, my mood sours even more. I can't believe how much I miss him, even after he messed with me the way he did. After he took my necklace and stole Aunt Grace's truck. Sure, he abandoned it in Athens with a lot of cash, which Aunt Grace gladly claimed. And it did help with some of my medical bills, but it wasn't enough.

Aunt Grace decided a few weeks ago to sell the house back to Celeste. She said the money would get her out of debt and give us a fresh start. I wish she'd move us somewhere new, but she likes it here. Probably because she's still hoping my dad will return.

Who knows? Maybe Bridger will come back too. Not for the first time, a nagging voice whispers, *What if he wasn't being a jerk?* What if he was telling the truth? That hallucination was so real. I felt the other version of me.

Or was it in my head?

Bridger's words come back to me. *You wished you could go back to before all this started, right?*

Before I can stop myself, I close my eyes. I wish to go back to the time when I was with my parents. I wish to go back to that day when I was six and see what awful thing happened to us.

The seconds become minutes and nothing happens. Feeling stupid for believing Bridger, I slam the yearbook shut and lean forward, resting my elbows in my lap. The best thing for me would be to let things go. Try to forget about the past. Get through the next two years, graduate, and get out of this town. Then I can truly start over.

The attic door creaks again and footsteps pad up the stairs. Just great. Now Aunt Grace is coming up here to get me. I need to go anyway. I gather Dad's things and stack them in the trunk. Aunt Grace offered to get someone to lug it down to my room, but I told her no. I like coming up here. It's comforting, having this space to myself.

The footsteps reach the top of the stairs and for some reason, the hairs stand up on the back of my neck.

"I'm coming," I say, glancing over my shoulder, expecting to see Aunt Grace standing there with her hands on her hips.

But nobody's there.

It feels like someone's up here with me, but that's impossible unless they're invisible. My mind's playing tricks on me. I hope I'm not going to have any more hallucinations or blackouts. I thought those were behind me.

I hurry out of the attic and down to the first floor, where the scent of freshly baked cake floats around me. My stomach lets out a loud growl.

"It's about time you got here," Aunt Grace says when I walk in the kitchen. She dips a spoon in the simmering barbecue sauce and tastes it. "Something's still not right," she mutters. "Come here. Tell me what's missing."

I glance longingly at a pound cake resting on the cooling rack as I take the spoon she offers me. The sauce is wonderful—somehow sweet and spicy at the same time. "It's good. I think this will win."

Aunt Grace shakes her head. "Good's not enough. It has to be perfect."

"So what do you need at the store?"

She points to a piece of paper on the counter. "Just a few things."

I snort as I pick up it up. Aunt Grace's "few things" consists of a full grocery list. Looks like I'll be gone for a while. Fun.

"Oh, let me add something before you go." Aunt Grace rummages through a drawer and pulls out a pen.

While I wait for her to finish, I try to figure out why she's so into the whole festival thing this year. It kicks off tomorrow morning with a parade and continues all day. The courthouse square looks like someone vomited red, white, and blue everywhere, complete with arts and crafts, greasy food, dinky rides for little kids, and several local bands performing one lousy song after another. The day is capped off when everyone migrates to the rec department for fireworks.

I still can't believe I'm actually going to the festival this year. Aunt Grace used to take me all the time when I was little, but the past few years I haven't felt like going. Instead we sat on the river dock, watching the fireworks exploding over the treetops and eating Aunt Grace's leftover birthday cake. I just didn't want to be the only teenager having to hang out with an adult because I didn't have any friends.

This year is going to be different. Aunt Grace decided we needed to join the celebration. She says I need to get out more. She thinks I'm being paranoid about everyone hating me in town, but I know better. I've seen the stares and heard the whispers, but I'm not going to ruin her birthday. If she wants to live it up at the festival, I'll be by her side. Even if I hate it.

"So are you gonna see if Sela can come over?" Aunt Grace asks as she hands me her debit card.

"I might," I say, just to get her off my back. "But she said something about helping her mom at the cook-off tomorrow." I don't know if that's true or not. I haven't talked to Sela since school got out.

Aunt Grace's nose wrinkles. "All the more reason for me to get this barbecue sauce just right. I can't let anyone get my prize."

I grab her keys, shaking my head. "I don't think you have to worry about anything." I start to head out the back door, then realize I left my purse upstairs. "Be right back," I call over my shoulder.

The doorbell rings as I get to the foyer. I open the door and try to keep my jaw from dropping.

Mr. Palmer is waiting on the other side.

"Hello there, Alora," he says, lifting his small suitcase. "It's nice to see you again." He crosses the threshold, forcing me to take a few steps back. "I sure have missed this place."

"What are you doing here?"

Mr. Palmer lets out a light laugh. "Work, my dear. I've been contracted to take pictures at the festival."

"Have you talked to Aunt Grace? She's selling the place so . . ."

A regretful expression crosses his face. "Yes. It's a shame. But she said since I'm only in town for two days I could stay."

"Oh. I didn't know." Great, now I get to see Aunt Grace flirting with him again.

"Are you here alone?" he asks.

"No, Aunt Grace is in the kitchen. I'll go get her."

Before he can say anything else, I fly out of the room toward the back of the house.

"Well that was fast," Aunt Grace says as soon as she sees me, and then she frowns. "What's the matter?"

"Mr. Palmer is here. Did you tell him he could stay with us?" I ask in a quiet voice.

She raises an eyebrow at me. "Yes. It's not a big deal."

"But why?"

Aunt Grace takes a deep breath. "I swear, I don't get you sometimes. What does it matter? It's a little more cash for us, and besides, I feel sorry for him. He told me he's been divorced for a long time, and he hasn't had any good cooking in years." Now she grins like she's pleased with herself.

I stand there a few minutes, feeling weird about the whole situation, while Aunt Grace greets Mr. Palmer. They make small talk for a moment, and then finally I hear their footsteps going upstairs.

I swear, if I catch Aunt Grace putting the moves on him, I'll puke.

39

The tiny cell I'm in is too bright. Bright white walls and floors. Crisp white linens on the narrow bed. Stark lights. I'm going blind. And nuts.

I figure I've been in here going on two, maybe three hours. After the Space Benders arrested me, they whisked me away to a five-story black building near the DTA headquarters.

The Black Hole.

The place where the Feds toss anyone who screws with the government. Once you go in, you don't come back out unless you're nulled. Or executed.

I pace the cell for what seems like the hundredth time. There's only one pitiful excuse for a window. Nothing that will allow prisoners to escape. The only other window in this room is a small one on the door. I can't even see out of it. I stop to stare at my reflection in it, wondering if anyone is out in the hallway observing me. Probably not. Two cameras are mounted in the room with me. They won't see me doing anything interesting. They shackled me with a thin metallic device around my neck, an Inhibitor, that prevents me from shifting.

I turn away and frown at my supper. The remains of the fishy-smelling paste concoction is smeared against the wall and floor. Courtesy of General Anderson. I cringe, remembering his visit.

To say he was pissed when he left earlier is a huge understatement.

He came in smiling at first. Nothing like the red-faced ranting lunatic I stunned a few weeks ago. But he didn't stay that way. He threw one question after another at me, but I wouldn't answer him. Then he flung my tray off the table.

Dad never told me the general has such anger management issues.

The door slides open. I make myself stay calm. If Anderson comes back for another round of crazy, I'll be ready to deal with him. Unless he's found a way to bypass a trial and have me nulled or killed right away. I hope it doesn't come to that. At least with a trial, I have a chance of getting a lighter sentence.

Professor March enters instead. I heave a sigh of relief.

He stands in the doorway and gives me a long, unreadable stare. My stomach drops. Finally he says, "I don't know what's going on in that head of yours, Bridger, but you don't have any idea of the trouble you're in."

The wanted picture of me on the Jumbotron flashes in my mind. I start pacing again and reply, "I do, actually."

He rubs a hand over his eyes. Then he strides to the table and takes one of the seats. Behind him, the door silently shuts. "Please sit," he says, nodding at the chair opposite him. "I can't stand watching you prowl around."

Anyone else, I would ignore, but I owe him. The chair scrapes across the floor as I pull it out. "Tell me the truth, Professor. Is there any way I can get out of this mess?"

"You tell me. I don't know what you've been doing." His eyes flick up to the camera behind me. "I don't know what possessed you to shoot General Anderson and me. I don't know why you decided to perform an illegal shift. It's like I don't even know you anymore."

I look at my lap. My hands start to twitch. I fist one hand and rub it with the other. "I'm sorry, sir."

I knew he would have to play innocent about the shooting incident. What I'm not prepared for is the guilt eating at my insides. I feel like I've let him down. I wish there was some way to disable those cameras so I can talk to him in private.

"Look, I know you're sorry. Maybe I can work something out with General Anderson. Just tell them what they want to know. That's all you have to do and this whole mess could go away," he says in a toneless voice.

No chance that'll happen. My guess is the general told Professor March to say that. I look down at my clenched fists, suddenly angry. Angry for being in this situation. Angry that they're forcing Professor March to play bad guy. Angry at my dad for illegally going back in time in the first place. Then somehow reappearing after he's supposed to be dead and asking me to finish what he started. My life was on a set course. Sitting in a prison cell was not part of the plan. "We both know that's not going to happen."

Calm yourself, Bridger.

I jerk my head up.

No! Look back down. Try to appear like you're having doubts.

What the hell is going on? How can I hear him in my mind? I force myself to breathe slowly.

Professor March keeps talking like nothing weird is happening. "You don't know that. After everything you've done, it's best for you to cooperate with us. Tell us what year you shifted to and why you went there." He relaxes his face and even smiles. "Maybe then I can work out a deal for you."

The words are pretty. Exactly what General Anderson would want him to say. But in my mind I hear something else.

Stay calm. Keep looking down and let me do the talking, but keep your mind open. I'm going to do everything I can to help you, but I need to know the truth. Just picture it, and I'll be able to see everything.

That's nearly impossible to do. I want to jump up and pummel him with questions. Namely, how is it that he's a Time Bender and a Mind Bender?

The Academy has always taught us that nobody can have more than one Talent. Now I know of three people who have dual abilities. It makes me wonder how many more exist. It also makes me wonder why the DTA's been lying to us.

Open your mind, Bridger.

I relax my muscles and clear my mind. Pressure builds in my head as Professor March attempts to access my memories. My instinct is to build up my mental barrier. I push it away so Professor March can read my thoughts. I want to recoil at the sensation. I've never had a Mind Bender extract information out of me. It's creepy, like I'm being violated.

It doesn't take long, maybe ten seconds or so. Finally, Professor March breaks the connection. His face shows a flash of astonishment before he slips on a mask of indifference.

"So, you don't have anything to tell me?" he asks.

"No, sir."

"Very well, then." He presses his mouth in a thin line.

My head throbs. Not only from letting the professor in my head, but from nerves. He knows exactly what I've been doing, but I have no clue how he feels about it. Or if he'll even help me to get out of here, much less get back to 2013 so I can finish what I started.

Don't worry, Bridger. I'm shocked, that's all.

That makes me feel a little better. Not much, but it's something. I swear, I don't think I'll ever get used to this side of Professor March. I've never dealt with Mind Benders before. They keep to themselves.

Then I think of something else that unnerves me.

Professor, did Dad know that you're a Dual Talent?

No. I've never told anyone. Can you imagine what would happen to me if the DTA found out?

He's got a point. There's no telling what their scientists would do to him. One thing is for sure—he'd never be free again.

So you didn't know what Dad was doing either?

No. He never said anything to me, and I'd never read someone's mind without their consent.

Okay. I get that. But tell me why hasn't the general ordered an investigation into Dad's actions prior to his death? Or even into what I did before I shifted?

Professor March looks away for a moment. *I don't know everything that's going on, Bridger. But what I do know is that General Anderson is trying to hide something from certain people at the DTA.*

Does it have to do with Dual Talents?

I think so. And that's the one reason he doesn't know what year you and your dad shifted to. He can't order a formal investigation without alerting everyone.

So what is he charging me with?

Running away while being investigated, performing an illegal shift, resisting arrest, and shooting superior officers.

I squeeze my eyes shut, my mind reeling. What is going on? And how did Dad get in the middle of it?

Professor March breaks into my thoughts. *Look, I've got to go now. Give me time and I'll see what I can do to get you out of here.*

How are you going to do that?

I might have to resort to other measures.

What's that supposed to mean?

Just trust me, Bridger.

He suddenly stands and plants his palms on the table. "I don't think you understand the full impact of your actions. If you don't change your mind, General Anderson will bring in an Extractor."

My blood turns to ice. Extractors are Mind Benders employed by the DTA to forcibly obtain information from individuals who can put up a mental barrier. It's a painful process when someone doesn't want their mind to be read. I've heard stories of people screaming in agony before falling unconscious or suffering from brain hemorrhages. They always end up dying.

Professor March stares like he's trying to intimidate me. I don't know what to say. I realize he's going to try to help me, but what if he can't?

Bridger, trust me. I'm going to do everything I can to help you. Let them continue to think you're going to resist them. It'll buy me some time to make arrangements.

I swallow hard. Then I lean back in my chair and cross my arms over my chest. I might as well play up the part of uncooperative prisoner. "Go ahead, Professor. Tell them to do their worst. I'm not saying a thing."

40

"I'm not so sure about this," Aunt Grace says as she takes the small container of fried Oreos from the snack vendor.

"Trust me, they're good," I say in between bites. This is the second time I've eaten them today. I think of how Sela would scold me if she were here. That's another good thing about not hanging out with her anymore. I can eat whatever I want without listening to her anti–junk food rants. I take another huge bite, relishing the explosion of powdered sugar, chocolate, and fried dough. Heaven in grease form.

"Lordy, this should be a sin," Aunt Grace says after she swallows. "I hate to think about how much weight I've probably put on today."

"Oh hush. It's your birthday. You deserve it."

"Yeah, you're right." She gives me the side-eye, grinning.

A warm feeling spreads inside me. Despite not wanting to come here today, I've had a good time. I haven't seen Trevor, which is a huge plus. Then I helped Aunt Grace sell her barbecue and we made about two hundred dollars profit. That was definitely a win. But I'm getting tired. Aunt Grace wants to stay for the fireworks show. I'm ready to go home.

I guess in the back of my mind, I was hoping Dad would show up again for Aunt Grace's birthday. It's stupid of me to think that, but whatever. I can always dream.

We weave through the crowd and head toward the front steps of the courthouse, where the judges are supposed to announce the winners of the cooking contests. Several kids from school pass us, shooting nasty looks at me. Aunt Grace doesn't notice. She's spotted Mrs. Randolph cleaning up her booth.

"Hey," Mrs. Randolph says. "I've been meaning to speak to y'all, but you know how it gets. Busy, busy, busy."

More people gather around us while Aunt Grace and Mrs. Randolph chat. I try to listen to them, but they're gossiping about something I don't give a crap about. Plus, I really need to go to the restroom, courtesy of the Dr Peppers I drank this afternoon.

"I'm going over to Java Jive."

Aunt Grace raises a brow at me. "Why?"

"Do I need to spell it out for you?"

Mrs. Randolph chuckles as the lightbulb goes off in Aunt Grace's head. "Oh, sorry. Yeah, but don't be too long, okay?"

"I might hang out over there for a while. There are too many people over here." No joke. I'm starting to feel claustrophobic even though we're outside.

"Fine. I'll meet you there in a half hour."

I hurry down the street to Java Jive. Of course, it's packed with people I don't want to be around. Sela. The Brainless Twins. Kate. Levi. Trevor. For a second I consider going to one of those disgusting porta-potties around the courthouse. Then I think, *hell no*. I'm not running from them. Not anymore. I square my shoulders and march to the restroom. It feels like their eyes sear into me as I pass.

When I'm done, I stop at the door, trying to get my nerve up to go back out there. I can do it. Just put one foot in front of the other and leave. Simple as that.

But when I near the table where all the jerks are sitting, Trevor says, "Well hey, Alora. You don't have time to speak?"

On cue, Trevor's minions laugh. That figures. I glare at them, noticing how Sela is the only one who's quiet. She's really interested in something on her phone.

I don't need this. I keep walking, but then he jumps up and follows me. Kill me now.

"What do you want?" I ask in a low voice.

"I thought we could bury the hatchet, so to speak." He gives me the smile that he reserves for trying to charm girls.

"Save it," I snarl. "Don't think I've forgotten about what you did to me."

The pretty smile fades and is replaced by an ugly expression, very similar to how he looked when he went psycho on me. "And don't you think I've forgotten about what you did to me, little girl. Your lies are gonna cost me a scholarship."

"Oh please," I say, rolling my eyes. "As if you have to depend on one of those."

"Well, it's not like you'll ever get one," he says with a malicious smirk.

I don't miss a beat. "Just like you'll never get me." I push past him, deciding I don't need to listen to his special brand of idiocy any more.

Before I can get to the glass door, Trevor calls out, "We'll see about that."

Chills crawl over my body, but I don't look back. I won't give him the satisfaction of seeing that he got to me.

I barely get across the parking lot when I spot Mr. Palmer standing on the other side of the street, aiming his camera at a group of girls I recognize from school. They're all dressed in really short shorts and too-tight shirts. The kind Aunt Grace would never let me wear in public.

I watch as Mr. Palmer snaps several pictures of them. Okay, so I know he's supposed to take pictures of everyone, but that seems a little creepy. Still, it's none of my business. His employer probably wants him to take a variety of shots.

So many people are still out. The arts and crafts vendors are packing up their stuff, and a lot of people are heading toward their cars, most of them probably going to the rec department for the fireworks show. I just want to find Aunt Grace and see if she'll take me home. I've had enough socializing for the day.

I start to cross the street, but someone standing maybe ten feet away catches my attention.

She looks like me.

For a moment, I wonder if I'm hallucinating again, like I did at The Gingerbread House.

The girl hurries away. I will my legs to follow. I have to catch up to her, see if she'll talk to me. Or if she's even real.

I almost lose her in the crowd, but then I catch sight of her turning into an alley. I shouldn't follow her there, especially since it's getting darker, but I keep going. I can't let her get away.

I pass the rear side of a restaurant and stop when I get to the dumpster. The girl is gone. That's impossible. My head swivels back and forth and I check around the dumpster. She's not there. She couldn't have gone in any of the rear doors to any of the stores on this block. They'd be locked.

I start to turn back, but a sharp pain pierces my neck.

Then there's nothing.

41

My head is throbbing like a heartbeat when I wake up. Something is stuffed in my mouth. I gag and try to spit it out.

"Ah, Sleeping Beauty awakens," a male voice says.

I'm swaddled in semidarkness. The only light shines from a candle on a small table next to the bed I'm on—or rather tied to. My arms are stretched out above my head, bound with a rough cord. It bites into my skin as I try to yank my arms back to my sides. My head thrashes from side to side, taking in the piles of old furniture, and dust and dirt everywhere. I recognize where I'm at. It's the abandoned house in the woods.

"No need for that," the voice says. It's smooth and threatening at the same time. "You're not going anywhere."

A figure moves from the shadows at the end of the bed. I stare at him in horror and try to scream, but I can't. What is he doing?

Mr. Palmer lets out a low chuckle and scrapes a chair across the floor, letting it rest next to the bed. He sits and stares at me as if he could devour me whole, a crazed gleam in his eyes. "I've been looking forward to this for a long time, my dear Jane."

Jane? Who is that?

He caresses the side of my face, but I jerk my head away and try to yell again. Pointless, but I try anyway. All I can think is *I trusted him.* Aunt Grace trusted him. And he's doing this?

The candlelight glints off his glasses as he takes them off and places them on the table. "Oh, yes, I'm going to enjoy myself tonight."

It feels like someone has sucked all the air out of the room as reality hits me.

I try to scream.

Palmer smiles and leans close, so close that I smell the staleness of his breath. He whispers in my ear, "Go ahead. Nobody's gonna hear you. Nobody's gonna save you."

And then he licks the side of my face. Bile rises in my throat, and I gag again.

"You better get used to it." He smile is sinister, showing crooked teeth. "Now, I'll take this out, but only if you promise to be quiet."

I force myself to nod.

He tugs out the rag, and I take in several gulps of air while I think. Could there be some way to get him to let me go? He did seem to share a bond with Aunt Grace.

"You don't have to do this." My voice is a hoarse whisper, and I force myself to speak a little louder. "I won't tell anybody. Not even Aunt Grace. I swear."

"No, you won't. You won't be telling anybody anything. Not when I'm finished. I'm going to make you pay for what you did to me. Just like I've already made the other one pay."

Other one? Could he be talking about Naomi?

He stands and places his hands on either side of me while licking his lower lip. I hold still, too scared to move. Too scared to breathe. But I make myself keep talking.

"Why are you doing this? What have I ever done to you?"

Palmer pauses and looks somewhere over me, as if he's really seeing something, or remembering something.

"You're all just alike. You and Fran. Nothing but lying whores."

"I don't know who Jane is or who Fran is, but you're mistaken. My name is Alora."

"Don't lie to me!" he shouts. "You and Fran ruined my life with your lies. I never touched either one of you, and yet because of you two I lost everything! My wife. My kids. My teaching career. My whole life!"

He reaches over and picks up something off the table. I want to shrink away—it's a knife. He stares at it almost lovingly as he says, "Oh yes, I'm going to take from you just what you took from me. A life for a life. Just like I took care of Fran a few months ago."

By now I'm shaking. I remember the first time I met Palmer, when he said I looked like somebody he knew. Apparently Palmer has completely lost touch with reality. So he did something to two girls and paid for it. Now he's taking it out on me—and possibly murdered Naomi.

He's not just a perv; he's a *killer*.

And I'm next.

He returns the knife to the table and places his hands on the sides of my face, stroking my cheeks. Then his hands trail down my neck.

Please stop.

But he's not going to stop. Nobody's going to help me. Nobody but me. A fire sparks deep inside me and flames throughout my body. I won't lie here like I'm already dead and let him get away with this. Not without giving him hell.

I draw my legs up and twist my hips toward Palmer while kicking out. My feet connect with his chest. He stumbles backward, his arms flailing. His hand knocks against the table and sweeps the candle over. It rolls against the rotting curtains, igniting them. The fire spreads rapidly.

While Palmer grabs a blanket and tries to smother the flames, I yank against my restraints. They won't give. I don't know what to do. I need to get outside.

Smoke fills the room and I begin to cough. I squeeze my eyes shut, visualizing the yard outside, wishing with all my might that I was there.

Suddenly, the smoke disappears.

I look up to find the stars overhead. I'm stretched out on the ground outside the house. I blink several times. What is going on?

Through the window, the flickering flames make the house look like a jack-o'-lantern I quickly stand up.

Before I can figure out what happened, the door flies open and Palmer rushes out. His eyes lock onto mine.

I don't think.

I turn around and run.

42

My footsteps slam against the floor as I stalk back and forth in my cell. I don't know what time it is. The sun isn't shining through the tiny excuse of a window anymore. It has to be late afternoon.

Closer to my sentence being carried out.

I didn't get a trial. And now I'm scheduled to have my memories extracted today. I'm going to be nulled.

Everyone I requested for my final visitation has come, except for Professor March.

Mom was the hardest to deal with. She alternated from ranting about Dad and how he ruined everything to swearing she was going to appeal the sentence. And then she did something new.

She blamed me.

Her words still ring in my ears. "You're just like your father, Bridger. You could've made something of yourself, but you had to ruin it, didn't you?"

I said some not-so-nice things to her. I'm not sure exactly what I said, but I remember using the word "bitch." I feel horrible about it now. Especially since Shan was with her.

Elijah and Zed visited next. I thought they would act all depressed or even pissed, but they weren't. They were both full of nervous energy, pacing the cell. They tried to make small talk, but I couldn't focus. Right before they had to leave, I finally asked, "Have you talked to Professor March?"

Zed and Elijah exchanged a look. Elijah shook his head. "Just in class."

"Did he say anything about coming to visit me?" I was really trying to find out if the professor had said anything about helping me, but I couldn't exactly say that out loud.

Zed glanced at one of the cameras. "No, not a word. Nothing."

Now I'm sitting on my cot and rubbing my fist. My mind is fixated on Professor March. Maybe he's still working on getting me out.

Or maybe he lied.

The door opens and my gut clenches. This is it. I'm ready to take action, but what if nothing happens? What if Professor March doesn't help me? I hate not knowing for sure.

I expect the guards to enter. Instead, General Anderson saunters in like he's on an evening stroll. He's dressed in a black uniform decorated with pins and medals. Furing show-off. "Time to go, Creed."

"What, are you here to gloat?"

The general pretends to think, stroking his chin. "Not at all. I'm just here to make sure your sentence is carried out." He marches across the room and cuffs my hands behind my back. His voice lowers as he says, "Nothing is going to stop it."

I swear, if I get out of this mess, one day I'll get him back. I can imagine how good it'll feel to wipe that damn smirk off his face.

I follow General Anderson to the outer courtyard while the two guards trail close behind us. Everything is bathed in the dull glow of the dying daylight. Now that I'm about to become a Null, a pang of regret pierces me. I'll never be able to go to the mountains again. Or if I do, it'll be as a mindless servant.

I'll never be me again.

After a short ride on the transport shuttle, we arrive at a squat building. The lights of the transport glitter off the glass walls. We descend to a circular landing pad surrounded by a landscaped area. Two Nulls are working in the flowerbeds.

The general exits first. The guards usher me out next. I'm shocked to find Professor March waiting outside. He's standing with a short woman dressed in a white uniform. She has bright blue hair.

The woman greets General Anderson with a slight bow. "I'm Dr. Santos. I'll be conducting the procedure following the extraction session."

I swallow hard and look at Professor March. He remains silent. I glare at him, but he continues to ignore me.

A cold sweat covers my body when we enter the building. Still, I check my surroundings, searching for an escape route. The lobby is large. A giant TeleNet screen takes up most of the left wall. A smiling woman appears on the screen as soon as we're in the room and recites how to get to the various offices in the building. Three elevators line the far wall, while several chairs are spaced out on our right. A hallway stretches on both sides of the elevators. I wonder what's down there.

"Don't bother looking for a way out," General Anderson says.

My head snaps in his direction and I snarl, "I wouldn't dream of it."

When we reach one of the elevators, Professor March finally enters my thoughts. *Bridger, it's time. Good luck.*

Adrenaline floods my body. But before I can ask what he means, I see a movement through the outer glass door. The two Nulls are heading in our direction. That's not normal—Nulls don't go anywhere without an overseer directing them to their next task.

They break into a run and crash through the entrance, firing stunners. They hit everyone except me. I start to run for the hallway, but one of the Nulls gets to me first. He grabs my arm and yells, "You idiot! Come with us."

We sprint across the courtyard and board the transport shuttle. Behind us, several guards appear from around the med facility. They fire their weapons at us.

Once we lift off, I peer at the ground. Someone will undoubtedly follow us. But nobody does.

I turn to the Nulls and grin. They've removed the helmets.

It's Elijah and Zed.

43

By the time I break out of the forest, I'm panting so hard I can barely breathe. I've got to get in the house. I need to get to the landline phone since mine is missing.

I run to the back porch and try to open the door, but it's locked. Aunt Grace never leaves the house open when she's gone. I close my eyes for a second. *Think. Think.* My eyes snap open as I remember the spare key under the back porch steps. A noise startles me, and I whirl around.

Palmer is tearing across the backyard, closing in fast.

My heart pounds as I run down the steps and race to the front of the inn. I know it's useless, but I have to try the front door. It's locked. I jump off the left side of the porch and duck behind the shrubs. Maybe Palmer will think I ran down the driveway and head that way. Then I can go back and get the spare key.

But I can't move until I know where he is.

The seconds stretch into infinity. Sweat trickles down my back and I start shaking. His footsteps grow louder and louder as he searches for me. His heavy breathing gets closer and closer.

"Come out, Jane. There's no point in hiding."

Oh, yes there is.

I wait until the footsteps start to fade. I wish I could see where he went.

My mind goes back to the cottage and how I got out. I wished I was outside, and then I was. Bridger was right—I have some kind of ability. But he said I could travel in time. I didn't do that. I just made myself go somewhere else, like I did every time I blacked out. I squeeze my eyes shut and wish to be with Aunt Grace.

Nothing happens.

Damn! Why didn't it work now? I try again and again, but still nothing happens. I want to scream. I want to get away from here.

After what feels like a century, I force myself to crawl out of the shrubs. I feel naked and exposed. I push away the urge to crawl back in there and stay hidden. Stay safe. Which is stupid, because I'll never be safe with Palmer prowling around.

I try to pretend I'm weightless as I make my way around back again. I crouch by the bottom step and feel under it. I can't find the key.

I sweep my hand back and forth, my head jerking in every direction. Every little sound I hear could be Palmer coming to get me.

Please don't let him come.

Finally, my fingers touch something small and smooth in the dirt. I snatch it out and almost gasp in relief. It's the key.

I fly up the steps, careful to avoid the second one from the bottom that always creaks. I'm almost to the door—almost inside—when Palmer rounds the side of the inn, his breathing labored.

I freeze. Maybe he won't see me.

But he does.

He bolts across the yard. I barely have time to register that he's holding something.

A gun.

My hands shake, and I nearly drop the key. It's so hard to see the lock. The shadows are no longer my friend. I fumble and finally the key slides in. I twist the handle, push open the door, and slam it shut just as Palmer reaches the top step.

He bangs on the door and screams, "You better let me in. I swear things will be a lot worse for you if you don't."

I back away, horrified. How can things get any worse?

My legs almost crumple as I hurry to Aunt Grace's study. That's where she keeps the landline. The pounding on the door is thunder throughout the house. I try to ignore it and open the study. But the knob won't turn. This can't be happening.

The thunder from the door grows louder, more forceful. Suddenly it bursts open and Palmer staggers inside.

I back away, but he's pointing the gun at me.

"I've got you."

Three little words, and yet they shatter me into a thousand pieces.

"Now come here," Palmer says. I don't move. I can't. He advances toward me, saying, "I *said, come here.*"

And then he's right in front of me. Before I can process what's about to happen, he slaps me. I fall to the floor, tasting blood on my lips. The blood does something to me, brings up a wild part of me that I didn't realize existed. He's going to kill me, but not without a fight.

I jump to my feet and lash out at him. My fists connect with his chest and his face.

My body feels electric. Maybe I can stop him. Maybe I can get the gun away.

I should have known better. All it takes is another powerful slap from him, and I'm back on the floor. This time I hit my head against something. I lay there, stunned, and stare up at him. He towers over me with an arrogant expression on his face.

I want to curl up and cry. So this is it. This is how I'm going to die. But something behind Palmer moves.

I cock my head to the side and gasp as someone steps into the hallway from the foyer.

It's the same girl I saw earlier, the one who looks so much like me.

44

"I can't believe you two just did that," I say.

"Don't look so shocked, man," Elijah says. He extracts a key card out of his pocket and swipes it across the cuffs binding my hands together. The lock releases with a click. I slide the cuffs off and then he does the same to the Inhibitor around my neck. When I remove it, I feel lighter.

Free.

"Yeah, you look like you've seen some real ghosts." Zed twists around from the pilot seat and laughs. "I wish I could've taken a digigraph."

"What . . . how did you do it?" I ask, sinking down on the nearest chair. I remember Professor March's message just before they burst in the med facility. "So Professor March helped, right?"

"I'd like to take credit for this whole ingenious plan, but I can't lie. Professor March was indeed the mastermind. We were merely his instruments of chaos." Zed puffs out his chest and waggles his eyebrows. "But I won't turn down any pledges of your undying gratitude."

"Hey, how about stick to the piloting?" Elijah shakes his head and takes the seat across the aisle from me. "So are you okay, man? I know all of this has to be a shock."

I don't speak for a few moments. Something isn't right. I ask Zed, "Are we being followed yet?"

"No. We're in the clear."

"Are you sure? They can track the transport."

"It's all part of the plan," Elijah interrupts. "Professor March made sure they wouldn't be able to track us. We're safe."

They're fired up about the plan, but I can't relax. The whole thing reeks. I know how much General Anderson wanted to have my memories extracted. He couldn't wait for me to become a Null. He'll move the heavens to get me back in his custody.

Unless he *wanted* me to escape. And if that's the case, then Professor March is working with him. Against me. I lean over like someone punched me in the gut.

"Are you sick?" Elijah asks.

"Not like you're thinking." I can't believe Professor March would betray me. My suspicions spill out like vomit.

Elijah lets out a low whistle. "So March didn't tell you anything? That is weird, but I don't think it means he's working with Anderson."

"But don't you think this is too easy?"

"Not if March is stalling them," Elijah reasons. "That's what he said he was going to do."

I want to believe him. Professor March was Dad's best friend. It doesn't make sense for him to use me to get info about where Dad went.

I go over everything I've learned so far about Alora. The pieces of the puzzle are sliding in place. If I could only find the last few. Adalyn mentioned that Nate thought he was cloned. Why would the DTA do that when cloning was outlawed so many years ago? And when did Dad shift to the Foster Assassination to tell me to save Alora? Before his death?

Or is he really dead?

I know Adalyn asked Dad to go back and save Alora, but I wonder if there's another reason he was there. I mean, he risked throwing his whole career away.

And I think of Alora's death date. My heartbeat quickens—that's where I'll find Dad. Alora doesn't belong in the past, but what if I can't save her? Dad obviously didn't. If he couldn't, how can I? Losing Dad and Vika so close together was the worst thing to ever happen to me. I'm not sure what I'm feeling for Alora, but the thought of losing her forever makes my stomach lurch.

"Hey, did Professor March happen to leave a Chronoband in here?" I ask, remembering the whole problem I had with free shifting.

Zed pipes up, "Yep, it's up here with me. Safe and sound. And he left a comm-set, too."

He tosses them back to me, one at a time. I fasten the Chronoband to my wrist and place the comm-set on the seat next to me.

So Professor March thought of everything. I should be glad. Instead, a sense of dread descends over me. I have to make myself say, "Okay then. Let's get to Georgia."

Two hours later we land behind the inn-slash-museum. Nobody from the DTA is there. I guess they were recalled after my capture. We make our way into the forest. I don't have a cloak, so I need to materialize where nobody will see me.

"We'll wait here for you," Elijah says. "Good luck."

"Yeah, ditto that," Zed says. He play punches me on the arm and then grows serious. "Just make sure you *do* come back."

I start to make a smart remark about Zed getting sentimental, but it suddenly hits me—I could die. Just like my dad.

But I've got to try. I place the comm-set on my head and force a smile as I say my goodbyes. Then I activate the Chronoband and shift.

45

Palmer notices I'm looking behind him. He glances back and hisses, "Who are you?"

The girl smiles—a cold smile that doesn't reach her eyes—and raises her arm. A small, silvery object glistens in her hand.

"Drop it or I'll shoot," Palmer says.

"I don't think so," she replies in a clipped voice with a trace of a weird accent. Her eyes close, and she vanishes.

Palmer yells, "What the hell!" He circles in place, while holding the gun ahead of him. I try to shrink myself into a ball on the floor.

"Who is she?" Palmer asks, now pointing the gun at me. I can't speak. All I see is the tip of the barrel. I imagine the bullet speeding out and hitting me. "Is she your sister? Answer me!" He yanks me up and drags me to the foyer, his head swiveling back and forth.

She suddenly reappears next to him. Palmer doesn't have time to react. She slams her fist into the side of his face and snatches the gun from his grip as he staggers.

Palmer quickly regains his balance and charges at her. A bright blast flashes between them, and then he collapses to the floor, twitching.

"That was wild." The girl kicks Palmer hard in the ribs. He grunts but otherwise doesn't say anything. "Don't worry," she says. "He's not going anywhere for a while. Furing psycho." She kicks him again, then looks at me. "Do you know he's murdered fifteen girls over the past five years? You were supposed to be number sixteen. All because he flirted with two of his former students and they turned him in."

I clutch my arms to my stomach as I stare at the scene. At the girl who just saved me. Who is she? How does she know all of that about Palmer?

I really look at her. She's dressed in my clothes. I hadn't noticed it until now, but she's wearing the same dress I wore to Levi's party back in April. I'd hid it in the back of my closet.

"It looks good on me, doesn't it?" she asks as she twirls. "Nice for something so archaic."

"Why are you wearing it?"

She gives me a flippant shrug. "Maybe I wanted to see what it felt like to be the favorite daughter."

Okay, now she's starting to freak me out. I take a few steps back, but she fixes me with a frosty gaze, her eyes narrowed to slits. "Stay where you are."

The words are a slap. "What? I don't understand."

"Of course you don't. You're blank."

"I'm what?"

"Blank. It means you're empty up here," she says, tapping the side of her forehead with the silver object. "You don't know anything."

I hate feeling like a trapped animal for the second time in the same night, for not understanding her. "What do you mean?"

The girl rolls her eyes. "This is so tedious. I'll say this so even a Null could get it. You are not from this time. You are from the future." She says each word slowly, like I'm too stupid to understand. "Our father broke the law. He brought you here and abandoned you to his sister. Our beloved aunt."

If anybody said this to me before I met Bridger, I would've laughed in their face. Not anymore. Remembering what he said about traveling in time and waking up in different places after blacking out . . . yeah, it doesn't sound so strange now.

"If that's the case, why are you so mad at me? I don't even know you," I say.

She fixes me with a contemptuous gaze. "That's because we've never met."

46

It's dark when I appear in 2013. Moonlight streaks through the trees, giving me just enough light to see. I was aiming for around eight o'clock. The article detailing Alora's death pinpointed it happening between nine and ten.

The smell of smoke and burning wood envelops me as I push my way through the branches and brambles. An orange glow flickers through the forest. It has to be the old abandoned house. My mouth grows dry. That's where Alora's body is supposed to be found.

I start to head in that direction, but my skin crawls with the feeling I'm not alone. I activate the comm-set and scan my perimeter. A Time Bender is here. And he's heading my way.

It's Dad.

And he looks pissed.

I've never been so glad to see him in my entire life. My legs fly as I run to meet him, and I practically tackle him. I want to laugh and cry. He's real. He's here. He's still alive.

Dad is rigid at first, but then he embraces me. I feel safe, like I did when I was a kid. He pulls away too soon. "What's going on, son? What are you doing here?"

"Where's Alora? Is she safe?"

"Whoa, wait a minute." Dad rubs the back of his head like he does when he's thinking. "First off, I just arrived here myself from July third. I've been following Alora to see if I can figure out a way to prevent her death. And second, how do you *even know* about Alora?"

I give him the abbreviated version of how I got dragged into this mess.

Dad's face morphs from shock to anger to disbelief. When I'm finished, he runs his hands along the sides of his face. "Bridger, I don't understand. I've never been to the Foster Assassination. I just found out about Alora a week ago from her mother. She gave me this." He extracts a DataDisk from his pocket.

"I know. I found it in your desk back at the apartment."

"I never left it in my desk." Dad closes his eyes. "I don't know what's going on, but you've got to go back to our time. Now."

I shake my head. "No. I'm not going anywhere. I've got to make sure Alora's safe."

"That's what I'm here for, son."

We stare at each other. I want to tell him he won't. Not if he's alone. But how do I tell him that from my perspective, I'm talking to a ghost? That he's been dead for two months?

A scream pierces the silence. Our heads jerk toward the inn. Dad whispers, "Alora."

47

I feel as if I'm outside my body, watching the scene in front of me. The girl takes three steps forward and grabs my arm. I try to snatch it back, but I can't. She's stronger than she looks.

"Why are you doing this?" I ask, trying to stall her. "Why would you want to kill me if we're sisters?"

"I have no attachment to you. I didn't even know you existed until a few months ago."

"What?"

"Let's just say I've had access to some interesting info lately. That's how I found you. How I found that our father always took you to Green Zones to play and gave you gifts when you were little. You know what he did for me? Nothing."

I take in her crazed expression and Palmer's gun shaking in her hand. If I didn't know better, I'd think she was jealous.

"You know, I shifted back here once before. I wanted to get to know you before you were supposed to die, but then I saw you making moves on *my* Bridger. So don't expect me to feel any love for you."

I blink a few times. *Her* Bridger? "What are you talking about? I never tried to hit on him."

"Don't lie. I saw the two of you getting all cozy at the river once, when I did a free shift."

I wonder if she's talking about the time he kissed me or one of the other times we were at the river. And then it hits me. Bridger must be her boyfriend. Bridger claimed he wanted to help me recover my memories, but I knew he liked me. What if he kissed me because I look like her?

I feel sick. I wish this was a nightmare and I'd wake up and find Aunt Grace making me hot chocolate and blueberry pancakes. I'd tell her about the nightmare and everything would be rainbows and sunshine again. Except this isn't a nightmare.

I should be afraid. I should beg her for my life. It's not my fault our father was involved in my life. And I can't even remember that. It all happened so long ago.

But you can't reason with someone who's nuts. I know that from dealing with Trevor. What can I do? She has a weapon. I have nothing.

Something beeps. The girl checks a band on her wrist, one that looks like Bridger's, and groans. "We have visitors."

I take the only chance I might have. I reach behind me and grab the flower vase on the foyer table. She turns back as I hurl the vase at her and she fires the gun. I drop to the floor, wishing I was outside. I picture it perfectly in my mind. Me in the front yard.

And then I am, still on my hands and knees.

I scramble to my feet, stunned to realize that I really can go where I want just by thinking about it.

The girl has the same abilities as me, but she knows how to control them. She'll kill me for sure if she catches me again. I have to get help. Now.

A booming sound like a cannon echoes behind the inn, and I jump. The sky over the treetops erupts in a kaleidoscope of red sparkles. The fireworks show has just started. Everyone is at the rec department.

That's the answer.

The rec department is on the other side of the river. All I have to do is get there.

If the girl—my so-called sister—doesn't find me first.

I close my eyes and concentrate on wishing myself there.

But it doesn't work this time.

48

ad gives me a stern look and says, "Stay here." Then he takes off for the house.

I stare after him for a few seconds before I follow him. Like hell I'm staying put. My feet pound across the grass. I gasp for air, trying to ignore the squeezing in my chest.

I catch up to Dad on the back porch. He glares at me. "I thought I told you to stay put."

"Couldn't do it."

We enter the house and find a man lying stunned on the floor in the foyer, surrounded by broken shards of glass. It's the guest who was here in April, Mr. Palmer. I wonder why he's here now. What he saw.

Dad activates the tracker on his DataLink. "Alora's in the woods behind the inn. She's moving fast toward the river."

He looks grim.

"What's the matter?" I ask.

"She's not alone. Someone just appeared ahead of her. I have a feeling whoever it is isn't here to help her."

"Let's go," I say, stepping toward the hallway.

"I don't want you to go. You don't know how serious this is."

I feel my face growing hot. "Yes, I do. More than you know."

"I don't know what that's supposed to mean, but you are *not* to follow me. I've got to be able to concentrate. I don't have time to worry about your safety." I start to argue, but Dad holds up a hand. "Enough. Stay here and I'll be back soon. With Alora."

"Well what about him?" I ask, pointing to Mr. Palmer.

Dad extracts a Mind Redeemer from his pocket. "Erase his last three hours."

49

Everything is a blur as I race along the forest path. I don't know why I couldn't wish myself to the rec department. Maybe there's a trick to it, something I haven't figured out yet.

I'm almost to the dock, ready to dive into the river, when a voice calls out, "It's about time you got here."

I skid to a stop and slowly turn around. The crazy girl steps out from the shadows, smiling in a way that makes me want to punch her. She's still holding the gun.

"What do you want from me?" I ask.

"I already told you," she says, sauntering closer to where I'm standing. "I'm here to make sure you die. That's your fate."

If I was smart, I'd try to stall her. But I'm pissed. I close my eyes and suck air through gritted teeth.

"Don't even think about shifting. I'll put a bullet in your brain before you figure out what to do."

"What does it matter? You're going to kill me anyway. For no damn reason." My voice snaps out in a snarl.

"Oh, but there is a reason. You're *supposed* to die today. But you know what, I'm feeling generous. I think it was cruel for our father to dump you in this hellhole, all alone. Poor little Alora having to grow up in a strange place away from her mommy and daddy." She lets out an eerie-sounding giggle. "Yeah, I'm going to be nice. You really should thank me." She advances closer and extracts a small black circular object from her pocket.

I step back.

"Stay still," she commands. The gun is now pointed at my heart. "It won't hurt. I promise."

"What is that thing?"

"This will help loosen up those old brain cells. It'll make you remember *everything* you're about to lose."

Ice-cold fear. crawls over every inch of my body. All I can do is watch helplessly as she extends her other hand and holds the object in front of my forehead. A bright green light blinds me, and a searing pain builds behind my eyes, burning into my skull. I try to scream, but I can't.

Just as quickly as it started, the pain vanishes, and forgotten memories start to emerge.

At first it's just fragmented images. Me as a little girl, squealing as my dad chases me through a Green Zone. My mom—the dark-haired woman from my dreams—helping me with a drawing. Both of them tucking me into bed at night. Birthday parties. So many memories consume me.

I start to smile, but it melts away as my last memories of them surface. Mom and Dad arguing. Dad saying we need to leave with him. Mom sending him away.

Later that night, some people from the DTA showed up. Mom ordered me to my bedroom. I was crying. Then I heard Mom yell, "Please, don't!" She had warned me not to come out, but I had to know what was wrong. I rushed to the living room and saw a blonde woman and two men. Mom was lying in a pool of blood.

I screamed at the same time Dad materialized behind me. He pulled me back into my room and locked us inside. "Do you have your Jewill?" he asked.

I reached up to my neck, touching it under my shirt. He just gave it to me a few days before. He told me not to tell Mom about it.

Dad kneeled and looked me directly in my eyes. "Alora, this is very important. We have to go."

"But, Mommy . . ."

"Close your eyes." He took both of my hands in his. "And whatever you do, don't let go. Do you understand?"

I couldn't stop shaking, but I nodded.

The next thing I knew, we were standing on the edge of a river at night. The heat was suffocating. He told me how much loved me and he needed to get Mom, but he had to leave me for a little while. I was going to stay with his sister—a sister I didn't know he had.

I shake my head, fully understanding what happened. Even though my shifting abilities hadn't emerged yet, Dad was still able to take me to 2003 because I was born with the time-bending gene. But Dad wasn't supposed to leave me with Aunt Grace this long. He was going to save Mom and bring her to this time. The perfect way to escape the DTA.

"What happened to my father?" I ask.

The girl's mouth curls into a cruel smile. "My mother made him pay for what he did."

I want to claw her eyes out. I'd give anything to hurt her, show her what it feels like to have your life ripped away from you.

From out of nowhere, a deep voice commands, "Put the gun down."

50

After I erase Mr. Palmer's last memories, leaving him unconscious, I race out of the inn. Lights flash behind me. I twist around in time to see headlights bouncing as a white auto speeds down the driveway. Grace is here.

The knot in my stomach grows tighter. She's going to find Mr. Palmer inside and wild out. Then she'll summon the authorities.

I can't deal with that. Alora is going to die soon. How can I keep her alive without changing history? Her death is on record. The only possible way I could save her without destroying the timeline is to somehow make everybody think she died tonight. But how can I do that when there won't be a body?

The smell of smoke fills the forest. My nails bite into my palms. It's just another reminder of Alora's impending death.

Voices greet me as I near the river. A familiar female's voice and Dad's. It sounds like they're arguing. A new wave of adrenaline explodes through my body. I run faster.

I stop before I reach the clearing by the river. Dad taught me never to rush into anything blind. I peer through the trees. Three figures are illuminated by the fireworks. Dad is standing a few feet away from two girls. Both of them with blonde hair. One looks terrified, hugging her arms against her chest. The other yells at Dad, pointing a weapon at the first girl.

I feel like someone blasted me with a stunner.

The girl with the weapon is Vika.

She's alive.

I sway a little. How is that possible, unless she shifted here before her death? But why didn't she tell me about it?

Behind me, footsteps close in on my position. "Alora!" Grace screams. "Where are you?"

Damn. She must have seen our footsteps on the dirt path leading to the forest. I've got to stop her before she ruins everything. Before she passes me, I deactivate my cloak and leap in front of her.

She starts to scream. I throw my hand over her mouth and whisper, "Be quiet. Alora's in danger."

Grace's eyes are huge. When I lower my hand, she says, "What's going on? I've been looking for her for hours."

I wish there was a way to make Grace go back. I think about taking the Mind Redeemer out and erasing her memories from the past few hours. Before I can, the voices behind me rise again. Grace's eyes shift from my face to behind me. Her mouth forms an O. "Holy Mother of God. They look so alike."

I turn around. While I was busy trying to stop Grace, Dad moved closer to Alora and Vika.

Vika points her weapon at Dad. "I don't want to hurt you. I'm only here to make sure Alora dies."

Raw fear pierces my heart. Why would Vika want to do that?

"You don't have to do that, Vika," Dad says in a soothing voice. "She's not supposed to be here. She needs to go back to our time."

Grace tries to pass me, but I hold her back. "Wait," I hiss. "That's my father out there."

"And that's my niece. I have to help her."

Another round of fireworks blasts at the same time. It casts everyone in a faint greenish glow for a moment. Vika pretends to think, tapping her chin. "You should know better. There's an obituary for Alora. She *has* to die."

"What does she mean?" Grace asks in a high-pitched voice.

"Nobody is going to die." I stare hard at Grace. "That's why I'm here."

But apparently Grace doesn't believe me. She kicks me. Pain rips up my leg and I bend over, letting go of her.

Which I should've never done because Grace brushes past me and bursts out of the forest.

Immediately, a shot rings out.

Grace crumples to the ground.

51

My legs nearly buckle. I scream and try to run to Aunt Grace, but the crazy girl—Vika—says, "Don't move or you're next."

I want to tear her heart out, like she's done to me. All I can do is watch as Aunt Grace curls her legs close to her body.

"See," Vika yells to the man. "You made me do that! She wasn't supposed to get hurt!"

"If you'd put the gun down nobody would get hurt," he says.

I can't take my eyes off Aunt Grace. "Please, let me check on her."

Vika seems unsure. She's breathing hard. "Fine. But don't try anything or I'll kill you right now."

I run over to Aunt Grace and kneel by her. She's clutching her right shoulder. "Can you hear me?"

Her eyes flutter open and she moans. "Yes."

"Let me look at it."

Aunt Grace's fingers shake as she lets go of her shoulder. The metallic smell of fresh blood hits me. I try not to gag as I inspect the shot. It doesn't look life threatening.

"How is she?" Vika asks.

"She needs to see a doctor."

I want to slap Vika when she says, "It'll have to wait."

She turns her attention back to the man. "Now, the best thing for you to do is leave. None of this concerns you."

"I can't do that," he says.

"This is interesting. My mother has given me access to a lot of info, and yet there's one thing I still don't know."

"What's that?"

"You're supposed to die, too, Mr. Creed. What I don't know is *how* it will happen." She tilts her head to the side. "I wonder if I'm supposed to do it."

Terror pools in my stomach. She said Mr. Creed. As in Bridger's father? How could she be so cold?

Vika straightens her spine like she's preparing to fire.

"You don't have to do that," the man says in a disbelieving voice.

"Oh, but I think I do," Vika answers.

Another voice penetrates the tense atmosphere. "Put that gun down. Now."

My heads whips around, searching for the source. Immediately I sag in relief.

It's Bridger.

52

BRIDGER
JULY 4, 2013

My body is shaking as I emerge from the shadows. This is not the Vika I know. Vika was always stubborn, but she was rational. She was kind. She was gentle. She'd never threaten to kill anyone, especially my father. She always admired him.

This girl is none of those things. She's not my Vika.

Dad twists around, looking shocked. "Get back, Bridger!"

Vika looks equally shocked. "What are you doing here?"

I can't look at Alora and Grace as I pass them. I have to focus on getting Vika to put the gun down. When I reach Dad I fight the impulse to throw him behind me. "Please," I begin, glancing from Dad to Vika. "Let everybody go. I don't know what's going on, but we can shift back to our own time and sort things out there."

"I can't do that," Vika says.

"Why not? Who says anybody has to die?"

"You don't understand. All I'm trying to do is make sure things happen as they're supposed to happen. You can't go messing with the past, Bridger."

"Isn't that what you're doing? Who says Alora has to die? If anything, it looks like it's going to happen *because* of your interference."

For a moment, I think I've gotten to her. She flinches as if my words are physical blows. Then she shakes her head. "That's not true. Her death is a part of history. If I hadn't interfered, that man at the inn would've done it. He abducted her this afternoon, not me."

I think of Mr. Palmer, unconscious back at the inn. Son of a bitch, it *was* him. But why would Vika save Alora just to turn around and kill her later? She's acting unstable. Crazy.

Like a clone.

The air rushes from my lungs as the final piece of the puzzle clicks in place. Vika *did* die. Just like Nate Walker died, then somehow reappeared, alive, over a century after his own death.

Someone has been illegally cloning Time Benders.

The image of Vika lying on the ground at the Foster Assassination flashes in my mind. I remember the cloaked Time Bender standing over her—the Unknown who could have been from our future. That person must have taken a sample of her DNA and extracted her consciousness.

And now all that's left is a shell of her.

Suddenly I want to punch something. I know Colonel Fairbanks and General Anderson have to be behind this. But for what reason?

"Bridger," Dad says. He's staring straight at Vika, as if he's steeling himself to do something. My blood turns to ice as he says, "Get Alora out of here."

53

ALORA
JULY 4, 2013

Bridger's father whispers something to him. Bridger shakes his head as if to say *no*.

The gun swings from Bridger to his father, and I realize this is my chance. If I can make myself appear behind Vika, I might be able to get the gun away from her.

I close my eyes and wish harder than I ever have before, concentrating on the area just behind Vika.

Please work.

When I open my eyes again, I'm there—behind her.

But I'm too late.

54

BRIDGER
JULY 4, 2013

Vika's attention shifts from Dad and me to where Alora is sitting by Grace. "Where is she?"

Alora isn't there anymore.

"Where did she go?" Vika yells, looking all around.

Alora materializes a few feet behind Vika. I almost allow myself to feel relief. Until Dad lunges toward Vika.

And Vika sees Dad coming.

In that very moment, I realize Alora is the reason Dad will die. I should stop him. Try to tackle him or something. But I don't. Something Dad told me once rings in my ears.

Everything happens for a reason.

Those few words make me stay still. A part of me dies as Vika fires the gun.

This time hitting my father.

55

'm too late. Mr. Creed flies back and falls to the ground. Bridger stares at him, frozen.

So I take the chance to subdue the psycho. I charge and slam into her back. We tumble to the ground, and I dig my fingers into her arms.

She twists away and kicks at me, knocking me in my stomach. An explosion of pain rips through me, but I keep fighting. My fists swing and connect with her face and chest.

Vika's weight suddenly disappears. She's gone. I sit up and ask, "Where is she?"

Bridger breaks out of his numbness long enough to grab the gun that's lying a few feet from me. "Do you see her?" he asks in a hollow voice.

"No," I say, my head twisting in every direction.

Suddenly Bridger's mouth drops open and his arm snaps up. He's pointing the gun in my direction. Before I can move, he fires.

The sound is deafening, even louder than the fireworks overhead.

Then I turn around. Vika is lying on the ground with a perfect circle in her forehead, her lifeless eyes fixated on me.

56

He's dead. He's dead. He's dead.

Those words echo in my mind as I study Dad's still form. I can't believe I did nothing to stop this. I'm a furing idiot.

It feels like everything is moving in slow motion as I walk over to him. It's like I'm here and not here. I'm numb. I might as well be a Null.

Before I can reach his body, a shimmer appears next to him. My comm-set searches through different cloaking frequencies. This one doesn't register.

It has to be a Time Bender from my future. The ones we're supposed to stay away from.

The shimmer hovers around Dad.

"What's wrong?" Alora asks. She's still sitting where she fought with Vika, as if she can't move.

"Someone's here with us," I say, keeping my eyes on Dad's body. I want to move closer, but something tells me stay put.

Alora jumps up and backs away. "What do they want?"

"I don't know."

All I know is that I let my father die. I could shift back and try to save him again, but I don't. That could create a paradox. I can't change what's part of my history. By all rights, Alora should be dead too. But Dad wanted to save her. She needs to return to her own time. I have to honor that even though I'm dying inside.

The shimmer moves to Vika's body and stays for a little while before vanishing.

"Whoever it is just left," I say.

Alora rushes over to Grace and checks on her.

"How is she?"

"She's alive, but she's unconscious. We need to get her to the doctor."

Alora stands, hugging her arms tight around her torso. "Why did this happen, Bridger? Why did that girl keep saying I was supposed to die?"

I don't want to tell her, but I'm done lying. It's caused too much pain. "Because you *are* supposed to die today. That's why I shifted back here in the first place. Your mom found your obituary and sent my dad back to save you." I stop, feeling a lump in my throat. "But he appeared to me on one of my time trips and told me to save you instead. So here I am."

"Oh no, Bridger, I'm so sorry. It's my fault." Her face crumples.

I feel like a jerk. I cross the distance and pull her against me. I know how she feels. It seems like everything is my fault. I hold her tight like she's the only thing keeping me anchored to the here and now.

"Well, isn't that sweet."

We jump apart. I spin around, more shocked than I ever thought I could be.

It's my dad. Alive.

57

I don't know who's more stunned—Alora or me. I wonder if she thinks she's looking at a ghost. I get the feeling. There are two versions of my dad here with us.

Alive Dad appears different. He doesn't have any wrinkles. No streaks of gray hair. And he's dressed in a gray jumpsuit.

He laughs. "You should see the looks on your faces."

Alora swipes at her tearstained cheeks. "After what I've seen today, I'd believe anything."

"Well I'm most certainly not a ghost." Dad steps forward and holds out his arm. "Go ahead, feel it."

I don't move. I can't believe it. My eyes dance between Dad's body lying on the ground and the version standing before me. I don't know how many times I've wished to have him back. But I'm not sure about this.

"You're a clone," I hear myself say.

I don't get it. Why would anyone do that?

Dad lowers his arm, his smile disappearing. "I know what you're thinking, son. I'm not going to wild out on you."

"You say that, but how can I know for sure?" I wave my arm toward Vika's body. "She tried to kill Alora. She *did* kill you!"

He sighs. "I wish I could tell you more. I really do. But what I can say is that I'm not from 2146." He pauses to let that sentence sink in.

I think of the cloaked Time Bender hovering over Dad's and Vika's bodies. Obviously uploading their consciousnesses. That means Clone Dad and Clone Vika are from *my* future. Holy fure. "What year are you from?"

"I'm sorry. I can't tell you everything. There are some things that you just can't know yet. I have to let things play out as they're supposed to."

"That doesn't make sense!" I shout. "You're here now. Obviously you shouldn't be doing that."

"You're right. I'm not supposed to be here, but I can say there are things I have to do to set certain events in motion."

Understanding dawns on me. "*You* followed me to the Foster Assassination?"

"Yes. And I also left the DataDisk and money in my desk. All because you told me that's where you found them." He smiles like he pulled some kind of prank. "Now, you need to listen to me. You have to take my body back to the date it was discovered in 2146, okay? I didn't use a regulation Chronoband, so my body won't automatically shift on its own. Let Alora take my body to just outside of New Denver. Show her how to send a distress signal from my DataLink to Telfair. He'll take care of the rest. Just don't let him find out who sent the message."

I relax. Professor March really was trying to help us. He must have been stalling Anderson to keep them from following us to Georgia after we stole the transport.

"What about her?" Alora asks, glancing toward Vika's body.

"Throw her in the burning house." Dad says. I look sharply at him. "What? Alora's body is supposed to be found in there. Nobody will question that it's not really her."

"Will I see you again?" I'm scared of his answer. Despite the fact that he's a clone, he's still my dad. And he's also not of my time anymore.

Dad's mouth tightens. "Not anytime soon."

My throat constricts. "At least I know you're alive."

"I know, son. You're safe and that's all that matters. Now go. You've got work to do before the authorities get here."

"I know you said you can't tell us anything, but I have to know. What's going to happen to me when we get back?" Alora asks.

Dad doesn't say anything for several long seconds. "I'm really not at liberty to tell you anything that could change what's supposed to happen. But I can say be careful about completely trusting the DTA."

I nod. That makes sense, especially knowing that General Anderson wasn't truthful with them, either.

Alora throws her hands up. "But why? And what about my father?"

"I'll just say the DTA isn't looking out for the best interest of Dual Talents." Before Alora can say something else, Dad smiles and firmly says, "That's all the info I can give you. Tell Adalyn I said hello when you get home."

He steps away and holds his finger over his Chronoband. "One more thing," he says before activating it. "Even though you have to send the distress to Telfair, don't *ever* trust him again."

58

We watch the burning house for a few minutes after throwing Vika's body inside. The flames have completely devoured the building, eating away at the frame in a cancerous inferno. We're so close that the fire is uncomfortably hot against my skin, and yet I feel dead on the inside.

Like I'm supposed to be.

It's weird, knowing that when the fire dies, everyone will think it's me in there. I look over at Aunt Grace. She's standing by me, hand clutched over her wound, breathing hard. She's lost too much blood, but she insisted on going with us to dispose of Vika's body. Explaining that was hard enough. Having to fill her in on everything else was worse. She didn't believe us at first, so I shifted for her a few times.

Now she's a believer.

"We should go," Bridger says, still staring at the flames. He's been quiet. What he learned about his father and Telfair, whoever that is, was a huge blow to him.

"We need to make sure Aunt Grace gets back to the house first. I don't want Palmer to hurt her," I say. I know Bridger said Palmer was unconscious when he left, but I don't want to take any chances. Especially knowing that he's a killer.

"No, it's fine. I can make it back on my own," she says. She sways a bit.

"No, you can't," I say. "You could pass out."

She doesn't protest as Bridger wraps his arm around her waist and helps her walk. My heart breaks. She's been a surrogate mother to me for most of my life. It hurts knowing I have to leave her behind. I wish there was some way to bring her to my time.

At the house, we're shocked to find that Palmer is gone. Aunt Grace is upset, but Bridger shares that he wiped his memories from the past few hours. Palmer probably woke up, not even remembering what he did to me, and fled. Still, he would have to remember what he was planning to do to me. I'm not worried for myself anymore. I just hope somehow he's caught before he kills again.

Bridger guides Aunt Grace to the sofa in the front parlor. I get a towel to press against her wound.

"Do you have your phone? I need to call 9-1-1 for you." Then I remember I'm supposed to be dead. "Wait, I can't. You'll have to make the call."

I feel horrible, watching Aunt Grace extract her phone from her pocket. Her brow scrunches up with the effort.

"What should I say?" she asks. "I can't exactly tell them the truth."

Bridger has been quiet until now. "Stick to the truth up until you got here. You realized Alora had gone missing and went home. Someone shot you outside, but you never saw who it was. According to the article, Alora's body isn't found until tomorrow morning."

"Why can't I tell them that Dave was the one to shoot me?" Grace asks.

Bridger hesitates before saying, "You can't because Palmer isn't supposed to be caught now. In my time, the article said Alora's murder was unsolved. It has to stay that way."

Grace frowns, and I don't blame her. But I get it. The timeline has to be preserved.

After a few moments, Aunt Grace shakes her head. "I don't know if I can do this. How can I pretend to be so upset if I know it's not really you?"

Bridger's eyes meet mine for a split second. I know what he's thinking. It would be better to erase her memories. But I can't do that to her. I can't leave her behind, thinking her family is dead. Even though Dad and I can't live here anymore, it would at least be comforting to her to know we're alive in the future.

"I know you'll be sad," I whisper. "You know I'm not really dead, but you also know I can't be here with you anymore."

Her eyes glisten with unshed tears. "This is so hard, sweetie. Why can't you just stay? We could move away and start over. Change our names. Nobody would have to know."

I sit next to her and gingerly hug her. "I wish we could, Aunt Grace. But I have to do this. I need to find my mom, and I have to find out what happened to Dad. And if I can, I'll come back to visit. Okay?"

She sniffs. "Okay. And if you find Nate, tell him he better come see me too. I miss him."

I pull away and blink back my own tears. "Yes, ma'am. That's the first thing I'll say to him."

She lets out a shaky puff of air. "I better make that phone call. I'm starting to feel kind of light-headed."

"Yeah, you need to do that. You've got to get better." When she's finished, I stand and glance at Bridger. "I guess we need to go."

As we walk out, Aunt Grace says, "Hey, Bridger."

He turns back. "Ma'am?"

"You do anything to hurt my girl, and I'll find a way to get you. Even if I have to haunt you."

Bridger gives her an almost-smile. "I'll remember that."

It's funny. As we head back to the river, the heavy feeling I had back at the house begins to fade. I try to figure out why. I could go back an hour and try to change things, but like Bridger said, the past has to remain intact. I have to accept it.

"Are you okay?" Bridger asks.

"I guess. How about you?"

"I don't know. I've got a lot of explaining to do when I get back. And I don't know who to trust anymore."

When we emerge from the forest at the clearing by the river, where Bridger has to retrieve his father's body, it finally hits me. I don't belong here. I'm a part of this time since Aunt Grace is here, but it's not *my* time. That's why I've never fully felt like I fit in.

I won't have to listen to Trevor complaining about not being able to play football anymore, which I'm pretty sure he will, or wonder if he'll continue to harass me. And it's a relief to know that the psychotic Palmer will never be able to hurt me again. Maybe I'll even be able to forget about how Palmer murdered Naomi, or at least put it behind me. It's something time will tell.

I'll miss Aunt Grace like crazy, but I'm ready to see my mom again. It's what I've wanted for so long. And I've got to find out what happened to my dad. I have to figure out what being a Dual Talent means. What the DTA wants with me.

I have my whole future to look forward to.

It's time to go home.

The End

ACKNOWLEDGMENTS

First, I'd like to thank my wonderful agent, Suzie Townsend. Thank you for finding that early version of my query letter at WriteOnCon and for believing in me and my book. Also, I want to thank the rest of the team at New Leaf Literary & Media. I'm so honored to be a part of the New Leaf family, and I look forward to many more years of working together.

I am eternally grateful to my editor, Kelsie Besaw, for loving my book from the beginning. And of course, I can't forget Julie Matysik and Adrienne Szpyrka for all your patience with answering my questions and for helping me make this book shine.

This book would have never existed without the help of my fabulous critique partners. To Christina Ferko, thank you for being there from the very beginning with this book. Thank you for not running away after reading that horrible first draft and for helping me whip this book into shape. I couldn't have done this without you! To Kimberly Chase, I'm so grateful that you helped me make this book even better and for all your encouragement. Also, I want to thank Melissa Blanco and Melissa King for reading early versions and giving me valuable feedback. You ladies rock! And I also want to give a shout out to The WrAHM girls (love you!) and the Fearless Fifteeners. *waves*

Finally, I want to mention my family. Thank you for your support over the years. It means the world to me. I love you!

YA 14 $\frac{99}{}$

616.1